Legend of the Oracle Runes
2

ALLEGORY OF THE MILIEU STONE

A fantasy novel
by Debbie Stansfield

Other books by Debbie Stansfield

Legend of the Oracle Runes 1: Nornien Odyssey

CONTENTS

Debbie Stansfield is the author of Legend of the Oracle runes and various other novels. When she is not lost in her next writing idea, she enjoys gardening, playing games and spending time with family. To learn more visit https://nyxnecrontyr1.wordpress.com

Dedication

Mom -

Thank you for encouraging the magic.

You will always be in my heart.

Legend of the Oracle Runes
2

ALLEGORY OF THE MILIEU STONE

A fantasy novel
by Debbie Stansfield

Chapter 1

Prologue

A year and a half have gone by since the centaurs called the ephemeral ceased fire. Things have not been peaceful; our old camp near McLeod's has been under constant attack. People and magical creatures alike fear for their lives. Some of them have found temporary happiness by getting married or having children, but I wonder how long the peace can last.

The centaurs are not known for their patience, sending small groups of warriors closer to our camps almost daily. We send a small contingent of our own warriors to counterattack, but more times than not they come back gravely injured or don't come back at all. There's an exception to this rule of course; Terri came to join us soon after McLeod's was destroyed. He's the one of the only centaurs I know of that came over to our side.

If only it was in my power to bring back the days where war was nothing but a myth. When people were still happy and not worried about their lives and families being in danger but unfortunately, it's not.

How can one explain to small children how all the legends about the trolls are completely wrong? That they're the ones that came to us for help when the centaurs attacked and killed some of their friends and families. How they aren't as evil as the old ones made them out to be.

And who can forget wonderful Shadick? The one and only Wolfane that I know of who came to our rescue when we needed him the most. He was the one that first told us about Justren being evil; if it had not been for him, we may have lost Alexandria by now.

Dear Alexandria whom I have not heard from in over a year and a half, I am so worried, but the last I heard from Starlansha she was fine. Yet, those letters have stopped some months ago, which worries me so much more. What reason is there to make her stop writing to me? It was reassuring when I got those letters.

The night when Alexandria and Shadick found out about Justren's deceit was the worst night of my life. I couldn't understand back then how such a friendly young man could be so deceptive about his life, but now I know that he was just playing everyone like they were some kind of toy. Then his family attacking the two people who are most important in my life.

When Alexandria found out that the centaurs massacred

the village where she lived almost her whole life, it was a very bad time for her because the house had been the only thing she had, had left of her parents, and I wish that I had some way of preserving those memories. I fear that time will erase all the memories of her parents.

At least something good happened that night. Alexandria and Shadick got closer and I do believe that both of them needed that, just someone who loves them completely. Even when they had to separate to retrieve the Trilate Amethyst, Septer Quartz and the Aquadious stones, their love grew stronger with every minute that passed and that they were apart. I never thought that either Shadick or Alex would find someone to spend their lives with, but I am glad that they found each other than someone who might hurt them. Sure, they will hurt each other but that happens in any relationship.

I had heard rumours of the dragons in Dragon Mountains, but I had never seen any until just before the war, when Chadromida came to our rescue with the dragons. Now, he's to a certain extent a handsome guy, but unfortunately nothing could happen between us what with me being the fairy queen.

My mother always talked about the Nornien stones and how she thought that, if ever there came a war, these stones would be our only saving grace. She had not told me how to combine the 3 stones that the Nornien stone was made up of, so when I tried unsuccessfully to combine them, it was with sadness in my heart that I started believing that my mother may have been mistaken about the stones' strength. Disappointed, I gave the stones to Alexandria for safe keeping. She in turn kept them on her while she was fighting and after the war when Shadick was killed that the stones united and gave her the power to revive him and heal all the other warriors that had been hurt during the war.

Just when we all thought that things would be quiet for a while, both Alexandria and Shadick had to leave, but once again they had things to do on their own. Shadick needed to return to his quest to find the Breastplate Solaar and the Glacier Sword. And Alexandria needed to get some training done so she could control her new powers.

So it was with a heavy heart that they both left us to go their separate ways even temporarily. Now I wish that there was some way that we never had to get separated, that we could have stayed together and get though these hardships together, but I know that it would not have been possible. Alexandria's powers were just too much to control without the proper training.

Now I sit and wait for two of the most important people in my life to come back to...

Chapter 2

Dream Oracle

Everyone in the palace was sleeping peacefully, all except one who was tossing and turning in her bed, plagued by nightmares.

Alone in an open field filled with light, she looked around her slowly; she had been here before. Or more accurately, she had visited this place in her dreams before, but it seemed different for some reason. The light seemed less bright than the previous times, and it felt as though she should be searching for something or someone, but she did not know who or what.

Hearing soft laughter from behind her, she spun around quickly only to find Justin standing 50 meters away from her with a self-satisfied grin on his face. This could not be right; they had found out a year and a half ago that he was actually a centaur. So how come he was suddenly human again? And why was he smiling as though he just achieved something spectacular?

Then as she blinked, Justin had disappeared only to be

replaced by Justren, an evil sneer on his face and a crude sword in his hands ready to use. He slowly started walking towards Alexandria, the sword held high above his head ready to strike. Backing up slowly, she realized that she had nowhere to go and that she was backed up against an invincible wall.

Closing her eyes, she waited for the blow from his sword. After a minute, she heard another sword being drawn from a scabbard and opened her eyes in surprise as she saw a black shape run past them. She looked around quickly to see if she could see who or what it was, but she only saw a wolf sliding to a halt a meter from where they were standing.

As she blinked, the wolf turned into Shadick, an impressive sword in his hands running towards them. Alexandria glanced quickly towards Justren to gauge his reaction, only to see an evil smile disappear from his morphed face as the sword that Shadick had been holding was thrust through Justren's abdomen.

As she looked at him, a drop of blood started running down the corner of his mouth eerily. Watching him drop to the ground, she looked up at the strong arms that pulled the sword out from Justren's now still form. She looked up slowly into the eyes she had been yearning for, for the past year and a half. Smiling happily, she ran into his arms tears silently running down her face. He held her tightly, not saying anything for a few minutes, then laughed softly lifting her face with his finger.

"You know I love you in my arms, but I didn't think that it would be such a tearful reunion."

Shaking her head against his chest, she took a deep breath then looked up at him expectantly. He immediately knew what she wanted lowering his face to hers and kissing her deeply pulling her closer with his left arm while she wound her arms around his neck, pulling his face closer. Lifting his face, he nuzzled her neck, placing kisses all over her neck.

"You have no idea how much I've missed you."

"And I've missed you too." Alexandria said, still hugging him.

Shadick pulled away slightly as they were surrounded by burning feathers twirling around and around them, the sky turning an evil shade of dark red and purple. Looking around her, Alexandria realised that there was an uncomfortable silence that was broken only by a weird swishing sound.

"What on earth is going on?" Alexandria wondered out loud.

"Whatever it is, it can't be good," Shadick replied, still holding his sword in his right hand.

Putting his arm around her shoulders, they looked around

still trying to find the source of the feathers, when they suddenly heard a new sound. It sounded like a million hooves were stomping their way closer to where they were standing transfixed.

Alexandria relaxed slightly when she saw a bull coming into view from over an invincible hill. Silently turning towards Shadick, she saw that he had not relaxed and was still looking towards the bull running towards them. Impatiently, she looked back towards the bull, realising that this time there was a whole herd of these bulls running towards them.

Surely, they couldn't do any harm; they were just migrating to a newer and greener field and they would swing out as soon as they realised that there was someone in their way. But as she looked closer at the nearest bull she saw a murderous look in its eyes, also noticing that it was running straight towards Shadick.

Opening her mouth to shout a warning at him, she realised that her voice had once again disappeared; although she shouted at him, nothing came out. Taking a step closer to him with the intention of pulling him away from danger, she watched in horror as the bull thrust its horns through Shadick's abdomen and saw how it raised its head, making its horns penetrate Shadick's heart.

Screaming in grief, she fell to the floor trying to block out the image of Shadick's surprised and incredulous look on his face. Mentally shaking herself, she stood up and walked towards Shadick's body, only to see him disappear into the distance the closer she tried to get to him. As she started running towards him, she was suddenly surrounded by strange women all of whom had wings.

Alexandria sat up screaming in bed, the thin satin bed cover sticking to her sweaty body. Clamping a hand over her mouth to silence the scream, she looked around the room, trying to orientate herself while ensuring that Shadick was not lying on the floor dead.

Taking a deep breath, she hugged her knees to her chest, looking out of the one window situated across her bed. Everything seemed calm and peaceful outside but on the inside she was still reeling from the realistic dream.

Impatiently, she threw the sheet from her body silently slipped into the slippers she had gotten as a present from the queen the second week that she had been here. A group of school kids had been attacked by two stray sharks, and luckily Alexandria had been close enough to defend them.

Slowly walking out of her room, she ran her hand against the smooth wall towards a hidden entrance that led to a large balcony. Climbing a few steps, she walked onto the open plan terrace. Looking around her, she took in the silent magnificence of her surroundings. The queen had ordered this balcony to be built specifically for her so that she could watch over her world without the need to enter the water.

She had also instructed some of the soldiers to bring down some exotic plants from the surface so that there could be a wide mixture of flowers and plants in her secret garden. Situated on her right and left hand there were two love seats made of a special coral, and Alexandria had found the queen sitting silently on these seats more than once during her stay at the palace.

Even though it had become a place of solace for Alexandria, she had always ensured that she was not disturbing the queen when she needed to be alone.

"Dreams can sometimes reveal our true feelings," a voice whispered

Alexandria looked around her in surprise, not remembering that she had seen anybody. Making sure that there was nobody around, she walked to the edge of the balcony. Lightly leaning on the ledge, she looked out at the population, most of whom were just starting to wake from their night's rest.

"Dreams have the ability to show you more than those around you, they can be more than just plain dreams," the same voice whispered

"I think it is rude to talk to someone when the other person can't see the speaker," Alexandria said while turning around, taking a slow, deep breath.

"Hmm... I believe that you are right," the voice said before a blinding light appeared in the middle of the courtyard. "I'm sorry, I seemed to have forgotten my manners today."

Alexandria stared at the new arrival in surprise.

"You... you're a lynx..." she whispered.

"Well, not exactly..."

"What exactly do you mean when you say, you aren't exactly a lynx?"

"You see, I am an Oracle, the Dream Oracle, to be exact."

"I'm not a 100% sure what it means for you to be an Oracle?"

"We are mythical creatures, all of us have our own kind of prowess, and each is as unique as the other."

"And you said that you are the Dream Oracle?"

"That is correct," the Oracle said, pacing around Alexandria agilely

"Are you the one that is responsible for giving me these... nightmares?"

"I am sorry to say it was unfortunately me, although I didn't send them to you as nightmares. But I had to get the message through to you, I am however bound to our codes, which in short, means that I cannot tell the person exactly what I want to. I can only show them in dreams, and then if there is no other choice, or they are simply not listening to their dreams, only then I am allowed to converse with them."

"What exactly was the message in these dreams? Is Shadick still alive?"

"That is something your consciousness added, it is your own fears of what will happen to the Wolfane that causes these dreams to turn into nightmares. But as far as I know, he is still alive. And the message in your dream is simple; you should not expect the centaurs, especially the one you know as Justren, to play fair in any way during this confrontation."

"What is new about that? We've realised that at the beginning of the war already especially when we realised, he was lying to us. And it is not as though there is any specific set of laws that would keep the centaurs from playing fair. On the contrary, their very existence is to break the law."

"But a person would think that even a centaur would know the risks of summoning these legendary creatures."

"If you mean the Cemlinos..."

"No... the monsters I'm talking about are even worse than them. None of the Oracles can even remember how to defeat these monsters."

"Alexandria? Are you out here?" the queen's voice drifted

up from the stairs.

"Yes, your majesty," Alexandria replied, turning towards the opening

"Who are you talking to, my dear?" she asked as she appeared at the top of the stairs

Turning slightly, Alexandria opened her mouth to introduce the queen to the Dream Oracle, but there was nobody there. "No one, I was just thinking out loud."

"Oh, I was sure that I heard another voice besides yours. Anyway, I just thought I would let you know that everyone is awake and breakfast will be ready in about half an hour."

"Thank you, your majesty. I appreciate that you came to let me know."

"How many times have I asked you to call me Arabella? You have been staying here for so long that you are like family. Now go get cleaned up before breakfast," the queen said, walking back into the palace.

Alexandria turned around gracefully, trying to see if the Oracle had reappeared but after a minute, she sighed softly and then walked towards her room to get dressed.

Chapter 3

Watery Reunion

They were sitting in the dining room two weeks after Alexandria had spoken to the Dream Oracle. Although she was a part of the conversation, she did not really pay attention to what was being said. They had finally decided that after a year and a half's training, she had accomplished what she had come down here for in the first place to get control of her new powers.

Now she was getting impatient with all the waiting. She was staring morosely at the wall, her head resting on her hand.

"Alex? Alex!" Starlansha's voice broke through her reverie

"Sorry?" Alexandria asked, looking at Starlansha

"Where did you go?"

"I was just lost in thought."

"Can your daydreams not wait until after our meeting? It is not as though I want to be here, you know." Roslata muttered

Alexandria ignored her "What was it that you were saying?"

"I was saying that we could leave as soon as you are ready. We just have to tell my grandparents so that we can inform them if we need a guard to the surface."

"There will be no need for a guard, if we run into trouble, we can defend ourselves. We are not weaklings. We've already imposed on them too much."

"You know that is not true, my dear." Queen Arabella said, gliding into the room

All three girls glanced towards her, the twins smiling at their grandmother.

"I have tried telling her that grams, but she is very insistent that we are imposing on you and gramps." Starlansha told her grandmother

"You are a very stubborn girl, Alex." the queen said, surprising Alexandria by kissing her cheek.

"I completely agree with that." Roslata said under her breath

"She won't listen to advice, even if it is for her own good." Starlansha said, laughing softly

"It was rather enjoyable to have youngsters in the palace again, and it would now be rather vacant without you three here."

"Gran, you know that you only have to ask, and we will come to visit again."

"Yes, I know dearest but with the uncertainty of the fighting against the centaurs, it may not be as soon as I would want it to be."

"If it is possible, I want to leave within the next few days. We need to seriously find out what is going on." Alexandria said forlornly

The twins glanced up at her in surprise.

"I thought that we would leave at the end of the month? I mean, there is no real rush." Starlansha said slowly

"I don't see the necessity of staying longer. Now, if you will excuse me." Alexandria said, standing up and walking out of the room.

* * *

She was waiting for the twins in the entrance hall by the end of the week. They had finally agreed, albeit reluctantly, that they had to leave. All that was left now was to say their goodbyes to the king and queen and then they could go.

She heard their voices and laughter coming from the throne room and wondered if they were going to be long. The door of the entrance hall suddenly burst open and a young man walked confidently into the palace.

He looked at her and walked quickly towards her smiling self-confidently.

"You, madam, tell me where the king and queen are!"

"Who exactly do you think I am?" Alexandria asked, shocked

"It is clear that you are a maid in the palace."

Alexandria gasped, standing up straighter.

"I am not a maid! And how dare you speak to me as though I am one of your slaves."

"I can speak to an insolent little beggar like you in any way that I deem necessary. I am the crown prince of Orlantha, and you better show me some respect before I have you thrown into the dungeon."

"I am not the one who should show some respect; you are the pompous ass around here!"

The guards looked at them uncertainly, not sure of what they should do. One of the guards ran to the throne room to get some help.

"I am not pompous; I just know that I am far more superior to you." the prince said haughtily.

"You clearly do not know to whom you are speaking." Alexandria replied.

"Prince Jacques! How wonderful of you to come visit us, especially on such short notice." Queen Arabella said, gliding into the foyer.

"Your majesty, I am glad I could come I have one complaint that I need to bring to your attention." he said bowing.

"And what is that?"

"This... street urchin thinks there is no need for her to bow down and show me respect."

"There is no need for her to bow down to you or anyone in the palace, Jacques."

Alexandria quickly hid her smile at the outrage on his face, then looked at the queen who winked at her surreptitiously.

"I beg your pardon?"

"She is not a citizen of the Atlantican Ocean, so she does not fall under its laws."

"If she is not from here, then where, and who exactly is she that she does not fall under the oceanic laws?"

"Her name is Alexandria, and she is from the small village McLeod."

"It used to be called McLeod's." Alexandria whispered sadly.

"I am sorry for reminding you of that."

"Everything is fine, do not worry about it."

"You are from the surface?!" Prince Jacques asked, surprised.

"Yes, she is." the queen said.

"Do not look so surprised, Jack." Starlansha said, walking towards them.

"It is so unbecoming of a crowned prince." Roslata added grinning

"How many..." he started, then saw the twins. "I thought your majesty never wanted to see these... traitors ever again."

"They are my granddaughters and not traitors." Queen Arabella retorted.

"But his majesty said that he never wants them near the palace after the last time they came here and caused trouble."

"We did not cause trouble, Jack. We were determined to make reparation with our grandparents." Roslata muttered. "Then why did you not let me know you are back here, Star? We could have gotten together sooner, caught up again."

"If you will excuse me and Rose, we still need to finish saying goodbye." the queen said, walking away with Roslata on her arm.

"What does she mean finish saying goodbye?" Prince Jacques asked

"We've been living with my grandparents for the last year

and a half, helping Alex with her training. We were just about to leave so we could get back to fighting the good fight when you got here." Starlansha said

"If you would excuse me, I need to go get something from my room." Alexandria said, turning away. "Star, we will leave in about an hour."

"Of course, I will be ready."

Alexandria jumped through the force field and into the ocean with a silent sigh of relief. They were finally going home. It was an hour later than she had planned, but Starlansha had looked so happy when she saw Jacques that she had given them some time alone.

It feels good to be in the water again, knowing that we are not going to someplace to train, Starlansha said.

I agree with you entirely. I have had enough training to last me quite a while, Alexandria replied

I can just imagine how much worse it was for you, as we only did minimal training. You had to train at night sometimes, right?

Yes, and those were the worst, but it helped me so much. It will really come in handy when the centaurs restart the war, none of us know unfortunately when exactly they will they decide to do that.

Night vision is the only weapon we will need if there is a big fight, so why even bother with anything else? Roslata said sarcastically, swimming ahead

Pay no mind to her. She is just a bit upset that we have to leave so quickly, especially since we were just starting to get close to our grandparents again. And she doesn't show it, but she does miss them, Starlansha said, then added, I am going to talk to her a bit if you do not mind.

No problem at all. I will just be back here lost in my own thoughts, Alexandria said, smiling.

She had learned early on that she should not interfere with what was going on between the sisters. The few times that she had tried to help, they had turned on her until she had hastily withdrawn from the room.

Queen Arabella had smiled saying that they were just like their mother had been when she had been their age. Yet, it was still a bit strange not to try and help someone. Shrugging slightly, she turned onto her back and looked back to the palace where the king and queen was now probably entertaining prince Jacques after their hasty departure.

Starlansha was hiding how much she felt for the prince by not talking about it when someone did bring him up, she ignored the person. Alexandria had tried to make the twins stay, but Starlansha had been very insistent that she could not make the journey on her own.

Vaguely wondering if Starlansha was in love with the prince, she turned back around and swam further. If she really thought about it, she could only guess what this split between the twins and their grandparents was doing to Starlansha's and Jacques relationship. She could tell that there was some kind of relationship between them. Maybe she should just not interfere in Starlansha's life, leave them to sort out their own relationship.

She was still thinking about how different relationships could be, when she noticed the twin's disappearance. She knew that they had finally reached the beach. Sighing in relief, she stood up. Before she could look around and really breathe, something furry jumped up, causing her to fall back into the water. Realizing that it was a wolf and that he was licking her face, she grabbed his fur and lightly pulled him off of her, standing up.

Hearing a soft, "Down Managwa." she stilled and looked up looking into the blue eyes that she had missed very much during the last year and a half.

Watching him, she looked him up and down but never looking away from his eyes for more than a few seconds. Opening his arms to her, she ran towards him not caring who saw her now. As he wrapped his arms around her body, she realised that this was what she had been working for. She had worked as hard as it was humanly possible, sometimes even pushing herself to the brink of exhaustion before calling it a day.

"Please honey... I need to hear your voice so that I can make sure that you are not just a figment of my imagination." Shadick said, holding her tightly

"I am just making sure that you are not the one of my mind's eyes." Alexandria replied.

"You want prove that I am real?"

Nodding, still holding him tight, she felt Shadick pulling away from her a bit kissing her, his arms around her body while her hands snaked up and around his neck pulling his head closer still.

"So sorry to interrupt what seems to be a very hot reunion, but I just want to know if you want some lunch before we continue onto the trolls' cave?" Starlansha asked.

"I would never say no to lunch." Shadick replied, still looking into Alexandria's eyes.

"Okay then... Alex, I was just wondering if you want to borrow this cloak. Unfortunately, we do not have any clothes that would fit you."

"Yes, please." Alexandria said, taking the cloak from Starlansha and letting Shadick hold it out for her so she could put it on, then turning back towards him and smiling at him. "Thank you."

"Then let us get going to our cottage, so we can start on lunch."

Shadick lightly took Alexandria's hand, kissing the back and then pulling her after him to the cottage, talking softly.

"Tell me, how did your mission go?" Alexandria asked.

"I would rather hear how your training has gone than talk about my mission." Shadick replied.

"Why do we not rather talk about our plans to get through the forest? I mean, we do not know if the centaurs have placed any sentries in the forest." Starlansha said, opening the door.

Pulling a face, Alexandria replied, "I have not even thought about that yet."

"I noticed nothing while coming here. The forest seemed quite peaceful compared to other times." Shadick assured her.

"That could only be a positive change."

"You can sit on the couch you two; I will take care of lunch." Starlansha said

They sat down and Shadick pulled Alexandria onto his lap, holding her close, resting his cheek against the top of her head.

"I missed you, Shadick." Alexandria said.

"You have no idea just how much I missed you. It was not the same fighting dragons without you being there." Shadick said joking

Punching him lightly on the arm, she gave him an incredulous look. Before she could say anything, he bent down and kissed her deeply. They heard something being thrown against the bedroom door and they looked up surprised.

"Is everything okay Rosy?" Starlansha asked.

"Oh yes, everything is fine." came the sarcastic reply.

"Do you think that she is okay?" Shadick asked, grinning hugely.

"Yes, she has grown used to throwing things the last while." Starlansha told him.

"Is that what I heard every night?" Alexandria asked.

"That as well as the slamming of different doors. Grams was so fed up after a while."

"The one night one of those doors almost broke my nose when my curiosity got the best of me."

"What?!" Shadick asked sitting up.

"Relax, nothing was broken. Roslata of course had been mad at me which has been nothing new, when I heard the doors slamming, I thought I would go and have a look only to find her so I stepped closer when she slammed the door. I was barely able to step back in time."

Alexandria turned a bit and kissed him passionately until she felt him relax.

"Can you two please stop hanging all over each other? Think about people around you the next time you start kissing each other." Roslata told them, frostily pounding into the room.

"Are you jealous, Rose?" Shadick asked smiling.

"Why would I be jealous of the two of you?"

"Just leave it Shadick; you know she would never admit to anything." Alexandria whispered.

"Lunch is ready so everyone can come and sit down, to enjoy the food." Starlansha told them.

They stood up and walked to the table and sat down, Shadick looking at the food appreciatively. Starting to eat, they did not really talk much only when necessary. Alexandria was lost in thought when she noticed Roslata shaking Starlansha's shoulder slightly.

"What is wrong, Star?" Shadick asked, concerned.

"I am just worrying about Amethyst." she admitted.

"Do you know something that we do not?"

"No, it is just that I was hoping there would be a letter for me here from Amethyst with an update on what was going on, but there isn't. She wrote me almost daily until about six months ago when the letters suddenly stopped. I kept writing, hoping to get a reply but nothing. I'm sure though that everything is okay and that there is nothing to worry about.

Alexandria stood up her chair falling over making the others jump. "We need to get back to the caves, now."

"There is no use for us running off to the caves when we are not even sure that there is any trouble." Shadick told her, pulling her onto his lap.

"But I cannot just sit here and not do something."

"We will do something; we just have to make some plans first. Rushing into a surprise attack situation is not the solution." Starlansha said.

"Okay, so we start planning an attack and then leave for the caves. No hasty decision making just simple planning in advance." Alexandria muttered as she relaxed in Shadick's arms...

Chapter 4

Update

They were walking swiftly towards the trolls' cave, Shadick easily keeping up with Alexandria. Roslata was muttering about not being able to see much in the forest with this speed, while Starlansha just shaking her head, trying not to tell her sister to keep quiet.

"Lexie, honey I am sure that nothing is wrong with Amethyst or anybody else." Shadick told her, taking her hand in his.

"I will not be able to relax until I know for sure, Shadick. I am getting a bad feeling." Alexandria said.

They broke through the last few trees a few minutes later and looked around expectantly, only to find the camp completely empty. Exclaiming softly, Alexandria fell lightly onto her knees her face in her hands.

"Are you absolutely sure that this is even the right camp?" Roslata asked softly.

"Lexie, I'm sure nothing happened to anyone they more

than likely just moved somewhere better." Shadick whispered softly, pulling her up and into the circle of his arms.

"But nobody is here! That can only mean that something bad happened to them." Alexandria said softly.

"Like I said, I'm sure they moved somewhere. Perhaps something happened to make them move without real warning."

"Why would they do that and not let one of us know? It isn't Amethysts usual way of doing things."

"She knows that you had to concentrate on your training and maybe she had to make a really quick decision and had no time to let anyone, besides the creatures and mortals here know that they had to move."

"I agree with Shadick, Alex. It could explain why I haven't been receiving any letters from her in as long as I have, moving on short notice not having time to let anyone outside of the village know what was happening." Starlansha said quickly.

Shaking her head, she slowly walked deeper into the camp leaving the three of them to speculate. She did not want to hear any more of their theories.

As she walked slowly around the camp, she heard a sudden noise from the cave. Not seeing anything, she ignored it and walked towards a long-ago burned-out fire. Bending and looking at the remains, hoping to find some kind of clue as to what had happened glancing up when another noise resonated from the cave. Straightening up and cautiously walking towards the entrance of the cave, she tried to distinguish the sound she had heard.

Looking into the dark entrance but not seeing anything, she turned her back on the cave with a soft sigh, without warning she felt a pair of hands snap over her mouth and waist pulling her back into the shadowy entranceway "do not even attempt to make a noise to let them know where you are.

"Lexi? Where did you disappear to?" Shadick's voice drifted towards her. "Lexi?"

"I'm sure she just walked into the cave, Shadick." Starlansha told him.

"She knows that there is still a possibility of danger as we didn't secure the area."

"You know Alex..." Starlansha started then stopped as she walked around the corner. "Shadick!"

Alexandria, who was still being held captive, groaned softly as Shadick ran around the corner of the cave. "Let go of her, you filthy beast."

"I am not a 'filthy beast' you half breed." the centaur muttered.

"That's rich coming from one of the foul creatures that has

been killing innocent creatures. Creatures who did not deserve to be killed for a mad man's gain."

"I agree with Shadick, that so called 'leader' will cause not only his own, but his whole clans' demise." Starlansha said still looking at Alexandria

"That is one of the biggest reasons why I left his side. He had no sense of right and wrong, he is only in it for his own selfish reasons." the centaur muttered.

"Terri...?" Starlansha asked softly.

Slowly letting go of Alexandria, the centaur asked in surprise, "How do you know my name?"

Shadick, who had quickly pulled Alexandria towards him, asked, "If you really are Terri, why did you attack Lexie?"

"Alexandria, is that really you?"

Nodding slowly, Alexandria threw herself into Terri's arms "It's been way to long."

"I am sorry if I scared or even hurt you, but you have changed so much since the last time I saw you. And I don't just mean in the physical sense but the attitude and the way you carry yourself." Terri said, holding Alexandria against him.

"You didn't scare me; it was just a shock to be attacked like that and I didn't really change." Alexandria said, stepping back into the comfort of Shadick's arms.

"I am sorry I called you a half breed, Shadick."

"And I am sorry I called you a foul creature." Shadick replied, smiling slightly

"Where is everyone? Are they okay? Or where they all killed?" Starlansha asked, fearfully.

"No one has been killed, at least not someone you would know." Terri said, slowly.

"What exactly does that mean, Terri? Could I please be more specific." Alexandria asked.

"I think we need to hear at least a short version of what has happened in the last year and a half before we do anything else." Shadick said, nodding.

"A lot has happened, Amethyst zoned out a few days after the two of you left. We had trouble getting her out of it as she didn't eat, drink or sleep. She barely spoke, only one-word replies even then we couldn't really figure out what was wrong with her. About a week after that she snapped out of it, as though someone had snapped their fingers. She was still distant, but at least she was doing her job as queen.

"The camp expanded a lot and everyone was getting along, and new people were arriving almost every day. Most with little kids or with pregnant wives but we accommodated them, only happy to help anyone. Everything was peaceful for about six months, we even called back some of the sentries within the forest.

"Some of the newer members were on guard duty the one night when a group of the centaurs and a small number of their army attacked us. It was in the middle of the night, unexpected. We might have had a chance if we hadn't pulled back some of the guards and some of the older fighters had been keeping an eye open. Unfortunately, it was not the case. We lost fifteen of the new members before we finally chased them off; they lost only five in the onslaught.

"And after that first initial attack, they sent groups every week. Amethyst was getting slightly desperate. She sent out fairies and unicorns to look for an open area where we could set up a new camp. Everywhere they went was a mess, towns destroyed, families wandering around hoping for something to eat. Some had to be killed as they were too far gone.

"No one wanted to do it but not even the elves could save them. That is when Chadromida sent us a message that he knew of an open area where we could set up a new camp. But the only thing was... it was close to the Wastelands. We managed to move the Dwarves and Elves and some of the humans there first so they could start up the camp. As soon as the first houses were built, we started moving the other people. The new camp is extremely fortified, and everyone has been happy with their new homes."

"Fifteen men died?!" Alexandria asked eyes wide.

"Yes, it was a sad night. Most of them had just started families, had new born babies."

"Oh my..." Starlansha started but all of them looked towards the trees as they heard a new noise.

Falling quiet, they watched as two centaurs walked through the trees.

"I'm telling you, Balditha just wants us out of the camp for some reason. Probably scared that we use his plans against him or something." the first said.

"He's not scared of anything; I agree with him. We need to make sure that there aren't any more of these filthy people left." the second replied.

"We already know that they moved to that other camp near the Wastelands; the spy is reliable."

"But if we can capture one of them and get more information about what is happening in the camp, it would be very useful. We can never have too much information."

Roslata slipped off a root of a tree, landing in a small puddle of water, causing the two centaurs look towards the cave. Growling softly, Shadick pulled out his sword shortly, followed by Starlansha and Terri. Alexandria looked at them amazed.

She couldn't let them fight the two centaurs. It was too

dangerous, and there could be more of them in the forest just waiting for some sign that there was trouble. Closing her eyes, hoping that she still knew how to do it, she turned into a squirrel and ran towards the fountain, barely noticing Shadick trying to catch her.

As the two centaurs walked around the corner, she made sure to make a lot of noise, drawing their attention towards her and successfully distracting them.

"It's just a damn squirrel; let's kill the little beast." The one centaur muttered

The other centaur grabbed his companion's shoulder.

"It is not worth getting your blood pressure up over a stupid critter that can do us no harm. You need to learn better control, Rona."

"It is just since these people moved that we have not had a good fight in more than a year, Garza. It frustrates me when I cannot put my sword to good use."

"Do you remember when we murdered that one human?"

"You mean the one we pushed two swords into his abdomen at the same time? That was a classic."

"Talking about the murders you've committed again when you are supposed to do your jobs! You were sent here to scout for survivors." a third centaur sneered, appearing from the trees

"We've already scouted the area, Brakwa. There is nothing but a cute, stupid squirrel to see around here."

"Yes, but just think of the mess if those pesky mortals and magical creatures came back and caught us off guard."

"It's not as though they could beat us with their current number of warriors. It would be suicide for them."

"If they are desperate enough and caught us off-guard, they could take out a few good numbers of our own warriors before we can group. Now stop playing, and let's get back to camp. Sir Justren wants to go over some strategies."

As soon as they were sure that the three centaurs had disappeared, Shadick ran to Alexandria just as she turned back into her human form.

"Never do that again! You could've been caught!" he said seriously.

"But they didn't, and that is what matters." Alexandria said, putting her hand against Shadick's cheek and smiling slightly.

"Just promise me not to do that again. You almost gave me a heart attack."

"I'm sorry to say it Alex, but it was quite a dangerous stunt." Starlansha said, fingering the pendant around her neck.

"Isn't that the pendant Prince Jacques gave you, Star?"

Alexandria asked quickly, changing the subject.

"Who is Prince Jacques?" Shadick asked frowning.

"Yes, it is." she replied, sighing softly. "It doesn't matter that he listened to my grandfather about us being 'traitors'. I still have strong feelings for him."

"Of course you do and as soon as this war is over you two can catch up with each other again." Alexandria said, smiling.

"I asked who this Jacques is?!" Shadick said a bit louder.

"I will tell you about Star's love when we are safe and camping sometime."

Nodding, Starlansha asked, "Do you wish me to ask my grandmother for some horses to borrow so we can travel to Valencia?"

"Yes please, it would go much faster on horseback."

"Okay, then please give me a few minutes to contact my grandmother and organise it."

Grabbing Alexandria's hand, Shadick started pulling her to a secluded spot, kissing her feverously. His hands bunched up in her hair, and her arms were behind his neck as they kissed as though there was no tomorrow.

"It's been way too long." he whispered, pulling back slightly.

"I know what you mean, but we can't right now, the others are too close." Alexandria replied.

Sighing softly, he nodded and then walked back towards the others.

Chapter 5

Spirit Melee

They were standing in a small group just talking about things that came to mind, trying to avoid topics about the war or what they had done the past year and a half. Shadick kept glancing at Alexandria; she seemed to not be completely there. Her eyes kept glazing over, only to be pulled back from whatever was on her mind when Starlansha touched her arm.

Had this been happening a lot while she was away with training? And that is why Starlansha knew what to do? Or was it the first time it happened? He wanted to ask them, but he didn't want to seem like he was interfering in whatever was happening.

Glancing at the wolves, he realised that they were also looking at Alexandria and acting as though something was amiss. They only acted like this when they were around people they didn't know, or if there was a magical disturbance somewhere close by. It couldn't be the latter as he didn't feel anything out of place.

"Alex? Did you hear me?" he heard Starlansha ask. "Alex!"

"Sorry, what did you say?" Alexandria asked, frowning.

"I was asking if you would like a sip of water. You are dreadfully pale."

"I feel fine. I haven't had much sun the last while, remember?"

Starlansha didn't reply, shaking her head helplessly.

"Lexie are you sure you are okay? I agree with Star; maybe you should lay down for a bit." Shadick said, stepping closer to Alexandria

"I'm fine, I promise." Alexandria replied.

"She's just looking for attention." Roslata muttered softly.

"No she is not, Rosy. If she was she would've mentioned something, not keep denying that something is wrong." Starlansha replied.

Without warning, a dark energy surrounded Alexandria. Shadick, who was closest to her, tried grabbing her. He only got thrown against a tree by the energy surrounding her. Then before all of their eyes, Alexandria disappeared, leaving an insignificant bit of power behind.

Landing lightly on what seemed to be the ground,

Alexandria glanced around, frowning slightly.

"Shadick!" she screamed. "Shadick, where are you?"

She couldn't understand it; she had been next to Shadick just a minute ago, and now she was standing in apparent nothingness. Not seeing or hearing anything except the lightning. Surely, she had just fallen asleep and was having a weird dream. Yet, this was nothing to what she had dreamt the last while.

Sighing softly, she tried to open a portal back to Shadick. It only glimmered slightly before disappearing. Shaking her head and trying to teleport back to her friends, she seemed to be in a magic isolated area, as her powers were not working at all.

"Your attempts to escape are quite amusing, but I think I should inform you that there is no way out of here..." a male voice said.

"I will find a way out of this place." Alexandria said, spinning around and looking for the owner of the voice.

"The only way out of this place is to battle and win in a fight against me. And I am sorry to inform you that no one has been able to defeat me in over a thousand battles. They all died of madness."

"Well, I am not them, and they did not have friends who would try everything to get me out. But even without them, you cannot keep me here. I will get out, even if I have to kill you in the process."

"If I was afraid that you would be able to defeat me, I would not have pulled you here. Although I must say, your attempt to resist my magic was rather entertaining, although entirely useless."

"Then why don't you show yourself so we can fight and I can get back to my friends."

"Oh yes, how rude of me." the voice said.

Before Alexandria's eyes, a tall young man stepped out from the nothingness, coming to a stop in front of her. She couldn't help but stare at the figure; he had to be over 6 feet and had black hair with blonde streaks; his emerald eyes had an evil glint in them, showing that he didn't care about what people thought.

"Strange..." the young man said.

"And what is so strange?" Alexandria asked, crossing her arms in front of her chest.

"When I show myself to someone, they get this instant fear in their eyes knowing that no matter what they did, they knew that they would not get out of here. You, on the other hand, show only confidence."

"Sorry to put a chip in your seemingly flawless ego, but I fear nothing; I know what I am capable of."

"Yes I am sure you do, but then again, so did the others."

"Maybe so, but I can see that me not bowing or showing fear at your appearance has knocked you off your ego trip slightly."

"Such confidence can only mean that I will have a good fight, which I have not had in centuries. I am quite excited."

Shaking her head in frustration, she pulled out the Coral Daggers on her hips, holding them at the ready.

"Oh yes, I forgot to mention..." he said, waving his hand and making the daggers disappear, "no weapons allowed, only magic."

"You could have mentioned that beforehand, but I can still beat you." Alexandria replied, then added, "I think before we start... Introductions are in order. I dislike killing someone if I do not know their name."

"Where are my manners today?! My name is Jace... I am a Spirit Warrior. Perhaps you have heard of my kind before?" Jace asked, and when she shook her head, "Oh! This is your first-time meeting someone like me?! Then you are lucky that you did not have to go through the other fights only to end up dying in this one. It's happened many times before."

"Other fights?"

"Well, of course! Did you think the elementals would let you gain all this power, all of their powers basically, without making sure that you really deserve it? No, dear you are quite mistaken."

"Let me just get this straight; I have to win to gain my freedom and 'the right' to use my powers? And if I don't win, I lose not only my powers but my life as well? That seems kind of unfair."

"When you win, you not only get your freedom and the right to use 'spirit', or whichever elemental you are fighting, but you will grow within your magic as well, as gaining a stone containing a lot of power. But it can only be activated when you put all five elemental stones together. But you are correct about the losing part, though. I get all your powers making me even stronger."

"I don't see how that is fair; But let's get this over with, shall we? So I can get back to my friends."

"Very well then..." Jace said, disappearing.

Alexandria looked around, slightly panicked, when she felt the energy around her change. How was she supposed to attack him when she couldn't even see him?

Without warning, three bolts of energy were thrown towards her. She had just enough time to put her arms in front of her face before they hit. Summoning her own energy, she threw it in the direction the bolts had come from, but it just disappeared.

Suddenly there were five balls of energy around her, taunting her by coming closer to her and then retreating over and over again. Getting a little frustrated at Jace's games, she didn't notice her blood starting to boil, making her spirit turn on itself. Thrusting her arms out on either side of her, she sent energy towards the balls surrounding her, destroying a few of them.

Out of breath and falling to her knees, shaking her head lightly, trying to make the fuzziness go away, she couldn't understand why she was suddenly so tired. Sitting down, trying to catch her breath, she put a shield around her body to stop the energy balls from hitting her. Closing her eyes, she tried finding the trigger of the sleepiness. At first, she found nothing, then realised that Jace was trying to make her destroy herself.

Grinning evilly and standing up slowly, gathering her energy around her, she lightly scanned the area, knowing that she could hit him if she put out just enough energy. His energy balls were still slamming against her shield without success. Closing her eyes once again, she quickly let out the shield of energy in all directions, not missing a single spot. She heard his groan before she saw him fall to the ground; he was immediately back on his feet.

She could see that he was now fighting at full power, still

trying to make her turn on herself. Sending a massive ball of energy towards her, she threw her hands out in front of her trying to stop it, only to be pushed back by the sheer force of it a few meters.

Slowly lifting her head towards him, her eyes flashing silver, she started running towards him, summoning two spirit swords in each hand, thrusting the energy into his abdomen, making them both lift into the air.

He grabbed the swords and made them disappear within him, in the same moment punching Alexandria in the face, which she was able to stop with her thoughts. She didn't see his leg coming towards her a second later, which hit her in the stomach and caused her to bend over double as the air left her lungs.

Knowing not to waste a minute, she grabbed his leg and started to spin around, gaining momentum with each turn, and when she felt him start to resist the force, she let him go watching him hit a wall and fall to the ground. She quickly appeared above him with her Coral Daggers now in hand, crossing them over his neck.

"Give up before I force them into your neck and kill you." she whispered softly "No one can control me, and no one can use my own powers against me."

"You're telling me if I keep fighting, I die?" he asked

through his teeth, breathing heavily.

Shrugging slightly, she said, "It's just about the same arrangement you made with me. But there is a difference between the two, if you are willing to listen."

"Let's hear it then."

"I am giving you a chance to change what you've been doing for centuries."

"You can have control of my powers; I am dead either way."

"I am not taking your powers. You are going to need them if you agree. But complete control over spirit would be helpful."

"I already told you; let's hear your deal."

"Help me, the magical creatures and mortals in the fight against the centaurs. Choose to join our side before they come for you and give you this option, although they will force you to join their side."

"You aren't going to take my powers or kill me?" he asked, smiling slightly.

"No, I will just take what you promised; and I have told you my deal, so decide."

Jumping up and hugging her tightly, completely pushing the daggers aside with his energy, he said, "I accept your deal, Alexandria! You are the nicest person I have ever met, not to mention the only person who was able to get me near defeat, and even if the others had been able to get me near defeat me know, they would've killed me without a second thought. And joining you in this war would be an honour."

Smiling slightly and taking a slow breath and glancing around, she replied, "So how do we get out of this place?"

"Oh, that's easy." Jace said, grinning while grabbing Alexandria's hand.

"Is the touching really necessary? Shadick won't be very happy if he sees you touching me." Alexandria muttered, shaking her head.

"Oh yes, your boyfriend! It is absolutely necessary, otherwise only I will teleport out of this world and to them, and you will be left behind."

Slightly pulling a face nodding slowly, "If it is absolutely necessary."

Jace, who still had a huge grin on his face, pulled Alexandria into a hug. As she was struggling to move away from him, everything started moving around them. She closed her eyes in surprise and held onto him, but just as she was about to complain that he hadn't warned her about this part, she felt her feet touch solid ground once again.

"Lexie!" she heard Shadick shout. "Let go of her, you miscreant."

"Oh, how delightful! It's the first time in centuries that someone has called me a miscreant." Jace said, grinning while still holding her.

Moving out of his arms quickly and accidentally stumbling slightly on a hidden root, she felt Shadick's arms moving around her. "I'm okay, Shadick. Just a bit winded."

"What happened? You just disappeared without warning, and who exactly is this... guy? And why are you holding your daggers?" Shadick asked, frowning.

"His name is Jace. He is the Spirit Melee; I had to fight him for my life as well as my freedom. When I won, I offered him a hand in friendship and that he joins us in the war, which he accepted."

"He didn't hurt you I hope." Shadick muttered, cupping her face in his hands

"I've been hurt worse." she said, sheathing the daggers.

"I could have killed her, but I spared her because she is such a nice person, and you told it completely wrong, Alexa!" Jace said, still grinning.

Growling softly, Shadick slowly stepped towards Jace but was stopped when he felt Alexandria's hand on his shoulder, "Just try ignoring Jace, it seems as though he is always in a mischievous mood."

"But Lexie, he just admitted to almost killing you!"

Shadick said.

"It was a death match, Shadick; I could've killed him but thought against it. There's been enough killing and more death still to come in this damned war."

"She's right, Shadick; there has been enough loss." Starlansha intervened

"Oh, how wonderful! The Mermalani twins!" Jace almost shouted.

"Hush!! Do you want the centaurs to catch us?" Roslata sneered.

"We have another person to travel with us? It is getting a rather big group not to mention large groups tend to become more noticeable." Terri added.

"That is why I will be turning into a small stone and meld with one of your daggers, Alexia!" Jace said, looking at Roslata appreciatively.

"It would be better that way; we don't want to be too noticeable; one more or one less could make the difference between getting to the new village or getting caught." Starlansha said, glancing between her sister and Jace, smiling slightly

"I see the horses have arrived while I was gone." Alexandria said, turning towards the four horses

"Yes, they did. I am, however slightly surprised at my

grandmother's choice."

"Why is that, Star?" Shadick asked, still holding Alexandria.

"Because the black horse is called Nightmare and the dark brown one is Fatum or Doom. The names are kind of self-explanatory."

As they watched, Nightmare slowly walked towards Alexandria and seemed to look her up and down. Then he sniffed, breathed deeply and let out a neigh before resting his head on her shoulder, completely oblivious to Shadick standing behind Alexandria.

Slowly stepping away from the duo, Shadick walked towards Fatum, who watched him through narrowed eyes. Fatum, who was obviously trying to scare Shadick, reared onto his hind legs while Shadick just watched him lazily until he got back onto all fours. He snorted softly before strolling towards Shadick in acceptance.

Looking at the two horses in surprise, Starlansha muttered, "I guess there is no problem with the horses after all."

"Please tell me you didn't expect them to hurt us." Alexandria joked.

"Knowing the horse's history, I am a bit surprised. But I am thankful that we have no problems."

Stepping forwards, still smiling, Jace said, "I think it's about time to start this journey."

Roslata, who had been quiet through the exchange, started walking past Jace and towards her horse, but he grabbed her arm and pulled her towards him before giving her a very affectionate kiss. Gasping softly and breaking free from the embrace, Roslata slapped Jace through the face and ran to her horse. He smiled contentedly, hugging a shocked Alexandria, while Shadick growled at him, stepping closer.

Jace slowly changed into a pitch-black stone before shooting to the dagger on her right hip.

Chapter 6

The Journey

"That is one fascinating character." Terri said, shaking his head as they watched Jace disappear.

"He is rude and uncouth and has absolutely no manners at all." Roslata said, slightly flustered.

"It looked like you were enjoying it actually." Starlansha commented.

"Lanshy, then you were clearly not looking properly. I slapped him, or did you miss that?"

"Let us not argue about it." Terri said quietly.

"I agree; Jace is just very enthusiastic about everything; even when I had the opportunity to kill him, he kept smiling." Alexandria said, jumping onto Nightmare's back. "Now shall we get started?"

Nodding slightly, Shadick, Starlansha and Roslata jumped on the horses' backs while Terri slowly walked towards Alexandria.

"Do you mind if we talk a bit while we travel, just so I can inform you of the new camp and the security?" he asked her quietly.

"Of course, I don't mind. I would really appreciate it. Just so we can see if any improvements are needed and if that is the case, we can come up with a few ideas to improve whatever needs improving." she replied.

Nodding in agreement, Terri led the way into the forest whispering to Alexandria. "It was an effort from Luanda; you remember her, I take it?"

"Yes, she was the butcher's daughter and was engaged to Michael, who became the general for the McLeod's group, if I remember correctly. But then again, it might have changed in the past year and a half that I was away."

"Indeed, you are correct they got married in the year and are expecting their first child."

"That's great! I am happy for them, although it is an awful time to have a child now, with the fighting and the uncertainty, it is rather hazardous. But knowing Michael, he will protect them with everything he can."

"Well, she is a very creative person; she had sketched Valencia without even knowing what it was. She was very shocked when Michael mentioned the layout, they were planning for the new camp one evening; she immediately ran to Amethyst with the drawings she had made."

"And what was Amethyst's take on the drawing?"

"She believes that Luanda is some kind of seer, which means that you are not the only individual with magical abilities. However, Amethyst is doing some research into the whole thing; she had made some kind of discovery before I came here but wouldn't say what it was."

"She can sometimes love her secrets, not to mention when she puts a lot of research into it."

"I agree with you on that one but going on to the actual layout of the camp, there are basically the four main camps, a fairy castle, homes for the generals and their families and a few extra houses. Then there are the training fields, ground were the dwarves make their weapons, general meeting area and fields for growing some of the vegetables etc., oh and an ocean was created for the mer-people if they are interested. It is not as big as Atlantican though, but it is big enough to be quite comfortable and, most importantly, safe."

"It sounds fantastic! Pretty well organised, but you haven't mentioned the security."

"There are four entrances, North, South, East and West, each has a guard tower with guards changing every six hours. And the whole of Valencia is surrounded by a river and can only be reached by draw bridges, and even if someone got across the river, they would suffer because of the desert."

"And Luanda drew the whole of Valencia without knowing any of the plans?"

"Indeed, she did."

"That is actually quite amazing; at least I don't have to feel left out anymore." Alexandria laughed softly.

"Hey, you two! We've reached the edge of the forest." Shadick told them, frowning.

"That went by rather quickly; I expected the journey to take longer." Alexandria said surprised.

"For you, yes; it felt like an eternity for me."

"I'm sorry for neglecting you, Shadick. I just really wanted to know the layout of the camp so that I know."

"It's ok...ay." Shadick said, stopping Doom and looking at a point past Alexandria's shoulder.

Turning around quickly, Alexandria gasped in surprise.

"What happened to this village? And more importantly, what is the village's name?"

"The centaurs showed it no respect, just like everything else that they come into contact with." Terri said sadly.

"And the village's name?"

"Domon dogou... Or as it used to be called Justren village. I do not know the original name."

"McLeod's, my home town. It is the village I was born and

raised in."

"Yes, the name sounds about right, it is now home of the damned, those few souls who died such a violent death that they could not move on. I suggest we continue; people have been known to have gotten hurt, and some even died when they entered the village."

"Lexie, let's go. I don't think we'll get anything useful from the village. And we have no resources if someone were to get hurt inside the village." Shadick said softly.

"I agree with Terri and Shadick, Alex. It does look very uninviting and dangerous." Starlansha said.

They all urged the horses forward once more, passing Alexandria slowly; she watched them pass her slowly then glanced back at her old village frowning, slightly. When she was sure that no one could stop her, she turned Nightmare towards the village and raced towards a corner, hearing faint screams from the others as she disappeared around the corner.

****

"Easy now, Night." Alexandria whispered, slowing the horse while glancing around.

She was sure that her parent's house had been around there somewhere. Taking a deep slow breath, she dismounted the horse, keeping the reigns in her hand. As she glanced around again, her eyes widened when she saw what had been her parent's home. It was a mess, and the centaurs had obliterated it, not leaving a wall intact.

She walked among the rubble and slowly let go of the horses' reigns while searching for something that had not been destroyed. She gasped softly, falling lightly to the floor by a picture frame, slowly picking it up and turning it around smiling when she saw that it had been her favourite picture. She had been about three years old. Her father had picked her up laughingly while her mom had looked on smiling. It had been one of the happiest days of her life.

Careful not to damage the picture more than it already was, she removed it from the ruined frame, frowning when a silver spiralled heart fell out of the frame along with a note. Picking up both, her fingers gently curling into her palm holding the necklace, she looked at the note more closely. It read 'The twin is with blood'.

That made absolutely no sense, but knowing that she didn't have much time to think about it at the moment, she put all three discoveries in a pouch by her one dagger. Without warning, she knew that she was not alone anymore. The air was cooler, she could smell something almost like mould, death, and she was sure that she could see movement from the corner of her eye, and Nightmare was very agitated.

"I do believe we have overstayed our welcome, Night." Alexandria muttered, taking the horses' reigns and slowly walking away from what had once been her home.

Suddenly she heard a sniffle coming from behind her, and spinning around quickly, she saw a young girl crouched where only moments before she had been standing.

"Little girl? Everything will be okay; just come over here so we can go look for your parents." Alexandria said, frowning when she got no reply, slowly taking a step towards the girl. "Sweetie, are you hurt?"

The girl slowly stood up, turning even slower and lowering a long grey cloak and revealing the face of an old woman, an evil grin on her face. The girl-woman laughed madly, pointing behind Alexandria, who spun around, instantly regretting that she had turned back to the house. A few steps away from Nightmare was a ghostly knight, his two-handed sword pointed towards Alexandria's chest. He was purposefully riding closer to them on his horse, grinning from underneath his armour.

Exclaiming softly, she quickly jumped onto Nightmare's back and, in the same movement, kicked his flanks racing back the way they had come. Glancing back, she saw that the ghostly numbers had grown and were chasing after her with a speed she had not expected from anyone, let alone the dead. She urged Nightmare forward as they rounded the corner, seeing Shadick riding slowly towards them.

"Shadick, move!" she shouted at him as she raced past him.

"Lexi what's...?" he started asking but saw the ghosts and quickly turned around and raced after her catching up quickly.

The two horses jumped over a fallen log in synchronisation and raced towards the group.

"You can slow down now; the ghosts can't pass that line. Amethyst put a spell around the perimeter when the ghosts started leaving the village and attacking anyone who passed close by." Terri told them.

Shadick and Alexandria stopped the horses, turning to look back at the village, watching the ghosts who were leering at them, making strange noises before disappearing one by one. The girl-woman was glaring balefully at Alexandria.

"That was way too close." Alexandria whispered.

"I did try warning you about the ghosts in the village, but you paid no attention." Terri muttered.

"What exactly did you go after, Alex?" Starlansha asked.

"I wanted to see if I couldn't perhaps retrieve or save something from my parent's home." Alexandria replied.

"And did you find anything worth risking your neck? And I mean something besides the ghosts that wanted to kill you."

"A picture of my parents and me not to mention a slight mystery that needs to be solved before it drives me crazy."

"What kind of mystery, honey?" Shadick asked.

Taking the picture, note and necklace out, she handed them to him.

"I found the necklace behind the picture, and I have no idea what the note means, but I know that it is my father who had written it."

"'The twin is with blood'. That doesn't make sense at all." he said frowning.

"If you think about it logically, everyone knows that Alex doesn't have a twin running around out there, and the necklace fell out as well; so, an identical necklace is with a family member. Someone you don't know about Alex." Starlansha said, thoughtfully.

"I'm sure my father would've told me if I had family somewhere."

"Not if he had shamed the family in some way." Shadick added.

"I was thinking more along the lines of an illegitimate child. An accident that your father never told your mother about because he was afraid of what she would do if she found out about him or her." Starlansha said.

"My father was not the kind of person who would cheat on his wife. He loved my mother and I way too much to do something so irresponsible." Alexandria retorted.

"I'm not trying to make you feel bad or talk bad about your father, Alex, but just think about it carefully."

"I will not think of my father in that light. Not now, not ever. he was an honourable man. Now, can we get moving, please?"

"I think we should look out for someplace to set up camp for the night, preferably away from the village and before nightfall, as one never knows what creatures wanders around here." Terri said, walking away from the village, the rest following slowly.

Chapter 7

Shadick's Tale

"I never thought my home village would be so abused and destroyed. I only saw it as a positive, good village where all the villagers stood together." Alexandria told Shadick sadly while they were travelling.

"No one expected that the centaurs would return after being banned. And you know that if the villagers had a chance to protect and fight for the village, they would've. I know that the villagers loved their homes." Shadick replied.

"I just wish I could've been there, maybe I could've stopped it from happening."

"I talked to some of the villagers before my trip. There was no warning at all; they came like thieves in the night."

"I'm sure that I could've stopped it."

"Stop beating yourself up, my love."

"I still wish..."

"I wish that we could have stopped it as well, and it's sad

that we couldn't."

"And I wish that we drop this depressing subject." Roslata added, faking a yawn.

"It is normal for her to want to talk about her home town, Rosy. Just like you would talk about the cottage or even grandmamma and granddad's kingdom." Starlansha said, frowning at her sister.

"I talk about the cottage because that is where our parents raised us. It was their home as much as it is ours. But if you had not noticed, they have been thrown aside ever since we had to start helping her on her impossible journey! They have been shoved aside, and we have been told that we should not keep going on about this subject as it happened. There was nothing that could have been done to save them."

"No one said that to us."

"Not when you were around perhaps, but all I have been hearing is that we should put her first and that is what our parents would have wanted. So, I should stop moaning and groaning about how my mom and dad gave their lives for people willing to sacrifice their own lives for the 'greater good'."

"I never had a chance to meet your parents, but from what I have heard, they were great people." Alexandria said frowning.

"Whatever you say, princess."

"Shall we set up camp for the night? It is getting rather late, and the sun will be setting soon." Terri asked.

"That is a good idea, I shall go find some logs for the fire, and perhaps I can catch something for dinner." Shadick added, jumping off his horse and walking into the nearby forest.

A few hours later, they were sitting next to the fire, each lost in their own thoughts; conversation was far and in-between.

Shadick glanced up at Alexandria's quiet form and sighed softly, "I guess the time has come that I tell you what happened on my journey. You have asked me multiple times that I tell you, but I kept dodging the subject." he said softly, lightly tucking a strand of hair behind her ear.

"If she does not want to hear, I am more than willing to lend an all too willing ear." Terri said with a grin, stepping closer.

"I want to hear what happened, but only if you want to tell us." Alexandria said, sitting up.

"It is not that I don't want to tell you; it is just that I had to work through a few things that had been weighing heavily on my mind. There were a few things that happened that I had to do, most of which I was not very happy with." Shadick said, smiling sadly.

"Everyone has had to do some things in the last few years that we regret and wish we could take back."

"True. I just sometimes wonder if we shouldn't try harder at not doing some of the stuff."

"What happened on the journey that made you wonder so hard about this?"

"When I left to start my quest shortly after our conversation, it was a hard journey, and I immediately knew that it was going to be difficult. For some reason, I had believed that the Centaurs had moved away from the Wastelands, but I quickly realised my wrong assumption when I reached Dragon Mountain and saw a forced march. It took me quite a while to find a way into the Wastelands. There were numerous fights, and I was just considering giving up when I was able to get through."

"At least you didn't get hurt too much during these fights." Alexandria said wide-eyed.

"These were mere scuffles than true fights, and I did get hurt by the end of my mission. But I was able to get help, and I healed quickly." he replied.

"Stop interrupting the man, Alexandria. We will never hear the whole story at this rate." Terri muttered.

"Sorry, I didn't mean to." Alexandria said, biting her lip.

"It is okay; I don't mind the questions. It gives me a chance to get my story straight." Shadick said, kissing her cheek. "When I was finally able to get into the Wastelands, I realised that I had not done enough research. I had no idea where the mountain area was that my father had spoken about. But there was no chance that I was turning around when I had worked so hard to get in, in the first place. Do you know that they have patrols around the entire Wasteland? They make sure that no one gets in or out without their knowledge or consent. I spent a few weeks just trying to figure out my next move. I made sure not to spend too long in one area so as not to make myself visible to the Centaurs.

"About three weeks later, I saw something that I had not expected. Signs of life, and I was a thousand times over sure that it was not Centaurs, as they lived in very rudimentary shacks that could and would be broken down on a weekly basis.

"I kept watch of this area for a few days, and when I finally saw movement, I approached the group. After some panic on their part, they welcomed me and allowed me into their burrow. I quickly realised that they consisted not just of humans but of fairies and many other different creatures. At first, I was shocked, but then they told me their histories.

"Turns out that they were chased out of their homes and villages because of their beliefs. When they realised that they had nowhere to go they made their homes together in the Wastelands. The Centaurs left them alone for the most part. Only when they felt murderous would they attack them, but mostly were left alone. I asked them if they would ever return to 'normal' civilisation, and they said that people weren't ready for unity as of yet.

"They were shocked to hear that there was a change happening because of the Centaurs. When I informed them that the creatures and humans were standing together and even living together, they seemed to reconsider their standing. I spent a while with them, just learning about them and even receiving some training.

"Their leader helped me figure out which mountain I was looking for; he told me that there were a few minor mountain ranges that were not natural, and they were not what I was searching for. He then told me about a place that even the Centaurs avoided. A dark mountain that if someone brave or stupid enough went there, they never returned. It was with some trepidation that I realised that this was what I wanted.

"My training increased as I wanted to be prepared for anything that might be thrown my way, and in return, I helped them defend their homes from the Centaurs. When I thought I was finally ready, we saddled some horses, and they took me to the mountain. I immediately knew that it was the right place. You could sense darkness coming from within, from miles away. When we were standing outside, they informed me that it was as far as they would go; they did not trust the place and would not put their people in danger when there was no need for it.

"They agreed to camp with me for just the night before returning to their camps. As we were unsure if the Centaurs ever travelled that far, we had two guards keeping watch. When we woke up the next morning, we had breakfast; then I gathered my things and walked into the cave.

"There were no lights, and I could not see anything. Just when I was starting to wonder how I would find my way around, one of the fairies appeared in front of me. She offered to help me as she was one of the few brave enough to go close enough."

"The fairies there are the same ones that live with Amethyst and the others?" Starlansha asked.

"For the most part they are yes, but their outfits are different and their lights changed to fit in with their surroundings. They are browner whereas Amethysts fairies are bright with happy colours."

"Guess that makes sense. They would really stand out if

they were that colourful."

"You are seriously telling us that there are places that even the Centaurs fear?" Terri asked, scratching his chin.

"Yes. At the time, I could not understand why anyone would fear mountains, but once I got into it I realised why they did not go there, why no one dares to venture that far.

"The destruction was clear even at the start of the cave, and it only got worse the deeper we travelled. We saw thousands of corpses and skeletons laying on the sides of the tunnels. There were hundreds of different tunnels, and most of them led to dead ends. This journey delayed us quite a lot as we had to turn around and follow another tunnel.

"When we finally found the right tunnel, we were exhausted and just wanted to die of hunger when the entire mountain shook as a roar erupted from ahead of us. We looked at each other and slowly inched forward. What we saw almost caused us to run back and not look back.

"I have heard rumours of the Minotaurs and how they were some of the fiercest of beasts still left over from the history books. But none of the rumours mentioned that they were as huge as this one, standing in front of us. I guessed that he was 15 feet tall, and its one arm was bigger than my whole body. I was unsure of how we would be able to fight this beast. To make things worse, he carried a sword as big as one of the horns on its head. A mage hanging on the wall, bigger than I thought was possible; before we could hide, he turned towards us with dark, pitiless eyes that seemed to cut into your whole body and soul."

"What did you do? And how did you know for sure that the Breastplate was even there?" Starlansha asked.

"At first I was unsure, but then I spotted it in the far corner of the cave. You see, my father had drawn a picture of the Breastplate as well as the sword, so I knew that it was what I had been looking for. It was unique, and even from a distance, I could see the outstanding craftsmanship that had gone into making it.

"As he walked towards us, the ground shook with each step. Lionella asked me if I thought he would surrender the Breastplate without causing a fight, something that we quickly realised was just a dream. He swung his sword at us, and we just rolled out of the way. I shouted at him that I just wanted the Breastplate and did not want to fight, but he just laughed and attacked again.

"It was a tough battle that went on for hours, and I finally got the upper hand when Lionella flew into his face and caused him to sneeze and lose his balance. I was able to run to the corner and grab the Breastplate and just got out in time when he got up. Luck was finally in our favour as he could not move out of the cave as he was too big.

"Not wanting to push our luck more than that, we ran until we got outside, and even then, we could hear the roars and groans coming from inside. We were shocked to see the rest of the group that we had left still there, seemingly just as shocked to see me alive. But as soon as their fear and shock faded, they handed us food and drinks. They wanted to leave immediately, but they quickly realised that I was too exhausted to move and would not make it more than a couple of steps. They gave up trying to get us to move and just let me rest for the next two days."

"You got the Breastplate, and your companions did not want to look at it?" Terri asked.

"They did want to look, but I refused to let them, informed them that it was mine, and for the next while, I did not want anyone to touch it in case it was just a dream. They grudgingly accepted."

"Sounds like you had a hard journey." Starlansha said seriously.

"It was, and when we returned to their camp, the leader banished Lionella for helping me as much as she did. Accused me of seducing her and putting her in danger that had not been hers to take on. I left shortly after that as they refused to listen to me about why she helped me. She told me that she would help me find the sword and flew off but promised to be back in time for the battle."

"And they were surprised that we have started getting along with the humans as well as magical creatures? They chased one of their own away because she was the only one brave enough to want to help." Alexandria said, shaking her head.

"It seems to be the attitude of most creatures except those that now live together, although I have seen that arguments still break out every now and then. But before it gets serious, it gets sorted out." Terri said matter-of-factly. "That is why the village was built the way it is. It gives everyone space and privacy, yet they can quickly run to others' help if needed."

"It sounds like it is perfect." Alexandria noted.

"Unfortunately, it is not perfect, but it will do until we get more opportunities to improve it and make it perfect."

"We will hopefully get a chance to do just that soon enough. Once we get there and we are able, I think we should start working on it."

"Do not get too excited or make too many plans. You never know if you will be disappointed when things go wrong, and it does not happen. And do not get me wrong, I want to make the village better just as much as you do. But we need to be realistic about all of this. The Centaurs can start up the war at any time, and we can't be busy with building houses or what not." Starlansha said, seriously.

"I think what Lexi is trying to do is great; think and concentrate on the positive. If everybody was only thinking about the negative things, then we would get nowhere. But you also have a valid point. We can't start something huge, but we can start improvements on the little things." Shadick quickly interrupted.

"As much as I like the positive attitude, we need to get to Valencia first, see what exactly has happened since I left and speak to Amethyst before we can do anything." Terri said, frowning and walking towards the horses.

"What is wrong with him? He was fine up until a little while ago." Shadick asked, confused.

"Let us leave him for now and get some rest." Alexandria said, shrugging.

"That sounds like a good idea. We have a long day ahead of us." Starlansha said, smiling.

"And hopefully this time, we will remember that there are more people in this group that matter than just two or three." Roslata said, turning her back on the group.

"No one said anything about only a few people being important. Everyone has a place in the group and has earned it in one way or another, Roslata." Shadick told her

"It sure as hell has not felt that way since she came into your life, Shadick. Others mattered a lot more to you then than and respect was shown. Now it is all about one person or maybe two, because they have a story on their hearts that needs to be told."

"Rosy, that is out of line, and you know it! No one in this group thinks that they matter more than anyone else. In fact, everyone is trying to make things better for everyone and not just themselves." Starlansha added, walking to her sister.

"Perhaps one of these days, I will see what you are talking about, but right now, I am not. If you will excuse me, I am going to sleep."

Alexandria watched in shock as Roslata walked away from the fire and sit down not too far from the horses. Starlansha ran after her sister putting her arm around her and whispering softly in her ear.

"Have I done something wrong?" she asked, turning to Shadick.

"You have done nothing, so you do not have to worry. Roslata just has a lot on her mind and is in fact used to people giving her all the attention and not others. Do not worry yourself about it. She will get over it just like everything else." Shadick told her, pulling her into his arms and holding her tightly, allowing her to fall asleep.

Chapter 8

Windy Well

"Tell me, when did you get over the whole need to tell Starlansha where you are going?" Shadick asked, holding her hand as they walked away from their temporary camp. "The last time we had any time together, most of it was spent telling everyone that we would be back in about an hour to do this or that."

"Since we were in Trilantican a week, Roslata very kindly told me that I didn't need to tell them where I was going, as they did not care. It was an irritating trait that I should have someone looked at. She suggested the monster in the hole, which I later found out was actually real, and even though nobody technically knew what was in the hole, it was just an accepted fact that it was a monster. They also used this trick on their young when they were misbehaving.

"I asked the Queen about it, but she said something about the monster as well as the hole had appeared randomly the one day a few days after the girls left to return to their parents' home. It had occurred to them to have it investigated, but they had heard reports from some of the villagers that they had seen some creatures disappearing when they had approached it." Alexandria said, taking a deep breath and pausing as she saw Shadick laughing. "What did I say wrong?"

"Not wrong, but I am happy to announce that you still babble and go off on a different subject from the main subject. The last few days, I have been wondering if you had completely changed from when you had left. You seem more confident, which is a fantastic thing but you have been so quiet that I was not sure if something had happened to make you change the babbling. If you ask me, it's a terrible thing, because that is who you are."

"During the training, there was not a lot of chance to talk. When we did have a break, Starlansha had to give all her attention to her sister, so I did not want to bother. Roslata was never happy being forced to be a part of the entire training thing, and she made sure that everyone knew it.

"I would end up swimming around and just observing some things to keep busy and not completely lose my mind. I actually spend some off time getting to know the people in and around the village and listen to them instead of talking their heads off each time."

"That was very sweet of you, although you didn't need to do that. I am sure that no one expected you to do that."

"I know that it was not expected of me, but it turned out that a lot of people needed someone to listen to them and not just reject them right off. The Queen actually called me into her 'business' room to thank me for bringing some of the issues to their notice."

"Then I am pleased that you did that and not just sat around arguing about a situation that could not change."

"Where are we?" she suddenly asked, looking around.

"We can't have gotten that far from the camp. We have only been walking for a few minutes! But I see what you mean, this village is not one I recognise. Although, if you think about it, the places have changed so much because of the Centaur attacks that this could be a well-known village. Perhaps we would not realise it because of attacks."

"Just when I think that I cannot be surprised by the actions of the Centaurs, I see something like this, and it just confirms that they have to be stopped. No amount of talking would make them change who and what they are.

"As if my hometown wasn't enough, they seem hellbent on destroying all the good things that exist in this world. If we can't stop them for whatever reason, what will happen to the places we know and those situated further away?"

"I acknowledge that, but there is no way for me to be sure, and I will not go out and guess at random."

"I get a feeling that the well over there is pulling us towards it, not that I'm sure why." she muttered as a wind whipped around them and seemed to force them closer. "I do not think that this is going to end up all too well."

Shadick grabbed her hand and together they tried to walk away from the well with the wind pulling them. With every successful step away from the well, they were pulled about five closer. When they glanced towards the well, they were only a few steps away. The glanced at each other and shook their heads. Making a decision, Alexandria took a deep breath and closed her eyes. She allowed the wind to take control of her body and stopped fighting a losing a battle.

"Well, that was a short trip. I was expecting to end up deep within a lava cave or something with the amount of power that had been put up to get us here." Shadick commented, and she opened her eyes.

"I was expecting to not still be alive if we gave up."

"We did not give up. We just decided that it would be for the best to rather face the enemy head-on than waste any more energy on fighting."

"Nice try, Shadick, but we both know that was not exactly

planned." She commented, glancing around.

"I am not sure why he is here, but that does not matter. My business is with you, Alexandria, and you alone." a voice whispered.

"I am here to help the love of my life! There was no way...." he started, but Alexandria put her hand on his arm.

"Am I to take it that you are one of the Elementals I need to fight? It is one of the most interesting traps I have seen. I assume that you are Wind?"

"You are correct. I considered just sending a wind to pick you up, but it did not seem very graceful. I do not want to be known as the Element that screwed up a mission because of something silly going completely wrong."

"That would be a tragedy. Now would it be at all possible for us to actually start fighting instead of just standing around here and talking as though we have not seen each other in years? It would be best, as I have not been known for patience the last while, and I do not want just attack, and you still had something to say."

A woman with ash blond hair was suddenly standing right in front of her, and she had a sneer on her face.

"This is not something that I am happy about. It was not by my choice that I came to this desolate place and live here as though I had a valid reason to, I don't believe having to fight you just to find out if you are worthy of my element.

"I was forced to come here by the 'higher ups' because they were bored, and no one had offered their lives or even a toe to come down here and do this. But it was decided that I, Meya, the most powerful of my kind, would be suited, and I was forcefully thrown here."

"I guess that you aren't the most powerful of your kind if they were still able to force you to come here then." Shadick commented.

"You insolent fool! What you do not know is that above me there are more people who are capable of things that I have not been able to because I am only bound by the wind. But it is good to know that you have made yourself known." she said and threw him against a wall sneering. "Now, stay there as my business is not with you. My business is with this witch who seems to be frozen in fear as she has not said anything."

"You guess wrong, I am not frozen in fear I was merely giving you a chance to get whatever is on your chest off and distracting you from everything around us." Alexandria said before punching Meya in the face and causing her to stumble a few feet backwards before running at her full speed, somersaulting over her head and kicking her again from behind.

She watched in satisfaction as she once again slid a few feet away, groaning when the Wind Element just stood up and took a deep breath, pulling all the air towards her and making breathing impossible. Shrugging she held her breath and ran towards her opponent once again, and as it seemed that she was too concentrated on what she was doing, it was easy to pretend to lose her balance so that she could effortlessly pull her opponents feet out from under her.

In doing that it caused the air to rush back into the room. She heard a grateful gasp coming from Shadick, but she knew that she should not let that distract her. As if in sync with her thoughts, Meya disappeared into the wind. She was left glancing around, trying to find her once again, ducking just in time as a punch was thrown at the back of her head. She quickly spun around on the spot and grabbed her hand and used her own momentum to help throw Meya across the room beside Shadick.

"How about we call it a win and we just go on with our business as though this was not happening?" she asked, sighing. "I know that there are going to be bigger fights in my future, and I also know that I am going to need all my strength for that."

"So, are you calling this a minor battle?" Meya shouted, forcing too much air into the room and causing them to take in too much air bending over double, coughing. "Unlike some of my 'relatives' I will not just decide to go easy on you because you are a nice person. I need to be heard, and it is too bad that you are the one that ended up being the one I am taking my anger out on as I will not go easy."

Alexandria glanced up at Shadick and flinched as he seemed to be in pain, but he was unable to do anything in his current position. She forced herself to stand up and make her body move when it seemed to shout to just give up. Once she was in motion, it became easier to move, and she ran towards Meya once again and threw a punch. It wasn't aimed at her face or her stomach, but at her throat.

Meya gasped in surprise as she was forced to fight for breath. While she was still struggling, Alexandria took advantage of her position and pulled her daggers from their scabbards and crossed them over Meya's throat, close enough to cut a little but not to cause the girl's head to roll off.

"I did not want to fight you or any of your 'siblings' this is being forced on me as well! I just want to spend my life with my best friend and those that have been part of our lives. I want to be given a chance to get to know Shadick more and to travel the world with him but not in fear of our lives! I wish that my parents weren't killed by Centaurs so that I could have spent more time with them and that they were able to meet a potential son-in-law and not leave me wondering every single time I kiss him whether or not they would be happy with my choices.

"I want to wake up in my bed, in my home and not have to rush out and fight something or in fear that something is going to happen to someone I love. I have lost a lot because of the Centaurs, and I have a feeling that I will lose a lot more before this fight is over. Yet, I force myself to keep going because that is what my parents would have wanted.

"They would not have been happy if I had just thrown my hands up in the air and gave up when they had literally given their lives to keep me alive and to make sure that I had at least a fighting chance! I wake up every day knowing that they depend on me to make sure that my family survives and that I did not just give up. That I gave the Centaurs a run for their lives. It is difficult, but I know that I am doing everything in my ability to stop them and give them a fight of their lives and not just shrugging and complaining about nobody doing anything about this and just accepting it.

"That is not how I was raised. I will give my last breath if it means that I can thrust my daggers into not only Balditha's gut but his son and his wife's!"

Meya looked up at her and smiled.

"Thank you for showing me that there is still hope in this

world, that someone is still trying to fight this battle and that the people on it had not just given up at the first sign of trouble. When I was given this task, I was told to choose a place where you would eventually show up at so that I could prepare. But as I was looking for a place, all I saw was people giving up and not caring that their homes were being destroyed."

"Then you have not seen the people fighting with me, they may have moved from their home, but by the sounds of it they have built themselves even better homes, and they are putting up a fight."

"I would love to see that..."

"Then join us and fight on the right side of this battle and not on those who feel that they have been wronged, when in truth it is their own fault that they are where they are."

"It would be the greatest of honours to join you in this fight." Meya said smiling waving her hand at Shadick and causing him to fall to his knees. "I apologise if I took my anger out on you. That was not part of my plan, but it seems that today was just a bad day to have met me."

Alexandria put her daggers away and held her hand towards the Elemental and smiled.

"Well I won't hold it against you, as we all have our off days, and it is understandable that one eventually snaps."

"Are the two of you done stroking each other's egos, and are we able to get out of here anytime soon? I suddenly hate being in cramped spaces." Shadick muttered, walking towards them

"I also apologise to you Shadick; my temper got the better of me this morning." Meya said, blushing.

"I will forgive you if you get us out of here."

She nodded and called the wind to lift them up and out of the well and let them lightly land not far from where they had started.

"I will travel with you, and before you say anything, I know that it needs to be inconspicuous. So, I will be transforming and melding with your daggers just as Jayce had. It will not physically change or alter them except to add a little stone on the handle. That way, you will know that I am always within calling range."

"Thank you, I appreciate it." Alexandria said just as Meya disappeared.

"I did not like that at all. I saw it all happening, but I could not move a muscle to try and help." Shadick muttered, shaking his head.

"That was her plan in a way, although I do believe her when she says that her emotions got the better of her. It happens to everyone in this life, especially when there is someone threatening you around every corner."

"It does not make it right."

"I have seen you lose your temper and expected no question as to why, so if you are judging her it is done in lies."

"Why do you always have to be right?" he said, shaking his head. "Not judging at all, just feeling useless as I have been thinking that if I ever end up with you when you were forced to fight another Elemental that I would help and that no one would be able to stop me, and I was unable to make any move to help."

"Do not think I blame you for not being able to help, as I know that you would have done your best to try and help me. But I have seen their power, so I know that it was not possible. Hold your head up high and move on, knowing that when it comes to the Centaurs, you will be right there helping me and not just sitting on the side of the battlefield watching what is happening. You will not be useless then."

"And I cannot wait for that day, and I give you my promise right now that I will do my best to prevent any deaths from happening, on our side at least. For the Centaurs surviving, I cannot promise anything at all as they deserve to go down bleeding."

"I do not disagree with you there at all; they have caused enough sadness to last a lifetime, and if they felt even a little of the hurt that they have sown, then I will be happy."

"While I was up there, I was still able to hear what was being said, and I could not help but hear that you wish that your parents were still around."

"I think that it would be anyone's wish, don't you think? That their dead family members were still around and that they could for at least one more time talk to them hug them and tell them that they are missed and loved."

"You do know that it is not your fault that your parents died, right?"

"I blamed myself for years, but I know now that it was not my fault, rather those who killed them who is at fault. When I was younger, I kept telling myself that if I had fought harder that they stayed home that they would have, that if I had been there, they would have taken me to kill and left my family. But I have realised that the Centaurs would have killed them anyway as they would not have been happy with just me. Not to mention that I had been too young to actually do anything to help them."

"That is good to know as I know my sister blamed herself for years, and no matter how much I argued that it hadn't been her fault she never listened."

"I have grown up and actually dealt with the Centaurs, so I now know that I could have done nothing to prevent it from happening."

He nodded and smiled.

"I am not sure how long that took, but we better get back to camp before a mass panic is started."

Chapter 9

Mermalani Split

"I am very proud of you for fighting so well against Meya. The energy that was coming from her was huge! Although, I still feel horrid for not being able to help you. But her wind attack took me by surprise, and even when I tried freeing myself, I could not even move." Shadick said as they walked back to the temporary camp.

"I know that you wanted to help, and you did try. I saw that. She was powerful, and her attacks hurt me." Alexandria replied, smiling slightly. "But I refused to give up."

"When she finally stopped attacking, I was happy that it was over. Seeing you being attacked and not being able to do anything to help was the most horrid experience ever. One that will not happen again. Hopefully, there will not be another test for a while, as I can see that is it taking its toll on you. You have not smiled and truly meant it since we reunited."

"Once I know that Amethyst and everybody else is safe and unharmed, I'll be able to relax. As for these tests I will deal with them as they are thrown at me."

"Terry swears up and down that everyone is in good health and nothing has happened in a few months."

"Yeah, but he had been away from Valencia for a few weeks and has admitted that he does not know for sure whether anything has happened since."

"I think that you worry a little too much at times." Shadick told her matter-of-factly, pushing her against a broken-down building and kissing her neck softly, lifting her arms above her head, trailing kisses from her neck to her mouth, nipping the corner of her mouth lightly.

Taking both her hands into one of his, he slowly started lifting her shirt up. Moaning softly lightly licking his lips, and silently asking him to deepen the kiss. He laughed softly before deepening the kiss, only stopping long enough to pull her shirt over her head.

"You...Why?" Starlansha's voice carried towards them.

Groaning in dismay, Alexandria slowly opened her eyes.

"Damn, and I was just getting warmed up", Shadick added to her silent complaint. "Perhaps we could just ignore it?"

"What do you think is going on this time?" Alexandria asked, bending down grabbing her shirt, pulling it on again.

"Knowing Rosy, it has something to do with her and it's life-threatening." Shadick answered, watching her closely as she ran her fingers through her hair.

Running her hands down the soft pants she was wearing, sighing softly before walked towards their camp. When they got there, they saw a troubling sight. Roslata and Starlansha stood a foot apart shouting at each other. Terry stood discreetly next to the fire looking somewhat confused and unsure of what to do.

He looked relieved when he noticed Alexandria and beckoned them forward.

"It started a few minutes ago. I am not even sure what they are arguing about." he informed them.

"You don't know what set it off?" Shadick asked.

"No, I was tending to breakfast. Only thing I was able to make out was your name Alexandria and the words 'given up on everything' then I cut them out and try to give them some privacy."

"Maybe we should intervene? There is enough fighting going on without us fighting amongst each other."

"The last time I tried stopping one of their fights, I almost got a door in my face."

"I don't see any objects that could be thrown at us", Shadick said, frowning.

"And we will pull you away from them before you can get hurt", Terry added.

"Why should I be the one to go break them up?" Alexandria asked, shocked. "You have known them the longest, Shadick!"

"Yes, but you have spent the last two years with them, so you know why they are fighting." Shadick said matter-of-factly.

"Rosy hates me and feels as though she had to sacrifice everything because Star wanted me to help. I offered her multiple opportunities to leave, but she refused. Saying that she couldn't leave her sister." Alexandria said, glancing at the twins.

"But they might actually listen to you, even if she doesn't like you." Terry said, pushing her towards the twins slightly.

Taking a deep breath and walking towards the twins, she lightly touched Starlansha's shoulder.

"Is there something I could do to help? You were arguing quite loudly, and we were getting worried."

"You can go jump into a very active volcano or a ravine where they can never recover the body." Roslata hissed at her.

"Rosy! You cannot talk to her in that way! Grandmamma

would be so upset that you would talk that way to anybody, especially to Alex." Starlansha said shocked.

"Well, I wouldn't know what Grandmamma would say because I have been forced to help someone I do not even like! And no, I could not let my sister go on her own because I know that anything bad could happen at any time. I also know that no one would try and protect her!"

"I would not let anything happen to your sister! She is my best friend, and I would do anything to keep her safe and protect her."

"You are more concerned about your own well-being and when you and wolf boy can sneak off for a roll in the hay! So do not even try and deny that isn't what you have been doing for the past few hours."

"Roslata, you are out of line! We thought that it would be a good idea to explore the area and see where we spent the night. Just in case we had to stay another night. It was also when Alexandria got attacked by another Elemental!" Shadick growled.

"That is a story that I have been hearing from her since we got back to land. Not one of us has actually seen one of those so-called Elementals. She is either on her own or with her lover when it happens."

"Why do you not stick with me then next time? Perhaps, I

have to do a trial while you're with me, and you'll believe me then." Alexandria said softly.

"We met Jayce, the spirit Elemental. Was he not proof enough for you?!" Starlansha asked her sister.

"You actually believe that story of him being an Elemental? Did you not notice how flushed and breathless the two of them were? It is only too obvious that she had somehow sneaked off for a quick lay. If I were you, Shadick, I would keep a very close eye on her. She seems to be cheating on you quite a bit." Roslata sneered, flipping her hair over her shoulder.

"She is not cheating on me, nor are we sneaking off for a little private time. I trust Lexie wholeheartedly and know that she is not the kind of person that would say she has feelings for someone and then turn around and screw his best friend." Shadick added, crossing his arms.

"Oh my word, you are still going on about events that happened when we were teenagers? I have moved past what happened back then, ages ago."

"That was because you were the heartless one. Not the one that had to get over having been cheated on."

"You make it sound like we had been dating for years or that we had been madly in love. You should remember that we had been seeing each other for only a month or so. And if you think back, you will remember that you only asked me because Star started seeing Prince Jacques."

"And you should have been honest with me. Or if it had been your plan to hurt me, to not have done it with my best friend."

"I do not remember Chad complaining at all when I started kissing him."

"Rosy, you were both drunk; no man in his sober mind would sleep with his best friend's girlfriend." Starlansha added quickly.

"At least he had the decency to come and apologise for what happened and accepted my anger. You just pretended nothing happened, and when I confronted you, you shrugged it off." Shadick said matter-of-factly.

"Wait a minute, let me get this straight. Roslata and you dated? And she then turned around and slept with Chadromida?" Alexandria asked, shocked.

"It was years ago. We were teenagers, and it didn't mean anything at all. After we had stayed with their family for a few weeks."

"And there you go, you said it yourself! It meant nothing. Me sleeping with Chad meant nothing; it was just a blip on your moral compass. Now, if you will excuse me, I have better things to do with my life than travel around the world fighting a losing battle." Roslata said, turning her back on everyone.

"Roslata! It is too dangerous to be on your own. Could we just not tolerate each other until we get to Valencia?" Alexandria asked her.

"No! Because I am done pretending to be someone that I am not." she said before slapping Alexandria through the face. "I have made up my mind ages ago that I will not stand around here and be treated like a lesser being just because you do not like me.

"I have now tried to convince my sister that it would be for the better if she joined me, but I have failed because of your manipulation. I will leave her here and I will not care what happens to her anymore. I have better things to do with my life. There are people in this world that respect me a lot more than any of you have shown me so far."

"But we are travelling with her to make sure that we can live in peace again." Starlansha said, crying softly. "Don't you want to go back to Trilantica and live with Grandmamma and not have to worry about any of this?"

"And how do you know that isn't exactly where I am going?"

"Just let her go. She was not bringing anything positive to this group anyway." Shadick said

"And the 'leader' has spoken. Now, if you will excuse me." She said before walking away while they all stared after her in shock.

Chapter 10

Alexandria's Tale

"Star, it is no use running after her when she's already made up her mind." Terri said, stepping closer to her. "Perhaps she will return once she has calmed down a bit."

"I know, my sister. Once she's made up her mind, there is no way that she will change it." Starlansha replied, staring after her sister. "I knew that our relationship had been strained the last year or so, but I did not expect her to storm off and not worry about me."

"Terri might be right, though... we will spend another night here just in case she decides to come back. It would not be very nice to come back and find that the people you had been travelling with had disappeared. We know the area a little better and know that there is no immediate danger here." Shadick said, turning to Alexandria who was holding her cheek. "I can't believe that she slapped you! If I had not been brought up a gentleman, I might have returned the favour."

"There is no need to drop your morals just for me, Shadick. She had every right to slap me. I haven't really spent a lot of time trying to make her feel better about any of this. It's been a constant thing where she had to help me. I made her sister spend more time with me just because I had to train and did not think twice about anything else." Alexandria said, looking at Starlansha. "I'm sorry that I am the cause of all of this, Star. I should have tried harder."

"You tried hard enough, and there is no reason why you should apologise for her actions and decisions. She knew from the start that I offered to help you, and I never go back on my word. Whenever you were asleep or not with me, I would spend time with her. But she had gotten so distant the last while that it was nearly impossible to get through to her. It was as though she had met someone and was listening more to them than she ever did listen to me. Grandmamma did mention that she had met someone, but we thought nothing more of it because we did not have any proof as to who it was." Starlansha said, smiling slightly. "If you will excuse me, I need a few minutes to myself. Just to gather myself again. But thank you for saying that we will stay another night just in case she does come back. It will mean a lot more than she would ever say."

Alexandria watched Starlansha walk towards the fire and

sit down. It had been a while since she had seen someone she cared about argue in such a way. There had been nothing that she could have done differently to have stopped it from happening, but it was still hard. It was not something she was used to, being slapped like that.

Not even when she had lived with Amethyst and Valencia had it ever ended up with either of them slapping each other. They would talk it through and ensure everyone was happy with what had been decided. Valencia had always insisted that violence never really solved anything.

"Lexie? Are you okay?" Shadick asked carefully.

"Yes, of course I am. Just a little surprised at the slap and everything that has happened so far today." she replied.

"When I awoke this morning, I thought that it would be a good day. Turns out that I was wrong in thinking that." Terri said before turning back to the fire.

"I didn't even think it would turn into this when we went for our walk."

"No one could have predicted this, honey. Unless of course, you had a vision to show you what would happen."

"True enough, but perhaps there had been signs? Just so that I could have prevented this in some way. I see how hurt Starlansha is even though she will just pretend that she is fine. She is; or rather was close to her sister."

"Everybody drifts apart at some point or another. Even family members. All you can do is wait for them to return to you and ask for forgiveness. Sometimes it is for the best to accept it, but other times it is better to just let them go their own way."

"Wish that we could go back to that abandoned village and just forget what has just happened."

"That would not be all too wise, unfortunately."

"I know, we need to stay here and make sure that nothing else goes wrong."

"Very smart decision that. Let us go have breakfast and hope that this day doesn't get any worse." Shadick said and turned to the fire as well.

Alexandria stayed where she was, staring at the place where Roslata had disappeared. It seemed that she was the cause of a lot of pain, and she felt terrible about it. If she could change everything that had happened the last few years, she would, but it was not in her hands.

"I have been wondering, Alexandria." Terri said. "What happened during your training? I did not ask before as you did not seem to want to talk about it. But I was hoping that you would be willing to tell us now?"

"It is not that I did not want to talk about it." Alexandria started frowning. "I was just not sure how to tell you what happened. No words seemed enough to explain it all so I just thought I would put it off until I found the right words."

"A lot happened, so I do not blame you for being unsure." Starlansha whispered.

"You know that I would like to know, but after the first time I asked and you said no, I have not been wanting to ask." Shadick added.

"Very well then, where to start?" she thought out loud.

"From the beginning is always a good place, I have found." Terri joked.

"Alright then after leaving the Caves with the twins, we went straight to Trilantica. Roslata, of course, tried stalling us by saying that she needed some things from their Cottage, but Starlansha told her that they could come back another day.

"We arrived to find the army seeming to return from a battle and found out that the Sea-witch had been sending some of her warriors to attack the Palace. It had not been anything severe yet, so they were not worried. It was more of a nuisance than anything else.

"The twins were happy to see their Grandfather still alive and well. He, of course, scoffed that they had been worried for nothing. Their Grandmother admitted to us later that evening that they had lost some of the guards, and he had been taking it hard. But she whisked us off to bed and told us it was not something we needed to worry about.

"The twins had their room that they had been staying in and the Queen had organised a room for me and had made sure that I had everything that I might need.

"I, of course, just wanted to start training, but they convinced me to get a good night's rest first. The guards could not understand why the King and Queen were being so nice to a 'human' when they had never shown a liking to them before. Until the first morning when some of the sharks got through the line, and I used my magic to stop them from attacking some of the Mer-people.

"They quickly changed their minds at that point. Anyway, I wasn't sure where we would be training, but I trusted Starlansha so I knew that she probably had a place in mind. We travelled for about an hour or so until we reached an open part of the ocean with a big cave system close by. There we would not be interrupted, and we would be free to do what we needed. I am impressed with Star's way of handling my training. Not really being a trainer of any kind, yet she pushed me hard.

"Some days we were so busy that we spent the nights there, in the cave. But most nights we travelled back to the Palace and slept there. As I improved my control over my powers, she was able to ensure that I was being challenged. A few times just as we were getting into our training, we had to fight sharks or a few Sirens that the Sea-witch kept sending our way.

"But it was never something dangerous enough that we were worried. Starlansha invited Roslata to join us during our training, but she refused outright and said that it was not her job to raise me."

"Well, that is a nice way to say it when in truth, she said it in a very mean way." Starlansha said, shaking her head.

"True enough, I just thought I would not talk bad about your sister."

"Thank you, I appreciate that. Please continue telling the story."

"The guards taught me a bit more about some of the weapons that they use and made sure that they could teach me something new whenever they could. The people in Trilantica also tried helping us by giving us some food to take with us or giving us advice on what to do. Of course, the latter wasn't very helpful, but we pretended to take it seriously as we did not want to insult them.

"Once or twice the King himself joined us and he would parry with me or tell us stories about the training his father had put him through when he had been young. I believe that it was a genuine effort to get closer to his granddaughter that he insisted on joining us, it was on those days that Roslata actually joined us while training. But it was good as I learned a lot from him on those few days.

"I noticed though that Roslata would stare at us as though we were planning something hideous or something, but we mostly ignored her. Although we both noticed that she seemed to be rather happy the one evening when we got home but did not question it. It was then that the Queen told us that she had gone swimming in a foul mood but had returned happier than she had been in a while.

"Starlansha called a break the next day and tried following her sister just to make sure that she did not get into trouble but was unable to follow her for long. That day I decided to explore not just the Palace but the village as well as the surrounding area. It had been about five months since we had started and this was the first day that I had a day to myself.

"The guards that had not been helpful in my training looked at me suspiciously, but they had orders from the King himself to leave me be. The Mer-people were a lot friendlier to me, and some offered me a snack or something that meant a lot to them. A few ignored me, but it did not really matter to me as I wasn't there to make everyone happy. I found out later from an old Mermaid that some of the others believed that I was just here to cause trouble for the King, which is why I was getting such a cold reception from them.

"As we got deeper into our training, we sometimes did some things on our own, but mostly we worked together. The time passed rather quickly from then on as we were too distracted by what we were doing to notice the passing of time.

"If it hadn't been for Queen Arabella, I'm not sure that we would have remembered to eat and spend time with them and not just train. The one evening the King and Queen organised a big banquet for us, much to both of our surprise. On this night, the King told the people how hard we had been working and that we have even taken some time to help the guards with the sharks and Sirens.

"He then handed me two new daggers that he had especially made for me. I was shocked, but he told me that it was because I had been protecting Starlansha through all of this and my other daggers had broken about a month before that." she said, handing one of the daggers to Shadick.

"Although he admitted to me that he was quite shocked that you had broken them." Starlansha said grinning.

"These are quite something! I can see that the same hilts have been used although they have been improved and changed a bit." Shadick commented, "And the blades are slightly curved, which I'm guessing you love."

"I love my daggers very much! And I promised that I will try and look after these more, if possible."

"As much as you can?"

"The blades of the other daggers broke during one of the battles we helped with against a group of Sirens. You should understand that the previous daggers were quite old and had not been looked after properly for the longest of times. Which is why my Grandfather had these made for Alex. He kind of felt a little guilty and felt that it was something he had to do."

"It seems that the blades of the daggers have been infused with something that gives it a slightly red glow if you turn it just right, the white stone and purple stones bring it out even more. Or was that because your powers fused with it?" Terri asked, handing the dagger back to her.

"The latter, even though we aren't sure how exactly it happened. I was just going through a training regimen while using the daggers and my powers. Starlansha stopped me when she noticed the glow, and we gawked at it for about an hour while poking it, of course." Alexandria said, laughing.

"And after that?" Shadick asked.

"Just more training, fighting Sirens, training, fighting with Roslata... you get the idea." Starlansha said, shaking her head.

"After a slight disagreement about when we would leave. Star wanted to leave at the end of the month, and I wanted to leave the next day. We settled on the end of the week, which was when I was tackled by a very happy wolf." Alexandria replied, grinning and rubbing Managwa's head.

"Truthfully, if he had not done it, I might have." Shadick joked. "I missed you a lot while you were gone."

"Just as I missed you, not sure how well it would have gone down if you had been the one to tackle me."

"Thank you for telling us your story, Alexandria. It is good to know that you pushed through the hardships that you faced." Terri said. "And I am glad that you were able to reconnect with your Grandparents, Star."

"I think that it is time for me to go to bed. It has been a long night, and I need to not think for a bit." Starlansha said, standing up and walking to the sleeping area.

"The whole thing with her sister is still getting to her, isn't it?"

"Yes, it is. And I'm not sure what to do to make it better for her." Alexandria said, sighing.

"Unfortunately, there is nothing you can do to change it, honey. It is up to Roslata to make a move and get back with her sister." Shadick said, and she nodded and they all slowly followed Starlansha.

Her last conscious thought was that it would be a great, although dangerous power to have. Being able to change people's minds about something.

Chapter 11

New Companion

Terri had woken them up, and it felt as though Starlansha was on some kind of mission. She was marching around the camp, grabbing things and stuffing them into bags. If it had not been for Terri, they would have been forced to start the journey on empty stomachs. Instead, they watched her mission around them, trying not to get in her way as she may just have run them over.

"Do you think we should ask her if she wants to talk about it?" Shadick asked frowning.

"I think that if we try to get in her way just to ask her something, she might just slap us or something." Alexandria muttered.

"And asking her about things does not work. I tried to do that before I woke you. She just glanced at me before continuing on whatever mission she was on." Terri added.

"I think that it might be because Roslata isn't back yet. She is probably scared that something bad has happened to her."

"We were all surprised when she just left like that. I don't think there is really anything to worry about though." Shadick said. "I have known the twins for years now, and Roslata is very capable of protecting herself in any situation."

"But just imagine if it had been your twin that had just suddenly disappeared! Slapped your friend and then walked off without a word as to where she was going."

"You shouldn't just blame Roslata in all of this. I was the one that kept them apart because of the training for the last year and a half. She tried numerous times to spend time with her sister but would get told that she was busy helping me. I am not surprised that she slapped me; in fact, I was shocked that it had not happened earlier." Alexandria said, smiling sadly.

"It was not as though you did not give her a chance to join you! She was the one that refused to join because she does not like you for some reason. You should stop blaming yourself for everything. Because you are not the one making the Centaurs attack the Creatures and Humans. You are not the one that made Roslata storm off in a rage. Nor are you to blame for your parents' death or Valencia's for that matter." Shadick said seriously.

"I do believe though that the Centaurs did not imagine

that the Creatures would actually stand up for themselves. That is because I have been the one pushing everyone to fight and stand up for themselves."

"Shadick is correct, Alexandria. The Centaurs have been holding this grudge for years now. It is a ridiculous reason for why they are feeling so self-imposed, but it is a good thing that the Creatures are standing up for themselves. I think that it has given them a pause in what they are doing." Terri said, shaking his head.

"They... I mean you, were thrown out of the forest as well as the villages because of always wanting to kill everyone who dared step in the way. My parents, for that matter were the ones who made sure that you were thrown out." Alexandria said.

"I may be a Centaur, Alexandria. But I do not blame your parents for what they had to do. If I had been older and stronger, I would have helped them banish the Centaurs."

"Some people's egos can get out of control at times, and that is when they think their feelings or grudges make sense. If you are lucky, they will realise their mistake and pull back. But sometimes it happens that they only see what is wrong and don't see the validity as to why something happened." Shadick added.

"Very true, just imagine for a second that you were not

the kind of person you are. Your parents are killed, and as you grow up, you hold a grudge against those responsible for their deaths. When you are older, you are determined to get back at them, you know that they are stronger than you, but you do not care.

"Maybe you get other people to join your cause, and in the end you get everyone killed. You would only then be held responsible. In this case, it is more that you are making the Creatures stand up for themselves and their families."

"That is true, I guess it just feels as though it is because of me that we have lost so many Creatures already. That those who have lost someone so far will see me and think that I should not have been born." she said sighing.

"Everyone has known from the very beginning that there were risks in joining us, but I can assure you that they have known that even if they did not join us that they would lose loved ones. And you were the one that risked yourself during the last battle to save that little boy. There was no need for you to have cared enough to run after him and to save him." Shadick said. "If you remember, his mother was very thankful that you had saved his life."

"While you have been away I have heard of that story, it has been told over and over again. The Creatures look up to you because of that. You could have just shrugged it off and pretended to not care, but you did not." Terri added. "Some even wanted to have a statue of sorts erected in memory of that day."

"Are we going to get back onto the road anytime soon or are we just going to be sitting here, talking the whole day?" Starlansha asked suddenly.

"We have been waiting for you as you seemed to be rather busy gathering everything."

"I was just trying to distract myself from, stuff. But I am ready to go whenever you guys are."

"Then I think it would be for the best that we get going then. We still have quite a journey ahead of us."

"Agreed..." Alexandria said, looking at Starlansha before standing up and walking over to the horses. "I do believe that Amethyst might just have a panic attack if we do not get back soon. And we all know her; that would result in her coming to look for us."

"She will be fine, Lexie." Shadick said as he got on his own horse, "It is not something that she is used to, being without her sister. Just give her some time, and she will be herself again. People handle things differently. If this had been you, you might have run after her and not stopped until you were dragging her along behind you. But Starlansha knows that her sister would only throw another tantrum before storming off again."

"There is really nothing that we could have done?"

"No, there wasn't, Alex. Shadick is right about my sister. She is stubborn, and once she has made up her mind there is no way to change it. I have tried and learned that the hard way. Even my Grandmother had to learn that lesson." Starlansha said, joining them. "I am worried about her, and I wish that there had been something that I could have done to have stopped her.

"But I know for the better. I do not blame you, either. This is all on my sister's shoulders, and I hope that we will find her safe in the village. If not then I will be worried, but I will know that she is big enough to deal with her own troubles."

"Thank you for saying that, Star. And I'm sure that she will catch up with us at some point." Alexandria said, smiling slightly, then urged her horse on.

"So, what is our next move? Are we travelling until we reach the village, or are we stopping somewhere along the way?"

"I think it would be best to get to the village as soon as possible. Just so we can find out what has been happening the last few days. And to assure Amethyst that we are still alive and well. But I do not think that it is a very smart idea to push ourselves too hard and not to be ready if we have to be.

"We do not know if we will run across the Centaurs or any of their little minions, so it would be for the best to be prepared for that just in case. I think that we should travel until we really feel we can't anymore and then rest."

"There is a village that sits between us and Valencia. If you wish we can stay over there tonight?" Terri said matter-of-factly. "Otherwise, we can just keep travelling until we deem fit."

"Let me put it this way, we have no definite plan until we get to that part."

"Sounds like a good plan. We may not be tired when we get to the village and have another hour or so of travel in us." Shadick agreed.

"That seems..." Starlansha started but stopped as the wolves began growling.

"Do they sense danger?" Terri asked, looking around.

"Not so much danger as something in the middle of the road." Shadick said, pointing ahead of them.

"Is it perhaps a trap from the Centaurs?"

"There is no place for them to be hiding out here, so I doubt it. Might just be an animal that wandered out here in search of food."

Alexandria frowned, staring at the dark spot ahead of them. She quickly jumped off her horse and ran towards it after only a second. Shadick tried grabbing her arm, but she dodged him and kept running. It had moved, whatever it was. That meant that it had just been hurt, and there was still a chance of them being able to help. As she got closer, she realised that it was a wolf pup and she sped up even more.

Quickly kneeling next to the animal and running her hands over its fur. There was a lot of blood, and it seemed that its legs had been badly hurt, but it was still breathing.

"You should really not race ahead like that Alexandria." Terri said as he reached her.

"I saw it move, and I knew that I had to help. It seems as though she has been attacked by someone. Not another creature as I do not see scratch marks but stab wounds." Alexandria replied.

"Do you think that Centaurs did this?"

"It might be, but I cannot be sure. What I am sure of is that this poor wolf pup needs some serious help. And if we do not help her, she will die."

"I'm not so sure that is such a good idea, Lexie. How do we know this is not just some kind of sinister plan of the Centaurs?" Shadick asked as the wolves kept growling.

"Then please continue on to Valencia, and I will meet you there. As for me, I am taking this wolf to the village that Terri mentioned so that this poor creature does not suffer too much."

"There has been enough loss of life; why should we not try and help?" Starlansha asked.

Shadick sighed but nodded. "Very well then. Let us get this wolf to the closest doctor."

Alexandria picked the wolf pup up carefully, whispering softly to it as she carried it. Terri lowered himself and allowed her to put the injured animal on his back. She quickly got back onto her horse, and they raced to the village.

"There has to be a doctor around here somewhere!" Alexandria said urgently, glancing around.

"Sir! Could you please point us in the direction of the village doctor?" Shadick asked a surprised man.

"I can take you there quicker than I can explain." said a woman glancing at Shadick up and down. "Please, follow me."

They followed the woman as she rushed ahead of them. Only pausing when there was a rush of people ahead of them. Alexandria glanced at Shadick and saw that he was frowning at the woman as though he recognised her.

"Doctor Kyros? I have some people here who have an injured animal here for you to look at." she shouted as she opened the door.

"I am over here, dear! At the back, if you will please." Doctor Kyros shouted, and they rushed back, glancing up as they got there. "Oh dear... what happened?"

"We found the pup not too far from here, and she was already hurt. Could you help?" Alexandria asked frowning.

"Please put the pup on the bed over there so that I can have a look."

She put the wolf on the bed, backing away so that the Doctor could look at the pup without bother. They watched as the Doctor inspected the pup up and down, moving some of her fur away while muttering.

"If I am to save her, I will need to operate. But I will need the lot of you to leave. You can return in two or so hours to see if I succeeded, as I cannot promise anything."

Shadick grabbed her arm and pulled her out of the Doctor's house as she was about to argue. She kept glancing back at the pup desperately as the Doctor got to work. The poor creature had to survive! In this bad world something good had to happen, even if it was just by a wolf pup surviving.

"You heard him, he needs space and not to be bothered while working on the pup. Besides, we need to make sure that the other wolves aren't too irritated with this new pup; otherwise, any and all work that goes into saving her will be for nothing. Managwa is very protective of not just me but you as well."

"Now I remember you!" the woman said suddenly and they glanced at her "Shadick, right? Remember me? Dreska? We met a few years ago in a pub I used to work in. You were with your friend when we met."

"Dreska?! I have not seen you in years! How have you been?"

"am I to take it, you know her?" Starlansha asked frowning.

"Yes, I do know her. It was quite a few years ago, and I had almost completely forgotten about those days."

"I have been well, thank you. I am still here where I have been all these years. Although I can see that not much has changed since the last time, I saw you." Dreska said, looking Alexandria and Starlansha up and down. "Seeing that you have to wait for news. We may as well do it at my home. Would you like to come over for a drink?"

"Sounds like a good plan." Shadick said, nodding then started following her.

Alexandria glanced at the Doctor's home before narrowing her eyes at Dreska. What was this woman up to? She was getting an evil vibe off of her. After so many years, how could you just invite someone to your home without wanting something? And what had she meant by 'he hadn't changed?'.

"Come on, Alex. It won't help anyone by just standing out here the whole time as it could take hours." Starlansha said.

"Right, let's go see what this woman has to say." she said and ignored Starlansha's questioning gaze.

Chapter 12

A Shadowed Past

"Lexie! Would you please stop walking away from me?" Shadick shouted after her.

She ignored him and kept walking. Without warning she walked into something and fell over. She looked up angrily and saw that Shadick was right above her. Glaringly she started getting up from the floor, but before she could properly get up his arms were pulling her up.

"Could you please just listen to what I have to say?"

"And why should I do that?"

"Because I am trying to have a conversation with you, which is being made difficult by your storming off."

"Why should I listen to your lies, yet again?" she asked shrugging away from him.

"Please tell me when it was I exactly lied to you? And if you could tell me what I have done to upset you this much it would greatly appreciated."

"Michael is one of my best friends from the village and that is how I greet someone when I was afraid for his life. And you acted as though I was a misbehaving child."

"Is that what all this is about? Just because I may be a little jealous if someone gets close to you?"

"There is no need to get jealous after last night! And it was a harmless hug, nothing to make a big deal of."

"I am still a person, and jealousy is part of the package. If that is such a big problem..."

"I never said that you aren't a person, if in fact if you think about it, I was the one trying to convince everyone that you are as human as I am. And the last time we checked, we weren't together."

"That is not what I meant either. Look I did not mean to come across as an unfeeling brute..." he started then stopped when a buzzing interrupted them.

He sighed when he realised that it was a group of Faeries flying towards Alexandria and knew the conversation would have to wait. The four rainbow Faeries flew around her head and he got dizzy watching the movement. Just as he was about to complain they flew a short distance away from them and transformed.

"Alexandria, the Queen request your presence in the cave,

along with Shadick's," the blue Faerie said.

"If you asked me it sounded very important," said the green Faerie as she sat down on a rock, resting her chin in her hands.

"We *are* on the brink of war in case you forgot, so of course it is important! They are busy discussing strategies," the violet Faerie replied.

"You should cheer up a little, V! In case you have forgotten, it is important to laugh when things get a little too serious. Because without laughter, life would be very monotonous," the yellow Faerie said from her spot in the tree branch.

"Well who asked for your opinion?" the green one replied angrily.

"Will the four of you stop it?!" Alexandria interceded just then. "You are the rainbow sisters and one would expect that you would get along and whatnot."

They looked shocked at Alexandria then at each other and burst into laughter. The yellow Faerie nearly fell out of the tree while her green sister rolled around on the ground. Shadick looked at them curiously then glanced at Alexandria who just shrugged.

"Why do you insist on taking us so seriously, Al? I thought that you would have gotten used to us bantering with each other like this by now," the violet Faerie said, clutching her stomach from laughter.

The Blue Faerie stopped laughing and wiped her eyes.

"We were serious about Amethyst looking for you though. And she sounded like it was quite urgent."

"Shadick, please meet the Rainbow sisters. Brittany, Georgia, Viora and Yolanda... Thank you for coming to get us. If you would tell Amethyst that we will be shortly it would be appreciated," Alexandria said and they nodded before transforming back into their miniature forms and flying away.

Before he could reply in anyway, they had disappeared and he was left with Alexandria. The tension was still thick in the air and he was not sure what to say to make it better. Why was she acting like this? Perhaps she was lying about Michael just being a friend. She was very defensive when he mentioned him.

Then again, why would she have allowed the previous evening to happen if she was seeing him? In the same breath it could be argued that he could have put a stop to it as well. It was not as she had seduced him... much. Why was it that her energy seemed to call to him and made him fall for her ever since their first meeting?

"We should probably get back to camp. If Amethyst sent the rainbow sisters after us it is quite important," Alexandria eventually commented, not looking at him.

"That might indeed be so, but we need to continue our conversation," Shadick stated.

"And what conversation would that be? The one where you talk and I just have to listen? Thank you but no thank you... I have a lot more important things to worry about than what problems we may have in our *non-existing relationship*! We slept together last night and it was fantastic, but we do not have the time to have a polite conversation about it."

"I think that we need to sort this out and that would include *both* of us talking... not just me."

"Right now, the looming war seems more important than a one silly conversation," she replied before storming off.

Shadick ran after her knowing that they will have to sort everything out before they got to Amethyst as the tension was just too much for anyone to handle. And she would then find out about everything that had happened the previous evening and he was not ready to face the consequences in that. He grabbed her arm and forced her to face him; he refused to move his arm even though she was throwing death glares at him.

"I think that it would be best if you let go of me, Shadick."

"No, I was serious when I said that we need to discuss this. In case you did not notice, the tension between us is so palpable that it might just come to life and bite anyone that might be around us. Do you have any idea how uncomfortable it would be if they found out about what happened between us?"

"Very well then! We will just pretend that last night never happened, that way there is no need to worry about them finding out. Not that I was planning on telling anyone about it. but alright then, if you want to talk, then talk.

"I have told you already that I do not regret last night at all, in fact I was a lot more relaxed than I had been in months. I kind of find it funny that you barely know me yet you judge me by my friends, even though you haven't met them. But just to give you some *food for thought*... I was the one that got Michael and Luanda together in the first place.

"In case you forgot the conversation that you overheard between myself and Amethyst, I am not planning on getting involved with anyone in the village, nor any other place for that matter. It would only mean trouble for myself as well as the magical Creatures that I call my friends and family.

"And yes, before you say it... I know things are changing and that soon it would probably not be such a *big deal* for them to know that I am a witch. But I want to tell them on my own conditions and hope that they won't hate me for it. So I think that it would be best if I were to just stay single and not have to deal with any of it."

He stared at her shocked and she slipped her arm out of his grasp before he could gather his wits. She stormed away and emerged from the forest and he knew that even if he would be able to catch up with her, he did not want to make a big mess for her.

He took a deep breath and followed her more slowly, trying to ignore the anger he felt still reverberating throughout the forest...

***

"Alex! There you are, we were waiting for you. Where is Shadick? The Rainbow Faeries said that they found you in the forest together," Amethyst said as soon as she walked into the caves.

"Oh... uhm... we were.. He.. Uh.." Alexandria stammered.

"I am right here. Sorry for my delay, I just had to speak with the wolves in the forest quick so I sent Alexandria ahead of me," Shadick said appearing behind them.

"Very well then, now that we are all here... you met the generals from the villages earlier and they kind of met you. Or rather, Alex knows Michael," Amethyst said frowning.

"I believe that you mentioned him briefly before but I

think that proper introductions are in order," Christopher said suspiciously.

"Shadick is a personal friend of mine and he has offered his help in this war and as you have mentioned before we will need all of the help that we can get. So please do not sound as though you do not trust him. But I will tell you this, Shadick is a Wolfane. Meaning that wherever he is the wolves will be, if that means anything to you," Amethyst said glaring at Christopher.

"And what exactly, in the high heavens, is a Wolfane?" Michael asked confused, sitting up straighter.

"The easy explanation would be that I was born from a werewolf mother but a human father," Shadick said shortly.

"But werewolves are uncontrollable beasts! They are vicious and attack anyone and anything that come into their way during the full moon!" Philiaps shouted.

"Just shows how much you know! As for him being an uncontrollable beast, you have no right to judge what you don't truly know. Perhaps the werewolves you ran across was murderous monsters, but please know that there is always a break in the rule. And honestly... if it was about who I trust more... it would be him and not you," Alexandria said, surprising everyone.

Three of the four representatives frowned at her as she

finished her speech then quickly stepped back again, slightly behind Amethyst. Shadick grinned, but no one noticed. He wanted to run to her and hug her fiercely, but kept control of himself.

"And why are we supposed to trust you? You are nothing but a mortal, just like we are. And it has been decided that women will not be part of this war, it is too dangerous," Philiaps said, banging on the table.

"Do not dare talk to Alex like that! Her father made sure that she knows everything about swordsmanship and I would take a guess that she may just know more than you do about any of it. I have seen her handling a sword and it is impressive," Michael said calmly.

"And for your information... she is not just another *mortal*. Yes, she is an excellent swordsman, but more importantly she has magic behind her. Which makes her stronger than almost anyone in this room," Amethyst added, shocking them all into silence, while Alexandria blanched.

"Magic? What is this rubbish you are talking about? Is she a Faerie or something?" Philiaps asked frowning.

"History made everyone forget about them, but there are still witches out there in the world," Alexandria said. "Just because people outlaw something does not mean that they just stop existing. We all just find a way to blend in and not be caught, so as not to be hung for being evil. Which is why, no one but the magical Creatures know about me. I hid it just because I knew that people would freak out."

Shadick grabbed her arm to stop her from saying what may harm the tentative peace that had been accomplished so far. She shrugged off his hand and crossed her arms, looking at Amethyst.

"Let me put this out on the table before this conversation goes any further... You have come into the *magical* forest to ask for our help in the battle. And that means that you will fight alongside various of magical Creatures. You need to accept that and not judge them just because of what your history books have taught you," Amethyst said seriously.

"We understand that and we accept it. This coming war won't just be us having to fight them but it will be *all* of us fighting against the same enemy," Michael said glancing at Alexandria who sighed softly.

"Was there something specific you wanted us to be here for? Or just to discuss strategies?" Alexandria asked Amethyst.

"Oh right! It was something more specific than just discussing strategies. While the discussions have been going on, I remembered something that may just help us during this war," Amethyst said putting her hand against her forehead.

"And what would that be?" Shadick asked leaning against

the cave wall.

"They are three stones... apart they may seem completely useless and powerless but if combined they can be very powerful."

"And you wish to send someone to retrieve these stones?

"Yes, I do, but it has to be done as fast as possible. You see if the stones were to fall into the wrong hands it may just cause more trouble for us as it could destroy everyone."

"And who did you have in mind, Am? And where exactly are these stones being kept?" Alexandria asked frowning.

"Well... the Trilate amethyst can be found in the far reaches of Trilantica, also known as Sorceral Deep. The Septer Quartz can be found deep within the Sangalon Mountains and the third stone is called Aquadious. If you do not know what you are looking for it could easily be passed over. It is normally handed down the family line by King Celeriac, who is also of Trilantica."

"Well there is no way that we can send mortals to any of those places," Philiaps commented. "It is not as though any of us can breathe underwater and who knows what dangers lay waiting in the oceans depths! As for Sangalon Mountains, it is known to be life threatening to anyone who got close."

"I had no intention of sending a mortal to retrieve these stones."

"So who exactly did you have in mind?" Shadick asked.

"I was thinking that I would send the two of you... I know that you would be able to retrieve the stones as soon as possible and that you would capable of dealing with any danger that may be thrown at you."

"That is very true. We are not scared to fight if it came down to it and together, we would make an excellent team."

"I have no doubt in my mind that you would make a great team... but you will have to test that theory out some other time. I need Alex to travel to Sorceral Deep for the Trilate amethyst and the Aquadious. While you, Shadick need to travel to Sangalon Mountains to retrieve the Septer Quartz."

"What?!" Alexandria asked, standing up straight.

"We need to retrieve the stones as soon as possible and if you were to go together it would take twice as long. And it will just be waste of time, time which I am sure you realise we do not have."

"And you trust the two of them enough to go on these missions? A witch and a wolf... whatever it was you called him?" Christopher asked.

"I would trust the both of them with my life and I know what they are capable of. And I know that they will do whatever is necessary to accomplish this. Unlike mortals who believe just because something goes wrong that it went wrong because of superstition."

"When... when did you want us to leave, Am?" Alexandria asked glancing at Shadick.

"As soon as the two of you are ready. The Centaurs know about these stones and I am sure that they are planning to retrieve the stones as well, so as to use it for themselves."

"We have all the necessary supplies that may be needed... or at least we have the supplies that Shadick will need. Alex will be going into the ocean and unfortunately we do not own anything will allow her to breathe underwater," Grog answered.

"Do not worry about that; I have already sent words to the Mermalani twins and asked for their help. And they have assured me that they will be able to help."

"What exactly is a Mermalani?" Michael asked, although he looked like nothing would surprise him.

"A Mermalani is someone who has been born from a human father and a Mermaid."

"Alright then, it kind of makes sense I guess."

"I am not sure that they would help me..." Alexandria said sighing.

"As I have already told you, Alex. They have already agreed to it. Or rather, Starlansha did. Roslata on the other hand is more difficult to convince, but her sister will be able to do just that. She is a funny one," Amethyst replied. "If she decides that she does not like someone she will not be the most pleasant person."

"She definitely does not like me then."

"Very well then, Shadick do you need any weapons or supplies?" Grog asked.

"I have my sword and that should suffice. If you were able to just give me some supplies and perhaps a horse to ride upon I would be grateful. It would be very difficult to carry supplies while in wolf form," Shadick replied.

"Would you be able to organise everything that he needs, Grog?" Amethyst asked.

"Yes, it will be organised within the hour. There is a horse that he can use and the provisions just need to be put in a satchel," Grog said nodding and disappeared outside.

"Thank you, Grog it is appreciated."

Alexandria frowned slightly as she watched Grog leaving. Why did she have to go alone on this quest when, if she thought about it, it would go quicker if they were together. And how was she supposed to retrieve a stone that was miles below the ocean?

"Is there anything that you think you may need, Alex?"

"How about the ability to breathe..." she started, but got distracted by the yellow Faerie that had just arrived.

She flew closer to Shadick and transformed into her human form and smiled suggestively at him. He did not move, but stared at the barely clad Faerie in surprise.

"Ariana.... How many times have I asked you to not dress so inadequately? That a Faerie should be respected not just by who they are but by their entire look?" Amethyst asked frowning at the Faerie.

"And I have told you that not all Faeries wish to look like nuns. If you ask me it should be more a case of *if you have it, flaunt it,*" Ariana answered still smiling.

"Do you have any other news from the Mermalani?"

"I do yes... Starlansha said that it would be the biggest of pleasures to help Alexandria. Roslata on the other hand said that it would only be a pleasure to let her drown or have the sharks eat her or perhaps let the Sirens get a hold of her to kill or change into one of them. But she would be happy to oblige with whichever option you choose."

"I have not seen her so sour in years... she needs to get her priorities sorted."

"She seemed pretty happy to me when she gave me the message. It was all laughs."

"Oh, I'm sure that she was. Alex, are you ready to travel and retrieve the stones?"

"Of course, I am, it is not as though I need that much to go underwater," she replied walking out of the cave, arms folded.

"What has gotten into her? When I arrived, she seemed to be so happy," Amethyst wondered out loud watching her friend.

"It is probably nothing... surprised that you are sending her on a mission. I think that she thought that she would be helping you here, organizing the troops and whatnot," Shadick fibbed.

"It is not as though I have much of a choice! We need to get those stones as soon as possible."

"And we both understand that, Amethyst. And we are both willing to do what is necessary."

"I know that, Shadick... but she just seemed really upset."

"I will go talk to her for you."

"Thank you, Shadick. I appreciate all the help that you are offering."

"It is no problem at all," he said and straightened up before walking out of the cave and looking around.

She was standing next to a newly constructed fountain that Amethyst had requested. Fresh water was being pumped from the stream so that they were able to refresh whenever they needed to. She seemed lost in thought as she ran her hand through the water.

"Amethyst is really upset that you just walked out of the

cave like that. She is really worried about you now."

"I have my reasons for why I walked out of the cave and I am sure that she will understand why, soon enough," she whispered trying to wipe her eyes before he noticed.

"Of all the things you are really good at, hiding your feelings isn't one of them. I know that you were crying just now, I'm just not sure why you were."

"I had just washed my face and the water dripping down my face must have looked like tears."

"Why were you crying, Lexie? And do not tell me that you were just washing your face because your eyes are red."

"I was just surprised that she wants us to go find the stones. And yes, I understand that they have to be retrieved as soon as possible, but I just would have thought that it would have been easier if we were to go together."

"You know that it would take twice as long to retrieve the stones if we were to go together. And I have a really bad feeling that the Centaurs are already trying to retrieve the stones for themselves."

"I am sorry if I am interrupting something, but I was just wondering if everything was okay? The two of you seemed happy enough last night and this morning," Grog asked walking towards them.

"Nothing to worry about, everything is absolutely fine,"

Alexandria replied smiling.

"There is a feeling of heaviness whenever the two of you are around each other."

"I assure you that everything is fine, but your concern is appreciated Grog. We were just talking about the stones," Shadick told him.

"Very well then... and just so that you know. The horse has been saddled and the provisions have been loaded. It is now just up to you when you wish to leave."

"The quicker I get on the way, the quicker I will be able to retrieve the stone. It would be better for everyone involved."

"I tend to agree with you there, Shadick. I do not wish to rush you or anything but we may not have the luxury of just sitting around," Amethyst said walking out of the cave.

"Then I shall get going."

"And what about you, Al..." she said turning towards where Alexandria was, but she was nowhere to be seen "Where did she disappear to?

"I believe that she has already started her journey to Atlantican Ocean as she had just disappeared through those trees," Grog said pointing.

"It is not like her to leave without even saying goodbye... but I guess she has her reasoning."

"I better get on the road as well... time isn't on our side

after all," Shadick added walking to the horse and mounting the horse and kicking it into movement. The wolves automatically followed him and Amethyst wondered if she had done the right thing "Thank you for inviting us over while we wait to hear if the wolf pup will survive. We could have found a bar to sit at while waiting, but this is so much more comfortable. And I would probably be the only one to drink a beer, so it would be kind of useless." Shadick said, glancing around Dreska's home. "You have done well for yourself. The last time I saw you, you were living in the hotel on a semi-permanent basis."

"Thank you, it means a lot coming from you. And yes, I did. I worked in the bar for years on end and saved every penny that I could until I was able to afford to buy out the barman. Of course, he was shocked when I handed him the cash to buy his bar with no questions asked. I think that he might have had a small heart attack when I told him to just take the money and walk away.

"He stuttered something about how that was his livelihood, and I couldn't expect him to just go, so I told him that if he goes to another village that he could use the cash that I had just given him to buy himself another bar. It was quite a giggle when he was escorted from the bar by the guards." Dreska said, grinning coldly.

"You did not even warn him about what you were going to do?"

"No, I did not, just like he never warned us when our hours got cut or one of us got fired."

"That is a rather cold way to look at things."

"I do not see it as cold. I see it as 'fair is fair'. Perhaps if he had treated us better, I would have been nicer about the whole thing, but things happened like they happened, and that is what he deserved."

"I won't argue your point as I never saw how he treated you. From what I saw the few times that I was there, he treated his staff very nicely. Gave them meals and helped them out if they were in trouble."

"What you saw was him buttering up his next 'victim', he only did those things when he wanted to sleep with them, and when he got tired of them, he treated them like dirt, and before long they were fired for some or other reason."

"As I said, I do not know the whole story so I cannot truly comment." Shadick said, glancing at Alexandria, smiling.

"So, tell me Shadick, what have you been up to since the last time I saw you?" Dreska asked Shadick as she served them drinks.

"I was living with my sister, ever since my parents died but the last couple of years, I have been helping Alexandria and her friends with the war with the Centaurs as well as trying to find something that my father had been searching for since he was a young boy." Shadick told her.

"I heard about the tragic accident that claimed your parent's lives, and I would have found you but you and given you my condolences, but you never did give me your address. And what of Chadromida? I have not seen him in years."

"He is still living with the Dragons as he did when we met you and I haven't really seen him for a few years as we were both busy with our own thing. When he heard that the magical creatures and humans were getting together, he was able to convince the Dragons to lend them their powers. They showed up there with no forewarning they caused quite some trouble until everybody got used to seeing the giant beasts.

"He along with the dragons returned to the mountains when things seemed to have calmed down for a bit so he is there right now helping them in their realms again."

"Nothing much has changed then from all those years ago? Still running around doing whatever you want and causing trouble everywhere you go. Not caring who gets hurt in the process."

"Dreska, this is not the time to bring up the past."

"I'm not sure what you are speaking of, but Shadick is a good guy and has only been helpful ever since I met him!"

Alexandria said frowning.

"I have known Shadick since I was a young girl, and he has always been a gentleman, so I have to agree with Alex when she says that he is a good and helpful guy." Starlansha said.

"Then I must have the wrong guy if the two of you are so positive that he is such a good guy." Dreska said, straightening in her chair.

"Do not bring up the past when it only causes trouble." Shadick pleaded.

"Now you are afraid of trouble? That is something that you never had a problem with before. If I remember correctly, you delighted in sleeping with people and then pretending that it never happened."

"Shadick, what is she talking about?" Alexandria asked, glancing at him.

"Nothing Lexie, she is just joking around. Like we used to when we were teenagers."

"Using me and then ignoring me and pretending that you have never met me as a joke?"

"Back then we did a lot of crazier things, as well as a lot more dangerous, so I am not even sure what you are talking about."

"Let me refresh your memory then, Shadick and please do

not interrupt me, as I am sure that your girlfriend would love to hear the story." Dreska said, turning towards Alexandria. "I met Shadick over here when we were 18 years old, he was with his friend Chadromida, and they sat down at my table at the restaurant we were talking about earlier.

"At first, they ignored me completely and pretended that a ghost was serving them their drinks, until the one day when they suddenly noticed me for some unexplainable reason. They seduced me, and we went up to my room. I am sure that I do not need to tell you what happened in that room, but let me just tell you that it went on well into the morning.

"I fell asleep, and when I woke up, I expected to find to very handsome young men sleeping next to me but they weren't there at all. Neither was there anything that belonged to them; they had taken everything with them, probably hoping that I would believe that I had dreamed everything up that had happened.

"I convinced myself that they had to go do something else and that was why they had left me there without a goodbye and that they would find me the next day and explain, so I went back to sleep.

"I woke up early in the afternoon, got dressed and walked down to the restaurant. It was not my shift to work, but I wanted to check if they had perhaps decided to find me there but they weren't there.

"I walked to the marketplace, and that was where I found them. I tried talking, catching their attention, but they did not see me waving my arms around. I approached them, and when I tried talking to them, Chadromida asked Shadick over here if he heard something.

"And he replied with 'No, I do not'. I laughed it off and kept trying to talk to them, but they ignored me and walked around so much that I kept losing them in the crowds. I admit that I had fallen for the two of them a little, and them not responding to me got to me. I had several breakdowns at work and almost lost my job in the process but luckily, my boss got what he wanted from me several times.

"I was able to keep my job. However, it took me a few months to realise that I had been used and dumped by two guys who thought that seducing someone, sleeping with them and then ignoring them completely is a game for them.

"When my ex-boss found out what had happened, he laughed at me and told me that it was what I deserved and that he was not surprised that it had happened. And it was too bad that nothing worse had happened to me. Of course, I tried going to the guards and telling them that I wanted to open a case against the two of them but they laughed in my face and told me that Shadick and Chadromida were good guys who would never do something like that. I just kept quiet and watched as they continued going on as though they had no worries in their lives."

Alexandria stared at Dreska in shock, her mouth hanging open slightly, slowly turning to Shadick wide-eyed.

"Please tell me that what she just told me is lies and that she just made it all up to mess with me!"

"I agree Shadick. That has to be a lie told by someone who wants to cause trouble." Starlansha said, putting her hand over Alexandria's.

"Oh yes, please tell them what lies I am telling, that I have never spoken the truth about anything." Dreska sneered at him.

"I am sorry that you had to hear it from her point of view Lexie. I was going to tell you about what happened in the past eventually, but I wanted to make sure that you would understand everything and not just what someone else tells you." Shadick said, glaring at Dreska. "What happened all those years ago was the worst thing that I have ever done, and both Chadromida and I have been feeling bad about it and have never done something like that ever again."

"So why did you not find her then and tell her you are sorry about what happened?" Alexandria asked shocked.

"Because back then we were too cocky and full of

ourselves to realise that what we had done was wrong, it was only a few years later when we spoke about it again that we realised what had happened and we tried talking to her but she ignored us this time so we just accepted that she had forgotten about what had happened and had moved on with her life as she seemed very happy."

"I seemed happy, but it was all an act. It took me years to get over and accept what had happened. I did not trust any guy ever since, and that has cost me a thousand relationships, all because of the two of you. And I ignored you in the hopes that you will realise how badly you hurt me." Dreska said matter-of-factly.

"And what about what she said about seeing you with other women every day?" Alexandria asked frowning.

"The local women of the night loved trying to get Chadromida to sleep with them, and even when he told them no a thousand and one times, they still hung around him like flies hoping that they would get lucky. And when they saw that we were friends, they split up between the two of us and tried with all their might to get together with us as we looked like a 'good lay'.

"The barman eventually banned them from ever entering the bar again, and that was when they finally got the message that we did not want them. Shortly after that, my parents sent us to Atlantican ocean so that we could think about what we had done, and that was when we met Starlansha and her sister." Shadick said, kneeling in front of Alexandria pleadingly.

"From what I have heard, you used Roslata and slept with Starlansha over there without a seconds thought." Dreska added.

"I told Alexandria that I slept with Shadick while she was busy with her training, and we sorted that all out. I even told her what happened with Roslata. That they were dating and that she cheated on him with Chadromida and did not even think twice about it." Starlansha said, shaking her head "it was also discussed a couple of nights ago, so she knows."

"Oh, you poor pathetic girl! You believe what they tell you because you have fallen in love with the user! One of these days, I will hear how you are lying in your room useless because he broke up with you for yet another girl who he just wanted to use and abuse. Perhaps I will send you a bouquet of 'told you so' flowers just to rub it in a little."

Alexandria suddenly stood up, shoving Shadick aside in the process before running out of the room without a backwards glance, her eyes filling with tears but not wanting Dreska to see that she had had an effect on her. What she did not see or hear was Starlansha getting up and slapping Dreska through the face before running after her.

"You do realise that she said that just to get a reaction out of you?" Starlansha asked Alexandria when she finally caught up with her friend.

"That I could have handled. What got to me was that Shadick actually admitted to doing the things she had accused him of." she replied, frowning and slowing down to a walk.

"But has he not told you about his past before?"

"Not in so much detail, but he did tell me that it was rather dark and that he regretted everything that had happened."

"Then why react so strongly?"

"Because of the way she said it! As though he was some kind of heartless beast that did not have any care at all, and when she mentioned that he would leave me the same way, it kind of just got to me because that is exactly what I have been worrying about ever since we got together."

"It wasn't really what she said but more how you have been feeling about it all?"

"Yes, and I know that I probably overreacted, but I just had to get out of there before I threw a spell at her or something."

"That was very wise then on your part. Shall we go to the clinic and see how the wolf pup is doing? I am getting a feeling that you will have a new admirer in the form of that gorgeous pup as soon as she wakes up. And she will refuse to leave your side."

"I doubt it, I don't mind though as long as I know she is no longer injured. Let us find our way back because I have no idea where we are." Alexandria said, glancing around the alleyway and frowning as the air changed around them.

Chapter 13

New Breed of Evil

"Are you doing this, Alex?" Starlansha asked, glancing around them. "I think that it would be for the best to get your anger under control before something terrible happens to us."

"I'm not doing anything, Star! And I can assure you that I would not do anything to hurt us." Alexandria replied, frowning. "it would probably be for the best if we were to get out of here before there is no way out."

"If this isn't your doing, then yes I agree we need to get out of here."

There was a quick blast of air before they could move. As they looked around, feathers seemed to rain down on them. Alexandria frowned and pulled her daggers out from the sheaths. Starlansha looked at her in shock, before pulling her sword out. It all seemed too familiar to her, as though she had seen this happen before. But she could not for sure say where she had seen it. It was as though her memory had been wiped, and she was just not able to reach those illusive memories.

"Alex, should we be worried about what is happening here? Perhaps we need to call for help, in case this turns into a big fight?"

"I think that the time for help has come and gone. No one will hear us now. And no one in their right mind would run into an alleyway without real cause."

"You say that in such a way that it scares me more than whatever is happening around us."

"Just stay positive that we will get out of here alive."

Alexandria said, shaking her head tensing slightly. A shimmer had appeared in front of them, and images were being revealed slowly. At first, all they could tell from what they were seeing was that whatever the creatures were, they had wings. A few seconds passed, and women stepped out from the shimmering portal.

Starlansha's mouth fell open as she recognised the creatures. They were Harpies, the things that they had only heard about a few hundred times. But as they had been told that these creatures did not exist anymore, it was difficult to accept what they were clearly seeing. They had bodies of humans, but that was about where the similarities ended. Their eyes were dark red, with wings bigger than their own bodies. At the end of each wings was a sharp claw that they could see was sharp and deadly.

Just as they thought that they would be able to fight the four Harpies, the portal seemed to change, and more figures appeared. A soft exclamation could be heard as two Minotaur's stepped through. The portal disappeared, and Alexandria knew that there would be no more interruptions.

In the same thought, she was not sure whether they would be able to take on all six of the creatures that were now in front of them. The Minotaur's were twice her size and she had to strain her neck to look at the horns on top of their heads. How was it possible for two mythical creatures to just appear like this, as though it was a normal occurrence?

From what she had learned when she was a young girl, she knew that they had been wiped out. Had Valencia been wrong? Had there been a few left? Clearly a mistake had been made, not to mention they seemed even stronger than the stories of old.

Twirling her daggers, she looked at first the Harpies and then at the Minotaur's. This would be nearly impossible, but she was determined to fight until her last breath. Starlansha was about to ask something but was interrupted by a Harpy who attacked her with its one claw. It seemed to be some kind of sign as all chaos broke loose.

Alexandria ran forward and slashed at the closest Harpy

while dodging a swipe from the Minotaur. She ducked and swiped at its legs, but it just jumped out of the way, causing the ground to shake slightly.

She frowned and tried to figure out what the best way would be to fight these beasts. She swiped at the Harpy again and successfully ran her blade along its wing, causing it to scream in pain. They were distracted enough that she was able to put some space between herself and the creatures.

Concentrating, she threw a wind ball at the Minotaur, but it just shook its head and disappeared. Well, that was absolutely useless. She was supposed to have all this power, yet they had no effect on these creatures.

From the corner of her eye, she noticed that Starlansha was not having much luck either. If they did not get out of here soon, they might just end up dead. Throwing another wind sphere, aiming for the Harpy who screeched and took to the air. It seemed that it was enough to distract them but the Minotaur's saw it as nothing more as an irritation. Biting her lip, she took a deep breath and concentrated on trying to pull the breath out of the Minotaur, hoping that it would not be able to get away from that.

It took a step towards her but paused as it realised that it could not breathe. It roared and reared its head in frustration, smacking its large chest and swinging around. It's one horn went through the Harpy that had flown into the air, and with a gush of blood and a screech, she died.

The Minotaur shook its head and, with a snort fell to the ground. Before she could get too happy, the other three Harpies as well as the remaining Minotaur turned towards her and rushed at her. As she was about to throw a blast of energy at them, a howl came from behind her, and she ducked just in time as the Wolf pup rushed at the creatures, not seeming to care that she was outnumbered. She bit the one Harpy's wing and pulled on it hard, causing it to fall to the ground scratching at the Wolf. Alexandria rushed forward and stabbed the downed Harpy in the heart.

"Lexie!" Shadick shouted, rushing into the alleyway, freezing as he noticed the creatures around them.

Ignoring the distraction, she swung her daggers at the Minotaur's hooves, but they seemed to be pulling away. The Harpies glared at her before picking the Minotaur up and taking to the sky, disappearing before any of them could do anything. Still on the floor, the Wolf pup crawled over to her and licked her cheek, and she smiled a little. Only then did she glanced at Starlansha, who was standing against the wall in shock.

"Did you really just kill a Minotaur as well as two Harpies?!" she asked wide-eyed. "From what I have heard, they are nearly impossible to kill."

"I think that I just killed them unless they are just pretending to be dead." she replied, smiling slightly.

"What the hell just happened?! I was walking to the clinic to find you when I saw the Wolf pup running in this direction. I had also noticed that there seemed to be an evil aura in town, and I was afraid for you." Shadick added, looking at the mess.

"We took a wrong turn and ended up here. I had just convinced Alexandria that we should turn around and find the clinic when we were suddenly surrounded by feathers or something. We tried to move, but that was when they appeared through some kind of portal." Starlansha said, wiping her forehead.

"From what I was taught, those creatures were extinct. So how is it that they just appeared here, of all places?" Alexandria asked lightly, scratching the Wolf.

"I am not sure as that is what I have been told as well. Is it possible that they were just in hiding and the Centaurs had been able to convince them to join them?"

"Anything is really possible with the Centaurs, so guess that we will not really know unless we ask them. What is amazing is that if this attack was from them, how did they know where we were? Have they got spies all over the villages?"

"That is the only plausible explanation, but there is no way that I will allow you to go and find out!" Shadick said frowning.

"And you really think that you have the right to tell me what I can or can't do? Especially after what we found out about Dreska? Come on, Starlansha. Let us go to the clinic just to make sure that there are no permanent injuries."

Starlansha nodded and took a step towards her. The Wolf pup stood up as well, growling softly as it stepped on its hurt front paw. Alexandria looked at it in concern, but she just kept walking back the way that she had come. Shadick tried putting his hand on her shoulder, but she shrugged it off following Starlansha and the Wolf pup.

Chapter 14

Forgiveness

"That was way too close for comfort." Starlansha said, sitting on a chair just outside of the clinic.

"You're telling me. I just wished you hadn't run out of Dreska's house like that, sweetie." Shadick told Alexandria. "There was really no need to do that."

"Star, do you know anything else about those creatures? What I have been told is very little, and it has been years since I was told." Alexandria asked, ignoring Shadick.

"Nothing much, I'm afraid. I just know that my Grandfather mentioned them a few years ago. He said something about they were rather deadly but as far as he knew, they had all gone. I tried once to find out more about them but could not find anything." Star replied.

"They are called 'Harpeia'. Winged women." Shadick told them.

"And what does that mean exactly? As I have only heard of them as Harpies."

"It is just a very fancy way to say Harpy. The history books were written by old fools more concerned about fancy names than facts."

"And what do you know about them?" Alexandria asked finally turning towards him

"My father told me about them, and when I researched them further, I came to the realisation that they were basically non-existent. They used to attack humans as well as magical creatures quite often, but it was taken care of. But everyone had assumed that they were all killed because of no attacks in the last hundred years or so."

"If Star could not find out anything about them, how is it that you were able to?"

"I had to dig really deep and go talk to people that have been considered dead for years."

"That would explain it. Am I right in assuming the bull-like creatures were Minotaur's?" Starlansha asked.

"Yes, they were, they also haven't been seen for decades and their appearance here today is rather disturbing as they are very dangerous beasts." Shadick told her them turning to Alexandria frowning. "You went quiet, Lexi. What's wrong?"

"I had a dream... A nightmare really, back at the palace

that I couldn't understand, but now I do." Alexandria said softly, absently scratching Freyja's head.

"You never told me about these dreams, Alex." Starlansha said, moving closer to Alexandria.

"I didn't want to put even more stress on you. And like I said, I didn't think anything about it until the Dream Oracle appeared to me. And even then, I didn't really worry about it as she never really got a chance to explain the dreams in full detail."

"A Dream Oracle appeared to you?!" Shadick asked, shocked "What exactly did it tell you?"

"Like I said, not much, as Queen Arabella interrupted us before we could really talk. But she did tell me that she gave me the dreams to warn me about the Centaurs and that they cannot be expected to 'play by the rules' as well as that the creatures in my dreams were going to be used in the war. But she never got to tell me more about the creatures."

"We were interrupted before we could finish our conversation, and I do apologise for leaving so hastily before. But it is against our laws to let anyone who is not our 'premeditated' target see us." a voice said before the Dream Oracle appeared in the middle of the room.

Shadick immediately pulled out his sword, and Starlansha exclaimed softly. Alexandria and Freyja were the only ones who did not react in surprise.

"Welcome back, Dream Oracle. I never did get your name at the palace." Alexandria said, smiling.

"I guess you could call me Rialey." the Dream Oracle tilted her head slightly in thought

"Are you really a Dream Oracle or are you just a trick sent by the Centaurs to confuse and give us false hope?" Shadick asked, slowly sheathing his sword.

"Shadick! How could you ask her something like that when you can clearly see that she is more than just a trick?" Alexandria said.

"He has a fair point, Alex. But to answer you, Shadick; No I am not a trick from your enemies, and yes I am really a Dream Oracle." Rialey told him, smiling slightly.

"What has triggered your appearance today, Rialey? Surely, it's not to talk about my dreams again? Seeing that we have already encountered the creatures from my dream."

"It seems that the other Oracles are wondering about this war and which side to choose to join or to stay at a distance. Most believe it would be better to join the side of the Centaurs as they seem stronger than your army, although we have not been able to see your army. The protection around Valencia is quite powerful, more so than what we thought."

"They want to join the Centaurs?!"

"Well they are considering it; most consider it the smartest thing to do."

"That is foolishness!" Starlansha exclaimed.

"That is why I am here, to offer you my allegiance. I do not want to join them in their idiotic pursuits. I offer you my assistance."

"A lynx would be a bit of a noticeable addition. It would make us stand out even more than we do right now." Shadick informed them.

"You have a very valid point there. If you accept my allegiance, then I will change my form."

"Of course, you are welcome to join us! You didn't even need to ask." Alexandria said smiling. "The more, the merrier."

A soft light slowly surrounded Rialey as she gradually changed shape, her lynx body becoming human, a young girl with light blond hair falling in ringlets to her waist her body covered by a light blue and purple dress that reached her ankles. "Is this a more appropriate form, Shadick?" she asked, turning towards him.

"Yes, that is much better." he said, staring a little.

Glaring at Shadick slightly, Alexandria stood up from the bed, Freyja following her as she walked out of the door. "We leave at dawn."

"Why did you leave so quickly last night?" Starlansha asked the next morning, sitting in the pub area waiting for the other two. "I think that Rialey still had something to say but kept quiet after your departure."

"I wasn't in the mood to watch Shadick gawking at someone else. I had enough when it happened with Dreska. I mean, if he loved me, he wouldn't let stuff like that bother him."

"He is just a guy. Maybe you should listen to his side of the story before making up your mind about what happened. You didn't exactly give him a chance to explain, and even I was staring when she changed like that."

They heard female laughter coming from the stairs, and as they glanced towards it, they saw Shadick and Rialey walking toward them.

"You were saying?" Alexandria asked, shaking her head.

"Morning Star, Sweetheart." Shadick said smiling, kissing Alexandria's cheek. "I trust you slept well?"

"It was acceptable thank you, Shadick, and yourself?" Starlansha replied.

"Very well, thank you. Are we ready to leave, or are you

two still busy eating?"

"No, we're ready." Alexandria said, standing up and walking outside to where Terry and the horses were waiting for them. "Morning Terry, how are you this morning?"

"Anxious to get on the road." Terry replied, looking at Rialey. "I see we have another person traveling with us?"

"That's Rialey, she joined us last night." Shadick told him.

"There is something magical about your energy Rialey, if I may say so."

"You are very perceptive Centaur; I am a Dream Oracle." Rialey told him frowning slightly, "I did not know that we would be traveling with a Centaur."

"He saved me when I was in trouble. I trust him with my life. He is also a close friend of ours." Alexandria told Rialey.

"I hope that he does not turn on you when you trust him so much."

"You can trust him Rialey." Shadick intervened before Terry or Alexandria could say anything.

"Shall we get going before it gets too late?" Terry asked the group "I went to the Doctor and was told he wouldn't be able to do anything as the wolf refuses to stay there. He has given her medicine and fixed what he was able to, so all we need to do is keep an eye on her."

"Thank you for going to check with the Doctor it is

appreciated. I agree; I want to get to Valencia now. I need to see for myself that Am is well." Alexandria said, jumping onto Nightmare's back and slowly urging the horse on.

She was riding next to Terry and Starlansha talking softly about Valencia and Trilantica, not really paying much attention to their surroundings. Alexandria glanced at Freyja every now and then to make sure the wolf pup was keeping up.

Still injured, she refused to leave her side since the Harpy and Minotaur attack even when she tried. She had temporarily left her at the doctor's house, but she had whined and refused to relax, so Alexandria had given up calling the pup to her side.

"The pup does seem to have bonded with you since the day before." Terry noted.

"She does not want to leave my side even though she knows that she isn't at full health. I just want to make sure she does not hurt herself more than she already is. And that she is well fed and stays hydrated. That is the best I can do for her until she feels better." Alexandria replied, smiling slightly.

"Managwa does not seem to like it much that you have someone besides him, Alex." Starlansha noted laughing softly and looking at the wolf running next to Shadick.

"The way he was acting, you would think that you are its mate and not just a companion." Terry added also laughing.

"It is probably because he does not know her. When she is asleep, he comes to me for some attention, the silly wolf." Alexandria added, joining in with the laughter.

Their laughter caught Shadick's attention, making him smile.

"You really care for her, don't you?" Rialey asked him softly.

"Yes, I do but we've had a few misunderstandings, and it seems that it is driving us apart. I want to make it up to her, but I am not sure how. She can be a very stubborn witch. I like seeing her smile like that, though. I don't think she's really smiled or laughed in a year or two."

"She has had a lot of hardships in her young life. I believe that she hides her feelings too much, and that is not healthy."

"I have gotten her to open up a bit, but it is hard when we both have things to do. She keeps closing up, and then I have to work all over again to get her to let me in."

"You will be surprised how easy that is with the right words at the right time."

"We're going to set up camp here! It is getting too dark to travel anymore today." Terry shouted at them from a few feet ahead of them.

They nodded, dismounting from the horses and tying them to a fallen tree, before starting to gather wood for a fire. Alexandria and Starlansha already picking fruits and berries for supper laughing softly.

"When everything is quiet, go talk to her and explain what has to be explained. Just have patience and do not raise your voice." Rialey whispered to him before walking to Terry, whom she was trying to get to know better.

"I never would have thought that traveling would get tiring after all the training we did. But seems I was wrong because I am exhausted." Starlansha said, sitting down yawning.

"Really? I feel absolutely fine." Alexandria replied. "You feeling okay Star? You seem a little distant."

"I'm feeling a little drained, and I am still worried about Rosy. We've never been separated for this long, and I'm scared she gets hurt."

"I am sure she will be fine. She just needs a little time to herself; then she'll catch up to us in a few days."

Starlansha nodded slowly and then lay down on the grass, staring absently into the fire. Everything had gone quiet now, night had truly fallen, and it was easy to hear if someone approached their little camp.

"Lexi, can you please come with me so we can talk for a

while? I think I owe you an explanation." Shadick asked from behind her.

"Is it really necessary, Shadick? It's over and done with." Alexandria replied

"Please?" he asked again, holding his hand out.

She sighed, nodding and taking his hand slowly, standing up and letting him lead her into the trees to talk.

"What Dreska said yesterday, I know it hurt, but she had one thing wrong, which I told her after you ran out. It is all in the past. I am not the same person anymore. I have changed. And I have matured a lot since then. And I truly do have feelings for you, strong feelings."

"You should have told me that before I heard it from someone else. I might have taken it better if you had told me." Alexandria told him

"And I apologise for that. I really should have told you, and I realise that now. I am just hoping that it isn't too late for us."

"I don't know what to say. Maybe if you hadn't reacted the way you did to Rialey, it would be easier to forgive you. But how do I know that you won't always respond that way to women?"

"You mean when she transformed into her human form?" Alexandria nodded in response. "I was just so surprised! It was the first time I'd even seen an Oracle, and then she surprised me even more by transforming in front of us. I didn't know what to do."

"So, you don't feel any attraction towards her then?"

"I admit that she isn't bad looking, but I would rather have you a million times over than take her."

"It just feels like there are just too many secrets between us. How will we ever work as a couple if we cannot trust each other."

"I agree with you. So why don't we just work on it? Ask me something, and I will try to answer." he said, pulling her down to sit on the grass

"That is not how I want it to work. I want you to tell me this stuff out of your own free will, not ask you questions about your past life."

"Fair enough, Lexi." he admitted, holding her tighter.

"How about we talk about our lives as we travel? No expectations and just one promise."

"What promise would that be?"

"That I will not leave anything out. I will tell you everything I think you need to know that I see as important and think you will find important."

"That sounds like a good idea." Alexandria said, cuddling closer against him. "Thank you for talking to me about it. I really appreciate it. And I think it is what we needed."

"I agree we haven't given each other enough attention since we got back together. We have been too worried about the war and everyone else that we have been neglecting each other."

"How about we make another deal?"

"Let's hear it."

"We have to make time for each other. Even if it is just to hold each other."

"I like your deal better than I like my own." he told her, laughing softly. Alexandria joining in a second later. "I missed your laugh."

"Missed it?"

"Yes, you haven't really laughed or smiled and meant it in way too long."

"Neither have you."

"Am I forgiven for what happened yesterday? Even though I would understand if you didn't want to forgive me."

"You are forgiven. I love you too much to not forgive you. As long as I feel assured that it won't happen again."

"You can hurt me with my own sword if that ever happens again."

"I haven't felt this relaxed since I felt your arms around me when I got out of the Atlantican." she said, laughing again softly at his statement, looking up at the stars

"I am at your service, milady." Shadick smiled.

"We should probably get back to the camp before they send out a search party."

"I believe they will let us be alone for a while. They all know that we need some time alone."

They heard a soft sniffling coming towards them, Shadick tensing a little and then relaxing when Freyja came bounding into the small clearing.

"She really has become attached to you." Shadick noted as Alexandria scratched Freyja's head.

"Managwa doesn't like it; he's jealous." Alexandria replied as the fore-mentioned wolf prowled in before lying at the foot of a tree watching them.

"I believe that it is because she is so young, and also due to not a part of his pack. He doesn't trust her yet, but hopefully, in time they'll get along."

"I just don't want them to fight each other and get hurt, especially as she is so young and already hurt."

"He won't hurt her unless he feels that we are threatened by her."

Nodding slowly, she watched as Managwa walked next to Shadick and lay down watching Freyja cautiously as she fell asleep.

"I sometimes wish I could just close my eyes and fall asleep as easily as the wolves fall asleep. Unfortunately, my dreams are filled with worry and horror." Alexandria said sighing

"You are having bad dreams, love?" Shadick asked worriedly.

"Just the same things over and over. You dying in some way, and I can't do anything about it."

"I already died, and you brought me back to life. We are now connected. And I won't just die as easily as that, you know. I am a lot tougher than I look; just ask the Centaurs."

"That does not mean that I am not afraid."

"I cannot make a promise that I may not be able to keep. But I will try and not be killed until I am old."

Smiling, she cuddled closer to Shadick, closing her eyes and shutting out the images of her constant night terrors.

Chapter 15

Valencia

It was late morning, and they were all very quiet. They were all getting rather tired of traveling so much, and she wished that it would stop for a while. She was excited to see Amethyst again after what felt like forever.

"Honey! You're pushing that poor horse to its absolute limit." Shadick shouted at her, and she looked around her.

"Oh, I didn't even realise!" she whispered, shaking her head and slowing the horse down. "I was thinking about finally being able to see Amethyst, and I was just kind of on automatic."

"We will get there soon enough; you do not have to worry about that."

"I think that there is also a part of you that wish to never travel ever again." Starlansha commented grinning.

"That is also what I was thinking. To wake up in the morning and know that you don't need to travel someplace. And more importantly, being able to just relax with friends and family." Alexandria said sighing.

"Are you living in a dream world, Alexandria?" Terri asked seriously. "There is no time to sit back and relax. We need to figure out what the next plan of attack is. We have no time to relax our guard."

"Well, there goes my slightly good mood."

"She was just wondering if that could have been a possibility, Terri. We all know that there is no chance of having a little bit of off time. But sometimes it is needed to think of what one could do if you did not have the world on your shoulders." Shadick said, smiling. "Have you never thought about what you would rather want to do instead of doing what you are busy doing?"

"Growing up with the Centaurs, there was no chance to relax or to want to do something else. If you weren't concentrating on the present and whatever you were busy doing, then you were in trouble. So, I do not know what it feels like, nor do I believe that I want to know."

"For right now, there is no immediate danger. We are allowed to try and relax when it is possible, as we all know that being stressed and worried during battle isn't a good thing. It could cause you to get distracted, which is not something we need." Rialey added. "That is why I prefer to take a long bath or to take a walk whenever I get the chance. Because I never know if I will ever get that chance again."

"Well, this has gone from hopeful to serious to morbid... fantastic." Alexandria muttered as they reached the walls.

"How is anyone supposed to get into Valencia when the walls are 8 feet tall?" Shadick asked, looking up at the walls.

"Actually, the walls are 10 feet tall. With 6 guards at each gate and an alarm close at hand if any danger was spotted. There has also been a shield put up around the wall. It wouldn't stand up against an all-out attack, but it would last long enough for the fighters to get ready." Terri said, pointing to the barely visible sheen on the walls.

"And how is someone who wishes to join the village supposed to get in with such security?" Starlansha asked, her eyes flashing all along the wall.

"It is possible to get in, but only into the security council."

"Security council?"

"It consists of several different Creatures, who ask the person or persons some questions. For example, where they come from and how they heard of Valencia. If they answer truthfully, they will be allowed to see Amethyst. She will speak with them, and if she is satisfied with what she found out, she assigns them a house as well as a job. You see, everyone has something to do. And every part of it is vital in the continued survival of the village."

"That sounds rather... intense." Alexandria said frowning.

"It wasn't so difficult to gain entrance about a year ago. But we discovered some trouble makers, and we had to then make sure that we were able to keep them out. Amethyst came up with the Security council, and it took her over 6 months to choose those on the council."

"And where did she come up with the idea of the Security council?" Shadick asked.

"A lady name Luanda. I do believe that you know her Alexandria?"

"Oh, yes! Her father used to be the town butcher when McLeod's still existed." Alexandria said nodding.

"She has been having some sort of visions the last couple of years. At first, everyone just shrugged it off and laughed at her. But one night, she predicted a Centaur attack, and it happened exactly as she had predicted. That was when Amethyst decided to take her seriously.

"In fact, she was the one that drew this entire village on a piece of parchment, with exact descriptions of what should go where. She was also able to tell Amethyst which people would be a good addition to the council as they were trustworthy."

"I do not recall her having visions before. From what I recall, she was a rather plain and quiet young lady."

"From the rumours that have been floating around, it seems that her parents had kept the visions quiet when they had still been alive. They had been afraid of being rejected and that everything going wrong would be blamed on her. They also convinced her to never talk about it to anyone. And she listened to them until the day she arrived at the Caves and realised that it would be more acceptable in the magical community."

"Even though visions aren't exactly a normal or even common power, I am sure that the humans would have shunted her." Shadick noted.

"In the beginning, she was, yes. But now she had people stopping her in the middle of the road asking that she predict their future."

"If it isn't frowned at and rejected, it is treated with disrespect and abused. I remember when my mom was asked for potions and things just because she had helped some of her 'friends'." Alexandria muttered angrily.

"The villagers knew that your parents had been witches?"

"Not exactly... but some of them suspected."

"Halt! Do not come any closer unless you drop all your weapons. This is not a place to cause trouble, especially when accompanied by a Centaur!" a voice sneered at them.

"Lower your weapons. We mean the village, no harm. It is I, Terri, returning from my journey." Terri said, stepping forward.

"I do not know anyone by the name of Terri, and I have been stationed here for two weeks!" the guard said, lifting his bow higher.

"Will you lower your weapon soldier! And treat that Centaur with some respect. He has helped this village many times over. Although I do have to admit that I do not recognise his companions." another voice said.

"It is good to see you again, Captain. And I have to thank you for the vote of confidence." Terri said, smiling and inclining his head.

"Call the Council to the room and lower the gates. We seem to have some new arrivals for the test."

"There is no need to call the Council together. These people will be welcomed back with open arms."

"Knowing Amethyst, it would be more like screams of excitement." Alexandria commented, grinning as they walked through the gates.

"No one calls the Queen by her name except a select few." The Captain said, stopping them. "Show her some respect before I have you thrown in jail... or worse, out there so that the Centaurs can deal with you."

"Captain, I do believe that you should be the one showing her some respect." Terri said frowning.

"And why do you believe I should be showing a commoner respect?"

"Because she is the furthest thing from a commoner you can get. She is, in fact, the Queen's adopted sister, Alexandria."

They watched as that fact ran through his mind. His eyes widened, and all the colour drained from his face. He glanced at her up and down, slowly seeming to realise who was looking at and what he had heard.

"Terri, I believe you may have shocked him into silence." Shadick noted grinning.

"At least he wasn't shocked to death." Starlansha added giggling.

"Please, forgive me, your majesty! I was not informed that you would be arriving today. But I will send a message to the Queen right away and inform her of your arrival." the Captain said, bowing.

"There is no need for you to call me 'majesty' as I am not royalty. Amethyst is the one with the title. Also, I wish to rather surprise her, and if you inform her of my arrival, it would just ruin it." Alexandria said smiling.

"Very well, mam. I will inform the guards of whom you are but to not tell the Queen. Just so that they do not stop you from entering the Palace."

"Thank you, that is greatly appreciated." Starlansha said.

As they started walking away from the gate, there was a soft clanking as the gate closed. Shadick glanced back and saw the guard sliding bolts in the door, securing it even more before turning back to look where they were going.

"I do believe that you shocked the Captain into proper silence, Starlansha. I can assure you that, that doesn't often happen." Terri said grinning.

"All I did was smile and say thank you!" Starlansha said surprised.

"Most women and even most of the men are terrified of the Captain. And they go out of their way to avoid him whenever possible. No one dares to speak to him, never mind thanking him for something."

"Is he a mean person or something?"

"Once you get to know him, he is a very nice person. He has a tough exterior, and most people notice the 'I will kill you' aura that seems to be around him."

"Perhaps when all of the fighting is over, you can ask him out for a drink. It might help the people realise that he isn't all that tough." Shadick commented straight-faced.

"He isn't really my type... but perhaps he is more your speed, Shadick. Don't let me stop you." she replied, rolling her eyes.

"I'm sorry to rush the two of you. But perhaps we can start moving again? I want to see Amethyst as soon as possible." Alexandria said sighing

"Very well then, Alexandria. Let us get going to the Palace." Terri said, glancing at her. "I just thought that you may want to see the village properly."

"It is already getting dark though, so it isn't as though we would be able to see very well. Perhaps you could show me in the morning? But right now, I think that we should get some proper rest and have a good meal."

Shadick glanced at her before looking at Terri, frowning. He shrugged in confusion before slowly following Terri towards the Palace. Every now and then he glanced around at something in the village that caught his eye.

* * *

"I do believe that it is important to have a patrol along the wall just as an extra precaution. There is no reason for us to be caught unawares." a voice drifted towards them.

"That is understandable, but we then have to make sure

that the patrols happen in such a way that the gates aren't left unmanned." Amethyst replied.

"Why do we not ask Luanda if she did not perhaps have a vision about this? To save us the trouble of coming up with these plans?"

"If you think it is a good thing to use a person as though they are some kind of weapon or as though they are expendable, then perhaps we should reconsider whether you belong on this team." Terri said, walking into the room.

"Your majesty, would you really let a Centaur tell us what we should or shouldn't do? When it has been his kind that has been killing us?"

"I do believe that Terri is correct. If you see this war as only being fought against Centaurs and the magical Creatures, then perhaps you do not belong here. If you look through the window right now, you will see Humans and magical Creatures working together. It has not been a case of 'you and them' for a while now. Instead, it is 'us and them'.

"I think that you should go take a walk around the village to get to know some of the others. Learn their stories and what brought them here before returning here." Alexandria said, stepping through the doors, Amethyst's eyes widening.

"You heard the Princess! Now get a move on." a guard said, stepping forward.

They all watched as the man froze in place and glanced at the new arrivals. He looked at Amethyst before rushing out of the room. They stepped closer to Amethyst as though one being and smiled.

"I think that it might be better for us to go out and come back in so that Amethyst can get over the shock of seeing us." Shadick joked. "Or perhaps we should call the doctor because it looks as though she has seen a ghost."

"So, this is real? This isn't just another sick trick that my mind has decided to play on me?" Amethyst asked slowly.

"I can assure you that this is very real, Am. Your mind isn't playing a trick on you." Alexandria said, stepping closer.

Without warning, she flung herself into Alexandria's arms with a soft exclamation. Shadick and Starlansha glanced at each before laughing softly and shaking their heads.

"It has been such a terrible time! I have been starting to wonder if something bad had happened to all of you and that there was no one left to tell me. I considered sending a message to Queen Arabella to find out what was happening. But I was scared that I would only be bothering you and that you would get mad." Amethyst babbled, still holding Alexandria tightly.

"You can relax, Am. We were busy with training until about two weeks ago, and then Queen Arabella insisted that we relax a bit first before getting back to you."

"If you know my Gran at all, then you should know how important rest is in her eyes. Especially after the amount of training that Alex had to go through." Starlansha said, then added, "And she insisted that we spend some time with her and my Granddad. And unfortunately, there is no way to argue with her when she wants something that badly."

"And if you remember, I promised you that I will escort them home once they returned. My journey was taking a little longer, so even if they had been finished earlier, I would not have been there to join them." Shadick reminded her seriously.

"Very well then. I guess that my timing is a bit off as I expected you back for about 2 months now. But I guess that I was wrong." Amethyst said, finally looking around at the rest. "Wait a minute, where is Roslata? Normally the two of you are almost attached at the hip, Star."

"She decided that she no longer wanted to travel with us. We have been traveling without her for a few days now. We are hoping that she had gone back to Atlantican, but we have no way of being sure of where she went. Nor do we have a way to send her a message and find out." Alexandria said sighing. "All of us tried talking her out of leaving. Which earned me a slap in the face. But her mind had been made up for quite a bit by the sounds of it."

"We even stayed an extra night in case she changed her mind." Starlansha added.

"I am so sorry to hear that, and I can only imagine how difficult it is for you." Amethyst said, letting go of Alexandria. "If it had been in my power, I would have assured you that she was safely back with your grandparents. But unfortunately, I cannot do that. I am sure that she is safe, though. She is a smart girl."

"Thank you, Am. I appreciate that you are trying to make me feel better about all of this. Although I have to admit that her actions were rather selfish. Before she left, I had spoken to her several times, and not once did she mention that she was unhappy. If she had said something, I am sure that we could have done something to make it better for her."

"I like your attitude about it, Star. But you know that she was unhappy with me, and me dying would have been the only thing that probably would have made her smile." Alexandria told her.

"Then she needs to learn that not everything in this world revolves around her. Other people also deserve to get the attention and love."

"Well, I for one am very happy that Terri had been at the Caves when we got there. Even if we almost killed each other in the process." Shadick said, leaning against the table.

"And how was I supposed to have guessed that it was you lot making an appearance? It could have been the Centaurs or some of their followers. If you recall, I let go of Alexandria as soon as I realised my mistake. No harm was done to any of you." Terri replied grinning.

"I take it that Terri has informed you of why we had to leave the Caves?" Amethyst asked.

"He did yes. We were just happy that everyone had gotten out alive." Shadick said then added, "Lexie had been starting to worry that something bad had happened. It was rather difficult to hold her back from running around the entire place."

"I was not that bad! I admit that I had been worried but I was nowhere close to panicking." she said pouting.

"I thought that it was very cute."

"We tried staying there, but when the attacks got more frequent and more serious, we had no choice. Some lives were lost, and it was getting difficult for everyone to stay there. It was not a choice that I relished having to do but there was no other option." Amethyst interjected.

"It took months of convincing not just her but some of the Creatures and Humans. And we had to weather a lot more attacks before she finally made up her mind." Terri said. "But

I do agree that it had been for the best."

"Please tell that to the families who lost their loved ones. And we could do nothing but watch it happen."

"Am, will you stop blaming yourself? It was not within your powers to stop them. It was the Centaurs who made the decision to kill innocent people. Just as it was their choice to rip families apart." Alexandria said, lightly touching her friend's shoulder.

"But I should have made triple sure that the Centaurs were not close at hand when we started moving camp."

"And I can assure you that the Centaurs would have made sure that they knew what was happening. Or fed you false information just so that the losses were even bigger. If you ask me, you caught them unaware."

"You really think that?" she asked, biting her lip.

"From what we have been told so far? Most definitely. The couple of Centaurs that attacked you were only stragglers."

"I have to agree with Lexie on this one. I shudder to think of the losses this group would have incurred if there had been more Centaurs around. Or if they had been organized in any way." Shadick said nodding

"If you guys insist, it is just that it has been feeling as though everyone has been blaming me. Because I didn't create a portal like I did when we first moved there. But I knew I would not have been able to sustain it for everyone. Not without Alex helping me, at least." Amethyst sighed.

"You should really stop blaming yourself so much. You did your best in a bad situation. As for those people who feel like blaming you should realise that it would have been so much worse if it had been just them." Alexandria said smiling.

"Alright then, I should inform the Faeries that you have returned so that they can get food ready for you. I know that they will be very excited to see you, Alex. They have been playing around with different outfits, especially for you."

"A new outfit as well as food. Sounds too good to be true. But I think that rest is just as important."

"If you ask me, I would take just the rest." Starlansha said sighing.

"Food first. We haven't eaten in a while, so it is necessary. Afterwards, you can go sleep to your heart's content."

"Yes mom." Starlansha said, rolling her eyes.

"Very well then, I will leave you for now so that I can go inform the Faeries. I will make sure that they know that they need to hurry." Amethyst said, smiling and walking out of the room.

Chapter 16

Nature Alive

Quietly standing up, she tried not to disturb Shadick or the wolves from their rest. It had been a week since they had arrived at Valencia and was still struggling to shake off the long travels. None of them had been able to properly relax or sleep well in the slightest.

Shadick had finally passed out about an hour before, and he was sleeping so deeply that she didn't want to wake him. Yet, she needed to walk and explore the village and the surrounding foresting area. She couldn't just lie quietly when she knew there was still so much that she needed to learn, Freyja walking close to her side.

"What's wrong with me Frey? I can't even relax when I know that everyone is comparatively safe." Alexandria whispered to the wolf pup to which she whined softly as though in reply. "It was never like this. Even when I knew there was danger, I could switch off and get some rest now I just can't."

"Is everything okay, Alexandria?" Shana asked, appearing from one of the rooms.

"Just a lot on my mind I guess." Alexandria sighed.

"I can ask Rhoicissus to make you a tonic to ease your mind?"

"Who is Rhoicissus? I haven't heard her name before, nor do I believe I've ever seen her around."

"She is new to our assemblage, a very interesting creature that few have heard of. A spirit of a young healer that was cursed eons ago, by a demon who had possessed a human tried to force her to heal his human host. As she was not only a healer but a clairvoyant, she sensed darkness and as she had dealt with demons before she knew immediately that he was only trouble.

"She pretended to go to her alter and said she was just mixing him a remedy that would help with his injuries, then proceeded to mix a potion that would rid the poor young man of his demon possession.

"As he took a mouthful of the 'remedy', the potions immediately started burning him from the inside. He threw the goblet against the wall stalking towards her and grabbed her by the throat, speaking in a foreign tongue and telling her that she had made the biggest mistake of her life trying to destroy him.

"However, the damage had been done, and as his last life left him, he put a spell on her a life destroying spell that made her and her whole 'apothecary' disappear into a nearby urn. It was only to be released the day, some person or animal gave his or her life willingly; only then would she be able to possess and in turn, feel how it had felt for him when she called him a life-sucking monster.

"Centuries had passed before, and she had almost given up hope when a cat sensed her and approached her ethereal form. You see, she had been able to cast a spell that made it possible for her to wander outside her urn. The cat was touched by her sad story and offered her own life for the healers.

"Only later did she find out that she could turn into a human as well. She chose what is known as Nekomusume, daughter of a cat. She thanked the young cat girl who gave up her life every day by leaving her a little feast.

"She does not like talking about that time, but she has told a few in the hopes that the questions about her existence would be brought to a stop."

"Wow, that is a really moving tale, and in some way, I know how she felt. It had to be terrible."

"It could have been worse had I not stayed positive and

kept learning and practicing my spells, even though it wasn't nearly powerful enough to make much of a difference in that form."

A voice drifted from behind them.

"Alex, I would like you to meet Rhoicissus. She is the one whose life story you just heard." Shana told her, smiling and turning to the cat.

"It is nice to meet you, Alexandria. I have heard so much about you!" Rhoicissus said, transforming into her human form.

"I feel so guilty that it's the first time I have heard about you. I should have made some time available to get to know all the newcomers." Alexandria said, frowning.

"Alex, no one is expecting you to do that. It is insane to go to every camp and learn who is new and who had a child or who died. It would take anyone's focus off what is more important, planning the next attack against those foul beasts." Shana told her, shocked.

"But I feel so out of touch since I returned. There seems so much that I need to catch up on."

"It is good then that I made this little potion. I had a feeling that it would come in handy." Rhoicissus said, laying a hand on Alexandria's arm.

"What potion? I'm not really in the mood to be forced to

sleep and relax by a drink."

"If it is, you need it." Shana muttered.

"That is definitely not what this is, dear. This will simply relax the mind and body so that one can deal with stress and worry. It won't make you pass out or fall asleep. I, for one, am against that as it is unnatural and if not used right it can be dangerous. This potion is completely natural, and I made it myself, so I can assure you there is nothing in it that might cause danger.

"I even made something for your wolf, as I heard she was badly hurt when you found her." Rhoicissus said, handing the potion to Alexandria before bending down next to Freyja and feeding her the potion. "It will help her healing process as well as refresh her mind and body."

"Thank you, I really appreciate it. Now if you two would excuse me, I was going for a short walk." Alexandria said, slowly walking away.

"That girl really needs to get a good night's rest and relaxation. She is way too stressed." Shana said, sighing.

"I agree, but you can't force someone to do something that they do not want to do, but that potion should relax her mind enough for easier sleep." Rhoicissus told Shana turning into a cat.

* * *

Alexandria and Freyja were walking along no particular path when something in the forest to her left caught her attention. But when she looked, she couldn't figure out what she had seen, so she adjusted her path to go and investigate. She had drunk the potion that Rhoicissus had given her even though she had objected, but she had been right. It did help relax her mind, and she felt more awake than she had been in quite a while, but not lethargic.

"And you seem to be in better spirits as well, Frey! We have to thank Rhoicissus in some way, maybe pick some flowers and herbs while we're in the forest." Alexandria said, petting Freyja's head as they entered the forest. "I ought to ask that she teach me a few of her potions, especially for those times we're out and about on whatever mission. Although, at the moment I have enough things to worry about without putting that task on my own shoulders as well."

They slowly picked their way through some of the lower bushes and headed deeper into the forest, gradually leaving the bustling settlements behind them in the forest and succeeding in completely locking out the sounds.

Taking a deep breath and smiling a little, she took in the magnificence of the forest. "I haven't been able to enjoy nature in so long and this just feels like heave..."

Alexandria started her sentence cut off by a slight exclamation as vines slowly wrapped around her legs before moving upwards, cocooning her whole body in vines. The last thing she saw was Freyja suffering the same fate.

She was suddenly woken by Freyja, who was frantically licking her face.

"That's enough Frey, I'm okay now." she said, gently pushing the wolf away from her and looking around. "Where in the world are, we?"

"You are in a world known as Terrae." a voice drifted towards her.

"I'm not on my world anymore?!"

"Sorry that I was not more expressive in my explanation. You are still in your world but within your world exists more magical worlds that have been forgotten by mostly everyone except for those few who still live today. For example, the Elementals and other ancient creatures. I have brought you here today to test your abilities." said an attractive young man with dark brown hair with green flashes in his hair and wearing dark pants and a black shirt, a green cloak around his neck.

"Whoa, how is it that I've not seen an unattractive Elemental yet." Alexandria said, standing up.

He grinned and walked towards her.

"And I have to say that the rumours about you have been greatly understated."

"What rumours would that be?"

He walked around her slowly and looked her up and down.

"The ones that said you aren't bad looking and that you're a fantastic fighter, I'm talking about. I have to say, you are dazzling."

"You are a charmer, one of the first I have dealt with."

"What does that mean, my dear?"

"Well... Spirit was a big mouth who loved talking. And Air was silent yet spoke volumes."

"Oh yes, my kinfolk. I also heard that they joined your cause after you beat them?"

"If you're family, don't you ever talk with each other or do you just communicate through gossip?"

"We are only family in the sense that we are all elementals, we are not related per se."

"That is rather confusing, but I doubt that is why I am here."

"You are right, of course. I summoned you here to determine if you are deserving of your new powers."

Alexandria pulled out her daggers and held them out to

the Nature spirit.

"Am I allowed to use these or are you going to take them away from me as well?"

"You are allowed to use them as I use my own form of 'modern' weapons."

"You would be the first then, as the other two refused blankly to use weapons not made of their element."

"This weapon is of my own element."

"Can we just get this over with? I have had a really long and tiring day, make that last few weeks."

Without warning, there was a sudden green flash throwing her back against a tree. Standing up and twirling her daggers, glancing around her and looking for the cause of the explosion, her eyes widening as she saw the Nature spirit who was surrounded by green lightning. It looked as though he was growing in size. After a minute, the dust and lightning settled down around him.

She stepped back, trying to estimate his true size. His true form was astonishing. It was as though he had become a gigantic tree monster made of metal, a dark green cloak tied around what was his neck, a huge staff held in his right-hand swirling with a potent energy that caused shivers to run up and down her spine.

He lifted the staff, pointing it at her. Before her eyes, the staff opened with a few metallic clicks; four tubes appeared, two with lightning swirling in them and the other two with some kind of invisible power that seemed to emit soft bursts of sound that was as fascinating as it was frightening.

A burst of green lightning shot towards her, and she could barely get out of the way before it hit the tree with a soft sizzle. She looked down at her arm and saw that the shirt's sleeve was blackened from the attack and was disintegrating as she watched.

She ripped the other sleeve off before charging the gigantic spirit, kicking him against the chest as she somersaulted before landing on the floor, winching slightly.

"It isn't just a show; it is really metal." she muttered as she stepped back a bit before ducking as another shot of energy flew towards her.

She transformed into a wolf and ran towards him, sliding under his legs and turning into her own form again, wedging her blades into the crooks of the machines leg pulling them out as she flipped onto his back thrusting the blades into the neck part of the machine. She kicked away from him landing a few feet away from him as his hands came crashing down on his own form.

With surprising speed, he spun around and hit out at her with his left hand sending her sprawling. Flinching, she stood up, immediately running towards him once again and sending a ball of wind at him, stopping short when the wind died even before leaving her hands.

She growled softly as she remembered that she had not been able to use any of the other elements the last two times either. She grabbed the staff as he aimed a hit towards her using his own momentum against him and sending him flying.

He stood up and ran towards her, staff aiming straight at her stomach, the lightning seeming to get brighter the more energy he put into it. He shot the energy towards her, and she was able to dodge it just in time, her skirt catching alight.

She quickly patted it out and ran towards him gathering her own energy and stopping in front of him releasing the attack into his abdomen, moving out of the way as he came crashing down.

She jumped into a tree and then concentrated on the roots, making them wrap around him as they had around her. He struggled to get free and a few of the vines snapped, she concentrated harder and the vines pulled his staff away from him and successfully enveloping him completely.

She relaxed slightly when she felt the whole ground start shaking, the terrain under the tree split opened and swallowed it completely while she transformed into an eagle to avoid falling down the hole as well. Gravity seemed to be determined to pull her down as she could barely keep afloat, her wings beating in time with her heart.

She lost the battle with gravity and plummeted to the ground turning into a cat and landing with a soft pounce next to the crack, slowly retaking her human form and looking around. The spirit sauntered towards her in his own human form, grinning like a little boy who had gotten a very big present.

"I have to say that I am impressed with your efforts, and if I wanted to keep fighting, I am not sure who would win." he told her matter-of-factly

"Are you telling me that you are giving up?" Alexandria asked, rubbing a spot on her arm where one of his blows had landed

"I was testing you to see if you could use the powers that are now yours, and the little battle we just had proved that to me more than adequately."

"So far, it has only been a fight for survival, and I barely beat them."

"They take it too seriously. If we kill you, then how would you be able to defeat the centaurs and bring peace back to your world? I have seen the destruction they have caused so far. What you have seen so far is only a fraction of the total damage that they have caused.

"The whole globe is under attack, and they are taking it over piece by piece, sometimes not even caring about how many casualties or fatalities they cause the people.

"They do not care if they hurt children or adults; they just kill, laughing all the way, thinking there will be no repercussions for what they do."

"You are quite certain about this?"

"I have travelled your whole world searching for some of the old magic that might still exist and put a stop to this madness, so I have seen the extent of their sovereignty."

"Have you seen any weakness in their army? Anything that could help me fight and ultimately destroy them?"

"Some of the warriors refuse to kill, and I have heard chatter about some of them wanting to get away from him and his relations. If you could get to those heading the rebellion, then you can convince them to join you to fight against him."

"You make it sound so easy." she told him despondently.

"I will join you, as my relatives have, but I will go to his camps and start whispering to them about how they can join you. This way, you will have some inkling of their army and have some of them turn on their leader and join you. If they agree to it, you can make it so that when the fighting starts, they turn on the head centaur and attack from the inside."

"That is a clever idea; do you really think you could convince some of his warriors to join us?"

"If whispered in the right ear, then yes I will be able to."

"Now that you have come up with that smart plan and a hopefully fool-proof way for you to infiltrate them. What is your name?"

"The name is Necrontyr. I am sorry I did not introduce myself to you before."

"Necrontyr, now that is a very unique and interesting name. My name is Alexandria, as you have most likely heard."

"I have yes, and I for one think that the name suits you." Necrontyr said, stepping closer to her, grinning.

Alexandria stepped back, straight into a tree that had appeared out of nowhere. "I should get back; my friends will be worried about me."

"I assure you they have not even realised that you are not next to your companion. Those who saw you walk into the forest are too busy to raise an alarm." he told her stepping closer putting his one arm next to her on the tree and the other on her hip

"Shadick will wake soon, and he will worry and search for me as soon as he realises how long I've been gone."

Necrontyr put a finger against her lips, silencing her, then slowly and gradually leaning towards her, their lips an inch apart before kissing her deeply and passionately.

At first she tried fighting him, punching his chest and trying to pull away, but soon she got lost in his kiss, wrapping her arms around his neck, pulling him closer and standing on her toes to deepen the kiss even more, his fingers lightly pulling her hair as they kissed.

Freyja growled and barked suddenly and jumped in between them, forcing them to break apart, both breathing hard.

"That is one insistent wolf you have there." Necrontyr said, glancing down at Freyja.

"Why do you say that?" Alexandria asked, touching her hair self-consciously.

"She was wining and barking the whole time, trying to get your attention."

"I didn't hear her. I am so sorry Frey!" Alexandria said, crouching and petting her wolf that was looking at her furiously.

"I believe that she just wanted to break that kiss we just shared. She seems rather faithful to someone."

"That is what I tried telling you before, me and Shad..."

"Yes, yes you and your companion are more than meets the eye, and you would rather not do anything to compromise that." he said saucily, pulling her up lightly, leaning down slightly, their lips an inch apart.

"Exactly..." she started saying, losing her train of thoughts as he kissed her again, even deeper this time pulling her close to him, her fingers going into his hair wanting to push him away but losing her thought pulling softly on his hair a soft moan escaping her lips.

Freyja who had enough of this pounced against Alexandria, and they all three tumbled to the floor.

"Okay wolf I get it. Your mistress is taken; she is just such a great kisser that I cannot stop myself."

"Like I said before." she said, standing up quickly. "I better get going."

"If you insist. I will transport you home." he told her, grinning then frowning slightly as she staggered a little. "Are you feeling okay?"

"Yes, I am feeling absolutely great, just tired. Can we get going now, please?"

"Of course." he said, grabbing her hand still frowning as they disappeared and reappeared in the forest. "I will take my leave for now, but I will see you in a few weeks. But all I ask is that you look after yourself you are the one who will rid this world of the evil in it."

She waved him off and watched him disappear, then

glanced around trying to find her bearings, feeling something in her hand and glancing down, realising it was a green and black stone frowning slightly wondering what kind of stone it was and when Necrontyr had given it to her, sighing she looked back up seeing light through some of the trees, slowly taking a step towards the fresh air but fainting before she walked two steps.

Freyja whined softly as she fell, lying down with her head on her stomach.

"I promise you, Shadick she will be back as soon as she feels that her head is clear enough to deal with what lies ahead." Starlansha said as she followed Shadick through the streets of the grounds.

"She would not have left the palace without telling someone where she's going, or when she will be back." Shadick argued, glancing into every alley.

"Shana told us that Alex was headed to the forest, so she is probably just practising some of her powers."

"She also said that it had been a few hours ago! Why would Alexandria leave for hours and not let us know where exactly she would be?!" Shadick said panicked, spotting Managwa running full speed towards them.

"He looks worried, if that is even possible for a wolf."

"For Managwa yes, it is."

The wolf barely stopped in front of them when he turned around and ran for the forest again, Shadick and Starlansha barely keeping up with him.

"At least he knows where he is going, and not fumbling around searching for a trail."

"Once he's gotten a scent he won't forget it easily, and I have a suspicion he knows exactly where Alexandria is but couldn't do anything about it."

"Why wouldn't he be able to do anything? I've seen him drag a full-grown human out of a burning house."

"I smell Freyja, which means she is preventing him from getting to Alex." Shadick told her, speeding up.

They sprinted into the opening where Alexandria and Freyja were, simultaneously stopping a few feet from her unconscious form.

"Alex!" Shadick shouted, bending next to her, Freyja growling softly as he reached out to her. "Stop Freyja!"

"Be nice Shadick. She is only protecting Alex."

"She is only preventing me from helping Alex and making sure that she is not hurt badly."

He touched Alexandria's cheek, lightly running his hands down her arms and sides, making sure that she had not broken anything, before lightly picking her up and walking towards the palace without a word to Starlansha

"Shadick, is she okay?!" she asked worried, following in his footsteps.

"As far as I can tell, she is perfectly well, just passed out from exhaustion and cold from exposure. But we won't be absolutely sure unless the doctors confirm it."

"Good girl Freyja! Now come on, let's get to the palace doctors so they can check you both out." Starlansha called to the wolf as they walked out of the forest.

Chapter 17

Tale of the Elements

"You should have woken me up when she didn't return an hour later!" Shadick told Shana heatedly. "She could have been hurt worse, if not killed."

"I lost track of time, and I did not think any harm would come to her within the village walls! We've had no attacks before." Shana said softly.

"Well, something got through the security, and not even the guards saw anything, meaning that either they are slacking in their duties or they are the ones that attacked Lexi."

"Shadick, calm down Shana said she was sorry. There is nothing we could have done to stop what had happened to Alex." Starlansha said, standing up from her seat.

Shadick turned on her, his eyes dark with worry "It could have been prevented had someone just paid attention to what was going on around them! Now we do not even know if she is going to wake up or not, nor what happened to her in the first place."

"I am worried about her as well, but shouting and laying blame on people that have no fault in this situation won't help her."

"I do believe she has just passed out from exhaustion. Her vitals are normal." Rhoicissus said as she walked into the small living area attached to Alexandria's room. "I gave her some of my remedies to help her with any healing process she might have to undergo as well as a little something that will give her more energy once she is awake."

"Do you know what caused her to pass out, if that is all that happened?" Shadick asked, walking closer to the healer.

"Shadick, interrogating Rhoicissus will not help the circumstances." Starlansha muttered, glancing apologetically at Rhoicissus.

"Why do you not wait for her to wake up, and then you can ask her yourself? It has never helped anyone to worry about something before there is a need for panic. I have a potion for you that you can drink to help you calm down." Rhoicissus told him, handing him a small vile before walking out of the room.

"Is Alexandria okay?! I heard only now, and I came back

as soon as possible." Amethyst asked as she stormed into the room, her wings lightly trailing behind her.

"You should have been around when I found her in the forest unconscious! But no, you were flying around somewhere, and no one could get a hold of you." Shadick shouted.

"Shadick, there is no need for you to be so rude to me; I was inspecting the new grounds, which have been put aside for Alex and you. But if you would rather live in a palace that is constantly full and never sees any quiet, go ahead. I am sure that the stables have an opening that can accommodate your lot."

Starlansha flinched and watched Amethyst walk into the bedroom where Alexandria was still passed out.

"That was rather... unmannerly of Amethyst. I have never seen her lose it like that." Shana said, then walked out of the room.

"Maybe you should apologise to Am, Shadick. You aren't the only one who is worried about Alex, and everyone handles it differently." Starlansha told Shadick, touching his arm.

Shadick sighed, then nodded as they walked into the bedroom too see Amethyst sitting next to Alexandria, her hand glowing slightly against her friend's forehead.

"If you want to continue the argument, Shadick, I do not have the energy for it. There are more important things going on right now than keeping a silly disagreement up." Amethyst told him, lifting her hand. "She is not hurt, just exhausted as I am sure Rhoicissus have already told you."

"That is such good news. We were all worried about her." Starlansha said, smiling in relief.

"I am sorry for taking my worry and anger our on you, Am. I'm just really worried about her. Since I got to know her, I have not seen her so defenceless, so fragile." Shadick said apologetically.

Before she could reply, Alexandria moved slightly, slowly waking up. She opened her eyes slowly and looked blurrily around her, lifting her hand towards Shadick, who immediately grabbed it and held it tightly. "Welcome back, love. You nearly scared us to death."

"How long was I out for?" she asked, sitting up shakily.

"A few hours since we found you. Before that we aren't sure for how long you were unconscious." Starlansha told Alexandria, handing her a glass of water.

"A few hours?"

"Six hours, give or take." Shadick told her, kissing her cheek. "We found you at 6 this evening, and the clock has just struck midnight."

"What happened? Can you remember anything?" Amethyst asked, watching her carefully.

Alexandria frowned slightly. "I had another trial against Necrontyr, the nature elemental. We had just finished the test, and he brought me back here when I passed out. I was trying to get back to the palace, but I had no energy. Where's the stone that I had in my hand?"

"It is right here on the table next to the bed, don't worry about it. So did you beat the nature spirit?"

"Yes, but he dislikes fighting very much, so it was just a minor skirmish. It barely took any energy to prove myself."

"Then why did you faint?"

"I haven't really slept in a few weeks. I have had so much on my mind that I just can't switch my brain off and get proper rest."

"Why have you not told me this, Lexie? I could have helped you relax someway." Shadick asked, frowning.

"I did not want to worry you; I know that you have been struggling to get proper rest for a while now as well. You needed a few hours' sleep."

He sighed as Starlansha spoke up. "Tell us more about the trial."

"You don't have to Alex. If you want to rest for a bit longer that is fine. No one is pressuring you to retell the story if you don't want to." Amethyst told her, glancing sternly at Starlansha.

"No, it's ok I can talk about it, and it wasn't as terrible as some fights are or even could be. Freyja and I were just walking around when vines surrounded us and teleported us to another place, I found out was called Terrae.

"A young man stepped out of the shadows and started telling me about his world; I had to remind him several times that we were supposed to be fighting and not talking. He also told me that I was allowed to use my daggers and not just the elements."

"That is a first." Shadick said, his frown deepening.

"Quiet Shad, let her finish the story." Amethyst told him.

Alexandria smiled slightly. "Well, he transformed into this kind of contraption thing made of metal and shot lightning at me. We fought for a few minutes and then as suddenly as we had started fighting, he stopped.

I enquired why he had stopped, and he told me that he had seen what he needed to have seen and that further fighting wouldn't be needed. He then spoke about whispers that had been heard through the Centaurs' camps and a plan that would allow him to infiltrate them. In doing so, he will get some of them to turn on the centaurs, and when time is right, they will fight against them and surprise those foul beasts."

"That is a smart idea! Does he believe he will be able to succeed in his mission?" Starlansha asked wide-eyed.

"He is an Elemental, and can turn into any shape or form thanks to his powers."

Amethyst unexpectedly stood up from her position next to Alexandria and ran out of the room.

"Amethyst? Am!" Alexandria called after her frowning, sitting up straighter.

"Don't you dare get up you still need to rest." Shadick warned her, putting his hand on her shoulder.

"I agree. We all need to get some more rest. Whatever got Am in such a flurry, she will tell us when she is ready to. No use in forcing her, you should know that." Starlansha said, standing up and then kissing Alexandria's cheek. "Get some sleep, Alex; I will see you in the morrow."

Shadick glanced at Alexandria and smiled slightly. "I was so worried about you when I woke up, and you weren't next to me. I almost tore the whole palace down before Shana ran to me and told me she had spoken to you a few hours before. Then I got furious with her for not waking me when you had not returned."

"I heard some of your argument earlier. I would have opened my eyes earlier but felt powerless." Alexandria said, grimacing pulling Shadick closer to her.

"You could hear us?"

"Not everything, just words here and there. Why wasn't Amethyst around when you found me?"

"I do not know. No one could find her, and then when she stormed in here, she told us that she was busy sorting out some land for us."

"That's curious..." she started, then grinned. "Can we worry about this in the morrow? Right now, I have more enjoyable things to think about."

"And what would that be?" Shadick asked, mocking innocently.

"Oh, you know... this." she kissed him lightly on the mouth, running her finger down his chest, "and that."

He pulled her closer so that she was half laying on top of him, kissing her deeply, running his hands lightly down her back, a sudden burst of radiant purple and pink shining energy exploding. Wings shot out of her back, light purple and white in colour, disappearing slowly as she threw Shadick's shirt to the floor just as they rolled over the kiss deepening even more.

"We should do that to relax more often." Alexandria said

the next morning, her head on Shadick's chest.

"We would never get out of bed if that was the case." Shadick replied laughingly.

There was a soft knock on the door.

"Alex, are you guys awake yet? Amethyst called a meeting and asked that I come to call you two."

"Give us a few minutes, Star, just putting on some more clothes. You can wait for us." Shadick told Starlansha, causing Alexandria to groan softly before standing up.

"Okay good. She sounded rather serious, although worried that Alex still needs some rest after yesterday."

"I am not as fragile as what she thinks, you know. She always worries too much!" Alexandria said outraged.

"She sees you as her sister Lexie; give her a break. All of us were worried yesterday." Shadick said, kissing her quickly as she pulled a short dress on.

"Are you ready yet? I can just feel Amethyst's impatience, and I am rather curious as to what she has to tell us." Starlansha's voice reached them.

Shadick opened the door to see a pacing Starlansha, pulling Alexandria behind him. "All done now, you should relax a bit more, especially on stressful days like these."

"Oh, hush Shad! There is no time these days for things like relaxing; you never know when there will be need for us or when the centaurs will attack."

Alexandria hugged her tightly without saying anything until she felt her friend relax a little.

"You just need to close your mind sometimes Star. I've learnt that if you don't, there will be major consequences. You also need to talk to us about what is bothering you; we might be able to help you with whatever is bothering you."

"Like you passing out in the middle of the forest when you were supposed to be next to Shadick? And I know that you guys have your own things to worry about hence why I don't talk to anyone about them."

"That is exactly what I am talking about, and we are always here to listen to you. You are our friend after all, and that is what friends are for."

"Lexie is right, Star. We are here for you, even when it sometimes seems that we don't have time or energy for something." Shadick told her

"Thank you, guys. I will definitely remember that when the thoughts in my head are more focused." Starlansha said, smiling and glancing at Freyja, who was at Alexandria's side devotedly.

A few minutes later, they walked into the throne room where Amethyst was waiting for them, pacing up and down in agitation. "You guys took your sweet time, and I told Starlansha that it was urgent!"

"Alexandria was still asleep when Star came to call us, she had to wake up first, and we both had to get dressed. We couldn't just get up and leave the room in our sleeping clothes. The guards are distracted enough without seeing Alex in almost next to nothing." Shadick intervened quickly, grinning.

"Enough of that! I have found out some information about Alex's trials, and I thought that you would find it more interesting than her nightwear."

"I thought you did not know anything about the trials?" Alexandria said frowning.

"I didn't, but I did some research in my mother's books and asked some of the older creatures. And through what I have heard, I have been able to piece together some basic and I use basic lightly as very few seemed to know about what is happening to you." Amethyst said, sitting down.

"Please continue Am. You have all of our attention."

"Well, from what I could put together is that it happens only at the turn of a millennium and only to one, maybe two people who they deem worthy are actually allowed to take part in these trials. So even if a person has been studying and practicing the elements his or her whole life, there is no assurance that they would get picked to participate in these trials to become master or mistress of the elements.

"And at times, they do not even choose a 'candidate' to participate in the trials, as they do not sense anyone 'worthwhile'. Or they realise that the person they originally wanted to take would only use it for evil and destruction rather in aid of the elements. And in a very rare occasion, they may choose up to 6 people, but that has happened once in known history."

"Where did you find this information Amethyst?" Shadick asked frowning.

"Like I told you, I asked around and did some deep research which took the whole night, which means I did not get any sleep, and my patience is on a short fuse. Now, as I was saying, it is an honour for you to have been chosen, and not many get the chance to go through the trial."

"Thank you, Amethyst. I really appreciate the information. Were you able to get information on what has been happening to me from the start, first the stones and now the elements?" Alexandria asked.

"Unfortunately, there has been nothing recorded about something like this. But I have found out where you guys can go to find out about these trials."

"What?! There is a place we can go out to get more information?! And when can we leave?" Shadick asked, sitting up straighter.

"Dragon Mountains."

"Chadromida's home? He would have told us if he had information about the trials had he known."

"I did not mention Chad; I mentioned his home. Within the mountains, there lives a legendary creature, as old as he is young. If he agrees to talk to you, he can give you the information that you require."

"Then we have to leave as soon as we're able to! There is no time to spare."

"You do not even know what creature you need to talk to, nor do you know if he is violent or friendly or neutral. You can't just storm off without doing proper research."

"You did the research Am, so we're not exactly storming off unprepared."

"Yet you do not think to ask me what creature it is? You would have stormed out of the village without asking for the information."

"Will you two please calm down? There is absolutely no reason for you to have an argument over this." Rialey said softly walking into the room

"Shadick, I thought you would be more concerned about Alexandria's safety than you are right now. Maybe I was wrong about you after all, wanting to run off without thinking about how this might affect my sanity or the safety of the other people."

"Stop it!!! Can you two not see that worrying about the Centaurs is affecting your rational thought! If we fight amongst ourselves, they win." Alexandria told them heatedly. "And maybe he was only thinking of running off to go talk to the creature, but you know what?

"At least he is thinking about my health and safety, whereas you seem only to think about only yourself and the other people, when your friend if not sister is in danger. Who knows what these trials and other power gains might mean? I might lose control and snap and destroy the whole village, if not the whole world. Do you want that on your conscious, Am?"

Amethyst looked shocked, her face falling slowly. "I never thought about it that way. I am sorry, Alex. I feel like I have disappointed you."

"Yes, you have, but if you'll excuse me, I need to go find out about what is happening to me. I don't feel like I can trust myself at the moment, never mind someone who only thinks about her own safety." Alexandria said, walking out of the throne room some of the Faeries flying after her.

"I guess we better follow Alex, before she leaves the village without us." Starlansha said seriously following

Alexandria.

Shadick followed slowly, glancing at Amethyst as she stood in the middle of the room, looking after them in shock and surprise.

Chapter 18

Legend of the Stones

"Just when I thought that we had travelled enough, we end up doing more travelling." Starlansha said as she climbed onto her horse's back "I have to admit the Faeries outdid themselves with your outfit and hair today."

"Don't remind me. I'm trying to convince myself this is just a terrible dream, and I will wake up any minute now." Alexandria added pulling lightly on the long braid that was her hair "yes they did, I'm mostly surprised with the hairstyle but starting to like it more and more."

"Stop whining you two and get a move on!" Shadick shouted at them from the stable doors. "The quicker we get going, the quicker we'll get to Dragon Mountains and the quicker we can talk to the keeper of legends."

"Keeper of Legends, is it? I thought we didn't know what he was or what he was called."

"Yes, as far as I know we didn't know what it was either." Starlansha added.

"We don't. I just thought calling it the keeper of legends would be better than saying he or it the whole time." Shadick told them, grabbing Nightmare's reigns and pulling him along with him.

"I can steer my own horse, you know." Alexandria laughed softly, lightly slapping Shadick's shoulder.

"Just giving you a head start so that we can get there before night falls.

Starlansha and Alexandria laughed softly at the look on Shadick's face urging the horses into a slow trot, still talking softly.

"I wonder what kind of creature we'll have to deal with when we get there. Hopefully, something that isn't too violent." Starlansha said, glancing at the far-off mountains.

"With our luck, it's some kind of monster that refuses to talk to anyone unless we prove something." Alexandria said, laughing softly.

"You're confusing your evaluations with other missions, Lexie." Shadick joked.

"Oh yes, you're right. I started forgetting my whole life isn't an evaluation, just certain parts of it."

"If you think about it, you already survived, passed and

gained the stone of three of the elementals. As well as their allegiance to the war against the centaurs, that has got to put your mind at ease a little bit." Starlansha said, tilting her head.

"It does up to a point. I mean, even when I think that I am now Mistress of three of the elements it still feels unreal, I don't always feel the power in me, and then other times, it is so present that I have no choice but to acknowledge it."

"It is completely understandable that you feel out of sorts, Lexie, expected even." Shadick said, touching her shoulder.

"What is not expected is for you guys ever to be on time and not waste a good meal." Chadromida's voice came from above them.

Shadick glanced up, grinning as a dragon's shadow hovered over them. "And we can never expect you to have patience when it comes to just about anything."

Chadromida jumped off the dragon's back and landed in front of them. "Well, when I know that there are two gorgeous ladies on their way to visit me, I can't help getting a little impatient."

Starlansha blushed, glancing away from Chadromida, looking straight into Alexandria's laughing eyes. "And here I thought Prince Jacques was the only one who could make you blush like that."

"It is not like that, Alex. The whole 'gorgeous women'

thing was unexpected." Starlansha muttered softly as they followed Chadromida into Dragon Mountains.

"Relax Star, I was just joking around."

"Sorry, the whole long-distance relationship isn't exactly helpful in our present situation."

"I understand how you feel, Star. It is how I felt while I was training in Atlantican."

"Is that why I found you staring at nothingness more than once while we were training?"

"Yes and no. I found it hard to always concentrate on training when I knew other things were going on around the world, even around me at that moment."

"What are the two of you gossiping about back here?" Shadick asked, pulling Nightmare to a halt.

"Nothing much, just this and that." Starlansha said quickly, blushing again.

Shadick glanced at Alexandria as he helped her off her horse, but she just shrugged, smiling slightly.

"Are you guy's hungry?" Chadromida asked as the horses were led into the stalls.

"Starving, we never ate before we left Valencia, and that was rather early." Shadick said, pulling Alexandria towards the entrance.

"Then you're in luck. Some of the dwarves that still reside

in the mountain cooked a huge meal, and as most of the dragons are in their worlds at the moment there is too much for just me and the dwarves."

"That sounds just great Chad." Alexandria said, laughing softly at the guy's enthusiasm.

"The way they're going on, it's as though they haven't been fed in months." Starlansha added laughingly.

"That was the best meal I have had in months!" Shadick said later that night leaning back against the wall

"I agree it was a really well-made meal, and after all the travelling and scrounging for food, it is nice to arrive somewhere and have the food already there." Alexandria agreed stretching.

"Thank the Dwarves for us, Chad. They disappeared so quickly after serving us." Starlansha said.

"They do not always like being around people, and they know that the fighters need weapons, and their quality of weapons is still top of the line and a lot of fighters request them. I believe your Coral Daggers were made by some of the forefathers of these very Dwarves."

"Really? All I knew of the daggers is that Star and Rosy gave them to me." Alexandria laughed softly.

"We received the daggers from an anonymous

contributor, and they had been lying around in our home for a month or so, and we didn't feel comfortable using them, so I thought it was worth a shot to give them to you so you can try them out. They were meant for you it seems. You've been very at ease with them." Starlansha said distantly.

"An anonymous contributor?" Shadick asked frowning.

"Yes, the person was a tallish man who had worn a cloak at the time, so we couldn't guess at his origin. But he said that the daggers are meant for someone out of the ordinary and would only truly work for that person. We still tried questioning him some more, but he disappeared, and we couldn't find him again."

"That is strange, but I have heard of tales about travellers having heard or seen about someone giving another individual a 'present', and it turns out that the person does amazing things with the gifts that they had received." Chadromida said

"Did you give the daggers a name or ever considered naming them?" Shadick asked.

"Well, we thought about it, but we did not know that we wouldn't become accustomed to the weapons. When I had given them to Alex, I didn't tell her anything about the origins of the daggers, just that she could use them." Starlansha told them.

"Then why did you name them Coral Daggers, Lex?"

"The design on the bottom of blades looks like some of the corals I've seen in Atlantican, and I thought that it would only be appropriate." Alexandria answered, unsheathing one of the daggers to show the group.

"I never noticed that! And I had those daggers for a month, and I examined them to make sure that they were balanced and sharp." Starlansha said, pulling the dagger closer and looking at the design, her eyes widening slowly. "I can't believe this!"

"What's wrong?" Shadick asked

"The one day, about a week before Alex joined us, I had taken the daggers to the ocean to clean them. The water had looked so inviting that I jumped in for a swim. I had put the daggers near some coral on the ocean floor while I swam so the tide could wash them clean, but I lost track of time. When I finally realised how much time had passed, it was already nightfall.

"Picking up the daggers, I sheathed them and put them away without inspecting the blades. Some of the coral must have fused with the blades that day. That would explain the unique markings on the blades."

"My daggers have the ability to absorb different objects, no matter if they strengthen or weaken them?"

"No, I believe that it only absorbs objects that strengthen it, hence making the wielder, you in this case, stronger and more powerful."

"I never knew that weapons had that ability!"

"Very few weapons can do that. And if it does happen, it only happens once... maybe twice."

"Perhaps we could ask some of the Dwarves to look at the daggers? To tell us more about them?"

"I am not sure whether they would talk about their craft. They can be very secretive, if they feel as though someone is asking too many questions about something, they might close up completely." Chadromida said seriously. "besides, if they were made by one of their kind that has been banished, they will cut you out even more as they consider that one of the biggest 'no-go's' you can ever get."

"I do not think that knowing their origin is that important if you ask me. You are able to use them, and they seem to respond rather well to you as well as your energy, so there is no need to question it.

"I have seen how some people struggle to find a weapon that works well with them and how frustrated they get when they go through weapon after weapon before giving up completely." Shadick said shrugging.

"I think that I agree with you Shadick. They have not let

you down so far and I do not think that they will, so there is no real need to find out their origins."

"Very well then, I will not go hound the Dwarves to find out more information. Besides, I do not want them to see me as some kind of enemy." Alexandria said, smiling.

"What are our plans for the rest of the evening?" Shadick asked grinning. "I think we should consider taking a couple of hours to just relax and do nothing. That seems like a fantastic plan if you ask me."

Starlansha glanced at them, then sighed shrugging "I thought that we would be going to find the keeper not just sit around with our feet up."

"I agree we need to get back to finding the keeper; time is catching up with us after all. And as much as I want us to relax, we honestly can't right now." Alexandria said, standing up and grabbing her daggers. "Not to mention we're not even sure where it is in the mountain."

"Actually, some of the Dragons have informed me of a cavern everyone has always been avoiding. When I questioned them as to why I've never come across it, they said it was because the energy would make me change direction. I have to admit it does make a lot of sense." Chadromida told them. "Most of them didn't even want to tell me where it was exactly. I was able to get a couple to spill the beans though.

With a very explicit warning, it may be the last thing I do, and they will then make sure to bring me back just to kill me."

"Not ominous at all." Starlansha muttered. "Were they at least able to tell you what we should be expecting?"

"None of them have ever been able to get to the cavern. Apparently, about 3 of them tried but failed spectacularly. Kind of makes me more excited to try; the amount of power over the Dragons it would give me would be glorious."

"It isn't as though a power play over the Dragons is something new for you, Chad." Shadick said with a shake of his head. "Now take the lead and show us to this cavern you mentioned."

"We should have some kind of plan of action. No one has been able to tell us much about the keeper. I mean, do we need to be ready to fight, or should we just be prepared to talk to it? I don't really feel like fighting all that much, but the possibility is always there, which is making me nervous." Starlansha said with a frown.

"That is a very easy question to answer. Always be ready to fight, no matter what. Even if it seems stupid, you can never be too wary." Alexandria replied, shrugging.

"You can't be wary all of the time."

"Lexie is always ready to jump up and fight, and yes, that includes the bedroom." Shadick said with a grin.

Alexandria's eyes widened as her cheeks slowly started turning red. As she tried to come up with a reply, they felt a tremble below their feet. Quickly turning around, she walked into one of the entrances doing her best to ignore their laughs. She would not let them get under her skin for their own entertainment, there was nothing wrong with always being ready to fight.

"I have one question, Alexandria. How is it that you suddenly know where we're supposed to be going?" Chadromida asked from right behind her. "Have you been keeping something from us?"

"Not a clue where I'm going, but I figured I would walk around until I felt the need to run in the opposite direction. Might take me a while, but I will eventually get there, unless of course, you would like to take the lead so we could get there sooner? That would of course be the preferred choice. But if that is too much to ask for, then you are more than welcome to go back and relax next to the fire." Alexandria said, stopping in her tracks as a wave of nausea hit her.

"Or you could just keep walking in the direction you already are, and you will get there. Before you started ranting, I was going to tell you there was no need for me to take the lead as you were already going in the right direction."

"Perhaps you should take a breath, Lexie. Your emotions

are going a little haywire." Shadick told her. "Or perhaps we should go and discuss this mission a bit more, as Starlansha suggested a little earlier."

"Yea, I have to agree with Shadick. We haven't really come up with a proper plan. And for us to properly take this on, we need to know exactly what our plan of action is." Starlansha muttered. "It wouldn't do us any good to walk in there blind only for one of us to get injured or worse, killed."

"The plan is simple; we get there and talk to it and find out what information it can give us. If it wants to fight, I am more than willing to do that while getting answers. However, if it is willing to talk without violence, then we go that route. The sudden hesitation you're feeling is because of the energy coming from the keeper. I think it is just a way for it to protect itself." Alexandria said, starting to walk forward again. "Besides, we've already gotten this far, so there is no reason for us to turn back now."

She heard Starlansha groan before rushing after her and the wolves. The feeling she had was one of nausea and the extreme need to run far away from here. But she refused to let it overwhelm her but she forced herself to keep going. When she had said they had already gone too far, she had been absolutely serious. Chadromida and the others kept talking to each other and how wrong all of this felt. She started noticing the animal and human bones, which was when she knew they were going in the right direction.

"Is it just me or is it getting warmer?" Shadick asked. "And do not give me a witty come back about how we're in a mountain full of dragons so of course it is, Chad."

"You take all the fun out of everything." Chadromida muttered.

"I may be wrong, but I think it's because the creature is made of fire. Considering this is the place it calls home it only makes sense."

"Assumptions are dangerous things to make." a voice said from ahead of them, making them all rush deeper into the cavern.

"You're a phoenix! But my parents said your kind had disappeared over a century ago." Alexandria said, wide-eyed.

"They weren't completely incorrect in thinking that." the phoenix replied. "We are few but we do make our appearance when we get a sense of someone worthy."

"I have heard legends but took them all as falsehoods, but from the stories you should be a lot smaller than you are right now." Shadick said, stepping closer only to have a ball of fire shot at him. "Hey!"

"The lot of you walked into my home and started demanding answers. Why in the world do you think I would tell you anything? You are not worthy to hear any of the stories of my kind."

"Then how would we go about proving our worthiness?" Alexandria asked as she looked around the cavern and the phoenix. "Surely there is a way for us to make you see that we are only here to help? Or at least mean you no harm?"

"There is no reason for me to reconsider anything."

"That doesn't seem like a very nice way to talk to people. This entire group has been fighting against creatures wishing to only bring harm to the world." Chadromida exclaimed.

"Keep it talking and distracted. I think I've figured out how to make it more cooperative." Alexandria whispered to Starlansha as she spotted a pair of shackles.

"What?! Why?!" Starlansha squeaked, but she had already turned into wind. "I must admit, it is rather disappointing to finally meet a phoenix only to have them be rude and inconsiderate. We mean you no harm yet we are being treated as though we are complete and utter garbage."

Alexandria moved towards the phoenix as quietly as she could. There was just this feeling in her chest that the shackles around its leg were making it act the way it was. All of her concentration was on what she was doing and she didn't pay any attention to the conversation. As she got closer, she calmed her mind before jumping into the space between its leg and the shackle, doing her best to ignore the heat its feathers were causing.

Hearing an exclamation from Shadick just as the phoenix realised where she had gotten to. Alexandria raised her energy to a level she had not had to use in a while. The shackles barely bent but slowly, so slowly, cracks started appearing. Taking that as a hint, she quickly added some of her earth powers as well, causing the shackles to splinter with a loud bang. A light appeared, so bright it blinded them all, making her fly towards a wall. Shadick quickly ran towards her and caught her before she could get too close to the wall.

"What did you just do?!" Shadick shouted.

"Those shackles were made from some kind of magic, and if I'm not mistaken, they were also what was keeping it from giving us a proper chance." Alexandria replied, sliding from Shadick's arms. "I may be completely wrong but I have a feeling that I'm right."

"Then by the gods, I hope you're correct."

"Freedom! After 5 centuries, I can finally think for myself again and not have to constantly fight." the phoenix shouted and they all watched in shock as it shrank. "Finally, I will be able to breathe fresh air and spread my wings."

"Before you fly off into the sunset, would you be willing to speak to us now?"

"Of course! You are free to ask me your questions."

"We were told that the keeper would be able to tell us more about the Elementals as well as the stones they've been giving me? Is it really a piece of themselves?

"Ah, yes. I can feel the energy coming off of you, Alexandria. I have to warn you, though, to be cautious. You may have a feeling as though you are in control, but you are not. The stones make things a little easier for you to control but they are fallible. Not to mention the being watching the Elementals is manipulative and power hungry, more so than even the centaurs. It is why you are being forced to take part in these tests.

"You see, he is afraid that the next worthy being would be able to defeat him. It has been a couple of millennia since someone was close to being able to stand against him. The ones that made him uncomfortable enough to believe he might be defeated, all disappeared. His cronies are afraid of what he would do to them and only bend their knees to follow his rules."

"And what would happen if someone was actually capable of defeating him?"

"They would either need to take his place or have the entire world fall into chaos. You see, he is not only the ruler of his dominion, but he also keeps the world's elements in check.

If you were to lose one, the world would slowly turn to disarray. If you were to take them all away, the world would meet its end within a couple of hours. The stones they've been giving you when you are able to beat them, is a show of loyalty towards you. Because it gives them hope you might be the one to be able to save them from eternal servitude under a ruler who cares nothing about them."

"Is there something we should be expecting during these trials? Or is it more a case of don't hold back kind of deal?" Shadick asked with a frown

"My advice is that you are ready for anything. My time in this mountain however has come to an end. Do not ask me to join in your fight, as my kind does not get involved in fights of the worlds unless my master were to demand it of me. As it stands, I don't have a master, so I bid you adieu and wish you the best of luck in the upcoming war."

"Wait…" Alexandria started but the phoenix had already disappeared into nothingness

"That was not what I was expecting, I'm glad however. We were lucky enough to have an opportunity to meet a phoenix." Chadromida said. "Let's get back to camp. That way, we can discuss everything that we just learned and at least be comfortable."

Chapter 19

Voice of the Undead

They were sitting around a fire within the caves, having a bite to eat and something to drink, talking softly among themselves about what the Phoenix had told them about not just the elementals but the stones they had been giving her.

"Ever since the battle ended, I had been trying to find out more about the elementals. Not to mention things they help people or creatures with even if it was rare for them to care enough.

"I couldn't really find much besides them being some kind of force that kept everything together. They stayed hidden though refusing to accept they were responsible for some of the things happening." Chadromida told the group.

"Where did you get this information? And why didn't you share it with us when we first started talking about the Elementals? Not to mention, you were told I was being left stones which merged with my daggers." Alexandria asked frowning.

"Because I could not be sure if it was truthful or just old wives' tales. Even the dragons weren't completely sure about the stones, and most of them were around when they were created."

"That was going to be my next question. Where exactly did you get your information about the stones as nobody on our world even knew about it, not even Amethyst? I know she's been talking to just about everyone to find out more about not just the Elementals but those stones as well." Shadick added.

"I had to travel to numerous worlds with the dragons before I even found an inkling of where to get the information from, and even then, I wasn't sure if it would turn up anything of value."

"It is just so strange that I never heard about any of the stones before today, but not one creature knew anything about it." Alexandria said softly.

"If everyone thought it was just a myth or a lie or nothing worthy within the story, they wouldn't tell others about it, they would just ignore it, and over the years, it would get lost."

"Shadick has a point Alex. That is how a lot of our

histories are lost or wrongly told; people stop telling it. And it's not written down." Chadromida agreed.

"I guess." Alexandria sighed.

"Even though my dearest brother and loving fiancé has a lot of bad parts and have huge egos, they have a point when they talk about lost histories. I mean my brother doesn't even know if he's the only wolfane in the world, because if there were any others tales about them, they have been lost." a voice said coming from within one of the tunnels.

Shadick fell off the log in shock as the voice was followed by a young well-built brunette, his food falling out of his hand, Alexandria staying seated only because she had sat up when she felt his body tighten in shock.

"Astarte!" Chadromida shouted, jumping up and running to the young woman. "I didn't expect you here until the end of the week."

"My horse as well as the boat I was travelling on was faster than I expected." she said, smiling and wrapping her arms around Chadromida's waist.

"I still say travelling by dragon would have been even faster."

"You know the dragons haven't exactly warmed up to me yet. They fly away when I get near them."

"Shadick?" Alexandria asked, bending next to him. "Are

you okay? You look like you've seen a ghost or something."

"I think I just did, or am I really seeing my little sister standing in Chad's arms?" Shadick asked, sitting up

"Yes bro it's me; you didn't see a ghost." she said, shaking her head.

He jumped up and ran toward her, picking her up and kissing her cheeks.

"My word, Ashy! You've grown up so quickly since the last time I saw you."

"You saw me a year ago, and I haven't grown up that much, just filled out a bit more."

"It feels a lot longer than just a year! What are you doing here?"

"Well I missed Chad, and I heard you were around here and will be for a while so I thought, why not. I'm moving here, and all my stuff will arrive within a week."

"Why didn't you tell me, Chad?! I almost had a heart attack hearing her voice just now."

"Well, we wanted to surprise you, so we agreed to not let you know of the plans, or the engagement for that matter." Chadromida told him, grinning.

"Engagement?! How long have you been engaged for?" Shadick asked as they sat down around the fire.

"About half a year now, I asked her on my last vacation,

and we've been seeing each other every other weekend since then."

"You went about it wrong. You were supposed to ask me for her hand first, you idiot!"

"Your parents are unfortunately not around anymore, so it's not needed for that."

"Her brother is still alive! So, it automatically reverts to you asking me."

"Shads, you should be a bit nicer! You would've said yes anyways, and if you hadn't, we would've gotten married anyways because you are not the boss of me." Astarte muttered.

"I'm only kidding sis, partly anyways." Shadick said laughingly. "I'm so happy for you, my little sister is finally settling down. Never thought I would ever live to see the day."

She punched Shadick's arm lightly and laughed. "Not funny bro. And I am only 3 years younger than you are, and you haven't settled down yet."

Alexandria stood up and silently slipped into one of the cavern tunnels walking away slowly, knowing they wouldn't miss her. She did not want to intrude on the family reunion they were having. Shadick had not seen his sister in months, so she knew that he would appreciate some alone time with her and Chad.

When her parents died and Valencia adopted her, it had never truly felt as though she was a part of something everyone wanted. A family. Yes, she had the Faeries and they only showed her love and tried to make her feel at home but even Valencia knew she would never have the home her parents would have given her.

When Valencia had realized what she had started doing, she had pushed her even harder to harness her powers. She didn't however make her feel bad about the decision or pretend that she was happier than what she was. Yes, she had been happy to have someone to look after her. But it hadn't been the love and attention she had craved.

She had been given a necklace in the shape of Valencia's wings when she had turned 16, and was told not to tell anyone about it as she was not supposed to share it with anyone not, even her own daughter.

She still had the necklace and kept it safe where she knew that no one would ever find it. Alexandria had always wondered what the significance of the necklace was but had never been given a chance to ask Valencia about it as she had died a few months later.

Alexandria froze in her steps as she heard voices coming from somewhere ahead of her. As far as she knew, there was no one here, not human anyway. The Dwarves were in the other direction. Most of the dragons were in their worlds, so she could not understand where these voices were coming from. Slowly walking forward, trying to distinguish the voices from where they were coming from.

Without warning, she fell into a hole that she had not seen. She exclaimed softly as she fell on her feet, her right foot twisting a little. Standing up slowly, she looked around trying to see where she had landed. All she could see were gravestones. From the corner of her eye, she saw movement and what seemed like a blade. She was about to scream but she realised that she recognised the young woman walking towards her, but she blinked, not wanting to believe what she saw.

"Mom? Is it really you, or did I hit my head during the fall?" Alexandria whispered.

"You still remember me! I am happily surprised by this discovery. Your father was convinced his little angel had forgotten how we looked and would try to run when we showed ourselves. But I knew that my little girl would never forget her parents." Thalia told her daughter, smiling sweetly.

"Dad is here as well?" Alexandria asked, shocked.

"It is only natural that I am here as well. I would never leave your mother and the love of my life alone, particularly when I know that she is seeing our beautiful daughter whom we have missed." Damon said, appearing by his wife's side.

Without thought, she ran into their open and waiting arms, not realising that she might have passed through them.

"My sweet dear girl, don't cry. There is no need for tears. We have no pain here where we are. Our only worry is for you and your well-being. So do not worry about us." Thalia said, hugging her close.

"How is it that I can touch you? As far as I know ghosts cannot be touched, they are ethereal." Alexandria asked, still holding onto her dad.

"Ghosts are, but you have this exceptional ability to be able to touch us, and it is strengthened by the fact that we are in one of the Dragon's worlds." Damon told her, touching the top of her head.

"Did you lead me here on purpose, or is it accidental that I ended up here?"

"A little bit of both, but it is not solely to do with what we can do. We had a little bit of help from Inara." her mother told her.

"Who is Inara?"

"That would be me." a beautiful gold unicorn said, walking out of the shadows.

"I have never seen a true gold unicorn before. I mean, I

have heard tales about them but never seen one personally."
Alexandria said, her eyes widening.

"My kin are still around; I believe you already know one
of my granddaughters."

"Who would that be?"

"Her name is Ashley. As far as I know, she lives with your
Faerie folk."

"But Ashley isn't a gold unicorn; she is more grey than
any other colour."

"We are few and have the ability to hide our true colour,
as many hunters whether they are human or magical would
give their firstborn to be able to hunt us."

"I am sorry to interrupt Inara, but we do not have time.
We need to tell Alex what we called her here for." Damon
interrupted, still holding his daughter tightly.

"He is correct Inara. The forces that keep us from
communicating with the over world draws closer." an old
man said, walking in slowly from the shadows.

"Alastor, why didn't you warn us earlier that this was
happening?! We could have rushed this a little more."

"I thought that you would feel how much weaker we have
been the last few days."

"We were too concerned about finally telling our daughter
what needed to be told we did not exactly concentrate on our

own energies."

"I felt it, but they had so much on their minds that I did not want to bother them with things like that." Inara said, her head drooping slightly

"The Centaurs are getting more powerful. They are calling beings that have not been seen for centuries." Alastor muttered.

"Do you mean the Harpies and Minotaurs?" Alexandria asked frowning.

"You've faced them already?" Thalia exclaimed softly, holding Alexandria tighter.

"I had a brief encounter with them, yes."

"Those are only some of them. There are more creatures coming out for this fight than any war has seen through the ages." Alastor said seriously.

"Indeed, the Orcs haven't been seen for centuries. And they have never been seen fighting together, only against those they consider their enemies which is all people, but a large number of all of these creatures were spotted near their old home, further east just beyond the Wastelands."

"That is really close to Valencia!" Alexandria said panicked.

"No, Alex. Valencia lives by Antithia waterfalls, where she's raised you most of your life. When last have you eaten or drank anything?" Thalia asked worriedly.

"Maybe it is this heat in the mountains; what with the dragons living here, it gets rather heated." Damon said frowning.

"You don't know?" Alexandria asked to which they shook their head. "Valencia was killed when I was 16; there were a few straggling Centaurs and hunters that caught her unsuspecting."

"In all the years that we have known her, she was never that distracted by something that she was hurt. She was always the one that made sure we were kept responsive." Thalia said.

Alexandria bit her lip then sighing said, "She was killed protecting me. Some of the fairies were mocking and attacking me again, although it had been the first time in months, and I had run to my hiding spot I had created when I was 6 when these Centaurs and hunters jumped out from behind a tree and attacked me.

"Valencia had seen and heard what the fairies had called me and had followed me, she stopped one of their blades from severing my head by mere inches. I was cut but she stopped it before it could pierce my skin too deep."

"Were you hurt badly?" Damon asked his daughter.

"Just the one cut on the back of my neck. I still have the

scar but what happened next was what hurt the most. Before Valencia could gather her powers and form some kind of protection, they had attacked again, cutting her wings and body. The one Centaur, the biggest of the group, severed her neck just as they had wanted to do to me. The guards arrived just as it happened and they couldn't stop it. They told everyone that I had stumbled upon it accidentally and was lucky to have survived. They knew that I would have been considered an outcast if they had told the truth, so they had protected me."

"That's terrible!" Thalia whimpered, ghostly tears running down her face.

"I have heard some of the passing unicorns talk about that event, but I never knew it was for Valencia." Inara said, stepping forward. "They spoke about the Faerie Queen who had sacrificed her life for one of her acquaintances and had died a horrifying death."

"If she was killed, then whom are you referring to when you say they are really close to Valencia?" Damon asked his daughter.

"While I was away, Amethyst and the villagers decided to abandon the home they had created by Troll Mountain as it was constantly under attack, so they moved everyone to a new, better village. She named it Valencia in memory of her mother." Alexandria replied.

"That was very sweet of her. I take it she was then made Faerie queen when her mother died?"

"Yes, a Faerie queen at the age of 16."

"Can we move this family reunion on a bit faster? Time is of the essence, and that time is only getting less." Alastor told them.

"He is right, of course." Inara said. "It is time you tell her what you wanted so we can move on."

"Tell me what exactly?"

"We have kept a secret from you, and it has been terrible to have kept it from you."

"When I was expectant with you, your father and I had a rather heated argument, and we split up for a few months."

"5 months, to be exact, and during that time, I was so distraught that I had hurt your mother that I had an affair with one of the villagers."

Alexandria opened her mouth to reply in shock, but her mother spoke over her. "Your father told me as soon as we got back together about it as he felt awful and did not want any more secrets between us."

"We never spoke about it again until your fourth birthday."

"What happened then?" Alexandria asked softly.

"Luanda, the daughter of the florist, drew a picture of Centaurs and fairies, and in the midst of the skirmish, she drew me and your mother with you in her arms."

"Marishina, her mother, immediately brought the picture to us, as she knew who and what we were as I had told her when your mother and I had been apart. She told us that she was certain with every inch of her body and soul that Luanda was mine but had never said anything until that moment as she had not wanted to cause trouble. She then told us that Luanda had always been able to predict the future in her drawings and it had been proven before."

"At first, we chased her out and spoke about it very little, but the drawings became more reasonable as the days passed. She even drew your father and yourself when you had spent time in the garden, but had told me to not share it until I knew the truth. The exact same sight happened only four days later, and I was so shocked that I ran out to your father and told him." Thalia told her.

"Then a few years later, we came to the shocking realisation once again that she was indeed half witch when we got caught in the exact same scenario, she had drawn the first time. We were on our way to try and make a deal with the Centaurs when we were attacked. That was the day we were killed by the Centaurs for fighting alongside the Fairies when they had expected us to join them."

"I have never heard the story like that. All I was told was that the Centaurs attacked and killed my parents." Alexandria said, crying softly.

"No Faerie survived the battle, and the one Centaur that did has never told the story to anyone, rather had retold it so that it sounded as though we were weak and had begged for our lives." Damon told her.

"Why can't I remember this? I was there. You've said it yourself."

"I did not want you to see the battle and experience the overwhelming loss, so I teleported you to Valencia who immediately knew what had happened, along with a note about Luanda's true heritage." Thalia said softly.

"She never told me about a note about that, never even mentioned it."

"I also made her promise in the note that she would not tell you until you were ready, and she never got a chance before she died, it seems."

"We did not want you to hate us, sweetheart. That is why we wanted to wait for you to be older. We were even planning on a few play dates before we died." Damon told her, hugging her tightly.

"I hope you can forgive us in time, baby girl."

"I don't need to forgive you." Alexandria said to the shock of her parents. "I was never mad at you. It was just a surprise to hear it. But nothing could ever make me hate my parents. I always tell my friends about you, and Shadick even said you two sounded like great parents."

"Who is this Shadick?!" Damon started.

"We do not have time for answering questions, Damon. The time for the final warning has come, and we are already fading from this world." Alastor growled softly.

"He is correct as always, Alexandria. We have some more news on the new creatures that will take part in this war, and we also have a warning." Inara said seriously.

"What kind of warning is it?" Alexandria asked frowning.

"There is a traitor in your camp, someone who has been silently feeding the Centaurs information about everything that has been happening in the village. And do not expect the obvious person as it is not that person. We do not know who exactly it is, but we do know that he is a danger to everyone's safety. So, try and get him out of the village as soon as possible, so that some secrets can be kept safe about what is being planned by your side in this war."

"And you say you do not know who this traitor is? Then how can we be sure we exile the right person?"

"No, we are not sure, as he has been keeping his powers

and intentions quiet to even those of us capable of seeing in another's mind. He is a creature of magic descent, but unfortunately, that is all the information we could gather. At least now you are forewarned and can try and do something about it."

Without warning, Freyja and Managwa jumped into the hole running towards Alexandria protectively.

"Our time almost arrives; we have one more warning for you, Alexandria. And one last message that might change your outlook on everything." Damon said hurriedly, "Now listen carefully, child.

"Power is being taken from everyone in your camp. It is done in such a way that no one realises it. So be wary. Also know that if you are not ready, do not start the war, as you will be killed. You will know when the right time is to start." Thalia said seriously as they started fading.

"While I was expectant with you, Valencia and I were attacked in the forest by a couple of Centaurs. It was just me and her. She thought I should get out while your father was hunting. They came out of nowhere and I got stabbed. We were able to chase them away and I would have healed myself but then realised that the sword had pierced the umbilical cord and I was at risk of losing you. She offered to help with the healing knowing that it would take a lot of power."

"What does that mean, mama? I'm a little confused." Alexandria asked frowning.

"What it means sweetheart is that, when they were healing you, some of Valencia's Faerie powers were mixed with your mothers' powers. By healing you with so much of her energy Valencia inadvertently gave you some of her powers." Damon told her smiling.

"That is why Valencia gave you the Faerie wing necklace. Because when the charm is close to you, the Faerie powers in you emerge. Making you stronger than you already are. I'm guessing that she would have told you that part if she had lived." Thalia said. "It is also why you were able to do so much Faerie magic when she was around and when you practised away from her, you failed at the very same magic."

"Does that mean I am part Faerie?" Alexandria asked frowning.

"No, you were given your powers during a fusion of Valencia's and my power when we were healing you."

"I have not noticed any difference in power while I was wearing the necklace. I'm sure that it would have been noticeable."

"Not when it starts manifesting. No one will notice or see anything different." Damon told her seriously, stepping closer to her.

Managwa ran to the hole and barked loudly, Freyja not moving from her defensive position in front of Alexandria.

Chapter 20

Rescue from the Grave

"Who would have ever believed that my little sister would get married to my best friend. I mean, I knew that you guys were dating on and off but never realised that it had gotten serious." Shadick said, still sitting around the fire.

"It was never just on and off, big bro. We started dating seriously three years ago, and since then, we've both been faithful to each other." Astarte told him smugly.

"But I have seen all the girls flocking around you! And you never discouraged them."

"You never paid that much attention to what was happening to me. You always had your own flock to deal with. What you never saw was the girls flocking around me dispersing as soon as I told them I was spoken for." Chadromida told him, laughing.

"And here I thought that you had been my right-hand

man when we went out for drinks."

"I was thinking that you stopped playing the field when you met Alexandria!" Astarte muttered.

"I have. I was talking about a few months ago, when we met up during my mission."

"You played around with other women while still technically with Alexandria?"

"Nothing happened! It was just innocent flirting, and that night, we went home alone."

"He's right, honey, he was just flirting but he wouldn't touch any of them in any way, especially now that Alex is in the picture." Chadromida intervened quickly.

"Shad..." Starlansha's voice drifted towards them from one of the tunnels.

"You were saying brother...?" Astarte asked, arching an eyebrow.

"She's a friend of ours, so there is no need for you to worry about that. Yes, Starlansha?"

"I can't find Alexandria! But I keep thinking that I hear her voice." Starlansha said, stepping into the light.

"She was here just a few minutes ago."

"I do believe that she was trying to subtly give us some 'family time'." Astarte said frowning.

"Even though she knows that she is always welcome."

"Can we stop talking about what she is allowed to do or not and actually find her?" Starlansha asked, walking away again.

"I don't think that she is in any danger... the Dragons would never hurt someone in the Caves unless they were here to steal their treasures." Chadromida said, standing up. "But let us go find her."

☐

"Our time has run out, and we have to go before all our powers are completely gone." Alastor muttered.

"Are you sure that this is where she walked to?" Shadick's voice drifted to them.

"I'm sure that I can hear voices, that can't be good in any shape or form! It has to mean that Alex is in danger." Starlansha's voice drifted closer.

"I hear Managwa howling and barking. It sounds urgent but not as though there is any immediate danger."

"Alastor is right. We cannot allow others to see the dead." Inara said urgently, glancing at the hole as the voices grew louder. "It is too dangerous not just for Alexandria but for everyone else that is still around."

"Watch out! There is a hole here that I have not noticed before." Chadromida shouted.

"And I can see Managwa down there! Which means Alex

and Freyja are down there as well." Starlansha added.

"I am sorry that we are not able to tell you more, my darling daughter. But our time in this world is done, and we need to go before others see us." Thalia told Alexandria, hugging her tightly just as Shadick jumped down the hole.

"But know that we have always loved you! And that we are always with you, even if it doesn't feel that way." Damon said, also hugging Alexandria before disappearing just as Shadick caught sight of them.

"Let go of he...!" Shadick shouted, running towards Alexandria. "I swore that I just saw someone touching you."

"You did see someone touching me. You saw my parents hugging me goodbye." Alexandria told him, crying softly.

"Your parents are dead, sweetie"." Starlansha said, jumping down the hole as well.

"I know that, but their ghosts appeared to me and spoke to me."

"If you say that it was them, then I believe you, sweetie." Shadick said hesitantly, wrapping his arms around her.

"I would believe her even if you lot didn't." Chadromida told them confidently as he walked up to them, "Stranger things than people seeing the dead have happened in Dragon Mountains. The magic in here is more palpable than in any other place because of the Dragons and their worlds."

"Thank you, Chad. It means a lot to me that someone doesn't doubt what I've just experienced. And they did mention something along those lines. Along with something about me being able to keep them here for a while longer." Alexandria said, smiling at Chadromida.

"The things we as a group have seen and also experienced should also account for us maybe being more attuned to the world of the dead than other people."

"Chad, you are making it sound like just another day. It cannot be normal to see things that aren't possible." Astarte said frowning.

"You know what, at least he tries to make me feel better about seeing my dead parents, instead of going on as though I've completely gone crazy." Alexandria shouted.

"Lexie, calm do. I believe you! The others just don't understand what it feels like to see the unbelievable." Shadick said, putting his hands against Alexandria's face. "You are one very special young woman and capable of fantastical things. Whether it be from the living or the dead. Or just from what you are doing to save our world right now. Never forget that I will stand by you through any and all times."

"Thank you, Shadick, that means a lot to me. Perhaps we could go back to the fire? It would be a lot more comfortable there than just standing here while I tell you what I just found out."

Nodding, they all filed back to the fire. Astarte kept glancing at Alexandria nervously as though she was about to spontaneously blow up. She tried concentrating on Shadick's hand, warm in hers. Starlansha was frowning but not saying anything. While Chadromida seemed to be the only one that did not think she was some kind of weirdo, smiling and bouncing slightly.

"Did they tell you something specific?" Starlansha asked as she sat down around the fire.

"They told me quite a bit some of it very shocking, truth be told." she replied sighing.

"Do you wish to talk about it? Or would you prefer to think about things first before talking?" Shadick asked.

"I know now why Luanda has those visions."

"They told you the reasons for her visions?!"

"They did indeed. It turns out that my father had an affair with Luanda's mother while my mom was expecting me. They had a big fight and split up for a bit. When they got back together, he told her all about it, not wanting to keep secrets between them. He had not expected that she had gotten pregnant, but they quickly noticed some obvious signs that she was indeed his. Especially when Luanda and I were four years old, she had her first vision then, and her mother immediately went to my parents."

"So, Luanda is your half-sister?"

"That means that she is half witch!" Starlansha said at the same time.

"Yes, on both accounts."

"You do not seem to be that upset about that news." Chadromida commented, "I wouldn't think you a bad person if you did react badly to the news. It is what any other person would feel."

"I am neither mad or upset at either of them for not telling me or even the Faeries about the news. They told me that her mother wished to keep it a secret. And they only foresaw her being rejected if people were to find out that she was someone else's child and not who they thought was her father. Add to that the fact that she was having visions... although they tried to keep it quiet. She was also told that she should never tell anyone what she sometimes saw."

"It kind of makes sense. What else did they tell you?" Shadick asked, squeezing her lightly.

"Before Valencia's death, she gave me a necklace. Not just any necklace... the necklace that they are not supposed to give to anyone."

"You mean the necklaces of their wings?" Starlansha asked shocked

"Yes."

"Valencia gave you the necklace of her wings? Why had she done that if it isn't allowed?" Astarte asked.

"She never told me why all those years ago. My mom told me that they had been walking in the forest the one day when they were attacked. It resulted in my umbilical cord being severed, and my mom almost lost me. If it hadn't been for Valencia using her powers to help my mother heal, I would not be standing here right now. And in doing so, she fused her powers with mine."

"So, you will have Faerie powers?"

"In a sense yes. When the powers start surfacing, it will react to the necklace, and I will become even stronger than ever."

"And will you be telling Amethyst about this?" Shadick asked.

"She deserves to know about everything that I was told."

"I'm not sure how she will react to hearing that." Starlansha said hesitantly

"It might hurt her for a while, but she will understand why her mother did it. In her eyes, it was a way of telling me without having to actually tell me."

"Was there anything else that they told you?" Chadromida asked, frowning slightly.

"They told me how they died and how my mom had teleported me to Valencia as soon as trouble started. Along with a note on Luanda's heritage and that I should not be told about any of it."

"It makes sense why they told her not to tell you, as it could have gone badly. Not on purpose, of course, but emotions get too much at times."

"I was also given a warning that I need to tell Amethyst and the entire council about as soon as it is possible."

"What is this warning they gave you?" Shadick asked, sitting up straight.

"To quote them exactly', 'There is a traitor in your camp, someone who has been silently feeding the Centaurs information about everything that has been happening in the village. And do not expect the obvious person as it is not that person. We do not know who exactly it is but we do know that he is a danger to everyone's safety. So, try and get him out of the village as soon as is possible, so that some secrets can be kept safe about what is being planned by your side in this war.'"

"But they could not tell you who it was giving the Centaurs inside information?"

"No, they had no time to investigate further. They have been having a hard time getting into people's minds as they do not have physical bodies anymore."

"Then I think that it would be for the best if we get back to Valencia as soon as possible so that we can talk to Amethyst about all of this." Starlansha said, standing up.

"As much as I agree with you that Amethyst needs to know, we would not be any use to her if we were to show up there exhausted." Shadick said seriously.

"I agree with Shadick, we have had a long journey here and have been busy the entire time. We need to at least get a night's rest before returning." Alexandria added sighing "Besides she would not be happy with us if we concentrated more on what might go wrong than ourselves."

"Then it is settled. You will spend the night here and set off first thing in the morning. That way, you know you will get back there as soon as possible while still being properly rested." Chadromida said grinning.

Starlansha shook her head and sighed, ignoring Chadromida as he tried making them all laugh.

Chapter 21

Fiery Lava Pits

It was a frustrated groan that could be heard as she paused for a second. She had been sure that after her encounter with the Ghosts that she would have a good night's sleep further. But here she was again, wandering around the caves because of something. What she was walking around for, she was not sure. All she knew was that something was bothering her, and she could not still it.

If she had not known better, she might have believed that her parents had wanted something else. But they had said their goodbyes, so she knew that it was not them. It was strangely quiet, though, and if you had asked her, she would have said that you should have been able to hear the Dragons breathing at least. But there was nothing but a strange humming.

She had considered waking the others but had felt like she

had put them through enough. But there was no way that she would put this on them if it turned out that she was being silly. They already looked at her as though she had completely lost it.

She froze in her steps as it felt as though she was suddenly surrounded by a wall of lava. Of course, an Elemental would choose now of all times to test her. It was with a twinge that she wished that she had any control over when it happened but knew that it was for nought. Closing her eyes and allowing the Element to pull it to its mate, she lightly jumped down the well situated there.

"That was easier than I thought." a childlike voice said from the darkness.

"For an Elemental that deals with Fire, it sure is dark in here." Alexandria replied sighing.

"Oh right! They told me that you aren't able to see that well in low light."

Alexandria blinked as they were suddenly surrounded by small fires. Her eyes lingered on the shape of a young girl a few feet ahead of her, and she tried to hide her shock. She knew that they could choose the form and age that they wanted, but this seemed a little... drastic.

"I know what you are thinking, by the way."

"Is that so?"

"I do yes... you are wondering why of all the shapes open to me, did I choose that of a young girl."

"Hmm... perhaps you do know. I was hesitant to believe that you really knew and expected a silly reply."

"Out of all of the Elementals, I am actually the most serious. Yet I have the youngest shape. I chose this shape as I never had a chance to experience what it was like to be a child. And the one day while I was walking among some of the humans, I saw a girl that looked almost exactly like this. I did however change a few things to make it a bit more me."

"Did the child die?"

"Not at all! It was not like that, at all. I just saw how her innocence pulled people in and made them trust her. Then when they weren't watching, she would kill them or steal from them. Depending on what she needed at that time."

"A child murdered people?"

"She was one of the elusive Vampires that roam the world."

"Was?"

"Probably still is. I just haven't had a lot of time to go and find her the last couple of years." she replied, smiling slightly. "As much as I love talking to you, I think that we are distracting ourselves from the whole reason why you are here this morning."

"Right. To 'prove' that I am worthy of using the Elements. That you guys haven't made a mistake by giving me these powers."

"I see that you have already had your battle with Jayce then."

"He was the first out of all of you, yes."

"He has always been such an impatient being! If it were to be done right, he needs to be last. But no... he insists on going when he feels he wants to."

"I'm not complaining. It at least gave me some warning as to what I should be expecting. If it had been Meya who had attacked me first, I'm not sure whether she would have told me why it was happening."

"That is one of the things about us, Elementals... our element does not dictate our personalities."

"So, I have come to realize. As far as I can tell, you aren't fiery and hot-headed."

"I will not attack if not necessary if that is what you mean."

"Kind of..."

"Perhaps the time for talking is not now." she said, glancing up at the roof as a Dragon roared.

Without a second's hesitation and while she was still distracted, Alexandria rushed towards Claudia and attacked her. The Elemental squealed before ducking, barely dodging the attack. She whirled around and threw a fireball at her. A soft hiss issued from behind her as she ducked down to avoid being burned to death.

Glancing behind her, she noticed that it had fallen into a pit of lava. Closing her eyes and concentrating for a second before hurling two fireballs at Claudia. As she seemed to let it surround her, Alexandria slowly started changing the composition of the Element. Alexandria ignored the darkening of the Elemental's eyes but blinked when she disappeared from sight.

"That was brilliant! And before you say it... I know that it was not much of a fight, but I am impressed with what I have seen."

"Why does it seem that I only need to show a little bit of talent for you guys to be happy?"

"We weren't told to have you near death before accepting that you are worthy."

"Told?"

"Never mind that! But if you wish to continue fighting, we can, of course, do that. I won't hold a girl back from fighting when it's needed. I do think on the other hand though that you will be fighting enough not too long from now though. And you can use all of the rest that you can get."

"Does that mean the Centaurs will be attacking us soon?"

"I do not really know. I just meant in general. As we can't ever be sure of what they are planning."

"I was hoping that you had infiltrated their camp or even had a snitch in their midst. And that was how you knew what was going on, as Necrontyr has."

"No, unfortunately not. I just had a guess in the dark, to be honest."

"Well, I guess one thing I can officially say is that I only have one more of you to fight. Then we can all call it a day." Claudia said before disappearing in a burst of fire, turning into a stone and fusing with her daggers.

Chapter 22

Written in the Stars

"Are you sure that you are okay, sweetheart? You still seem shaken and very pale." Shadick asked, concerned, holding Alexandria tightly.

"Yes, just still trying to get over it. It was just so unexpected, the fight seeing my parents' ghosts, not to mention an attack from an elemental." Alexandria replied.

"Well, we knew to expect a fight. We just didn't know from which element, although the mountains should have been enough of a sign."

"No one could have predicted what had happened. I am just happy that all of us came out of it without being injured." Chadromida said softly.

Standing up slowly, Alexandria whispered, "I need some time alone, just to process all of this, it feels like everything is piling up and my brain isn't handling it right."

"I don't think that it is safe for you to be alone right now, sweetie." Shadick said.

"Let her go bro; she won't have another trial so quickly after the last one. I promise she'll be safe wherever she decides to relax and gather her wits." Astarte told her brother softly.

"I won't go far, I promise, Shadick. I just need time." Alexandria said, disappearing into one of the passages.

"What if something happens while she is on her own? We won't hear her screams if she goes outside or anywhere in this cave." Shadick muttered.

"She will be fine bro. Haven't you noticed that there are pixies surrounding her?"

"What pixies?"

"Hmm, strange she doesn't even seem to notice them, but why can I see them?"

"You've always been special Asti." Chadromida said smiling.

Shadick smiled, slightly relaxed. "True enough, I remember when we were younger, you used to see all the water fairies and nature sprites and no one else would see them."

"I guess I never grew out of that little flair. But I quite like it!" Astarte said glowing.

Alexandria lightly strode through the passages letting the whispers from the others fade.

* * *

A few hours later she was still sitting on top of the cave, staring into the night sky, trying to decipher what the stars were trying to say to her. She had climbed up here to clear her mind, but it had only caused even more questions to pop into her head.

Why had she ever been under the delusion that she would be able to accomplish something in this Odyssey? She had not even told Shadick about the realisation that she had been chosen for this, but so much seemed to have happened after the appearance of her parents.

"There seems to be a lot on your mind, you didn't even hear me climb up here and usually, you are super aware of everything that happens around you." Chadromida said, appearing in front of her.

"I'm just trying to figure things out that have been happening." Alexandria replied not to mention Freyja would have alerted me if there was danger."

"It helps to talk about these kinds of things, you know, and not always keep it hidden inside you; it can really eat you up. A hard lesson I had to learn when I was first chosen as the Dragon proviso. I kept everything inside thinking that it would be fine and that I didn't have to worry about talking to anyone. Then one day, I couldn't anymore, and I just snapped.

"It would have been a disaster if I had not been near the dragons at the time; you see, it was also then that I, along with the dragons realised just how much power comes with my new title."

"I never heard your story before, Chad. Shadick seemed to think that it wasn't my business to know unless you told me, so I kept quiet."

Chadromida sat down next to her, looking at her carefully before letting out a slow breath. "It isn't a very happy story, you know."

"You're the one that just said people have to talk about what's on their mind."

Laughingly he said, "Touché Lex! I was 16 when it first happened in a village long forgotten and long burnt down by people. Just like your unfortunate village."

"Burnt down by whom?"

"Oh yes, I forgot not everyone knows the stories. It was burnt down by a group of werewolves that considered the land theirs even though they were thrown out by the villagers."

"Werewolves?! How come you and Shadick get along so well with what he is?"

"Patience Lex, don't get ahead of me. Anyway, the village was burnt down the same year I was... nominated to join the dragons. I was playing games with some of my friends when the first dragon appeared to me and made its announcement, landed in the middle of the village where we were playing and called me forward.

"The villagers pushed me towards the dragon hoping if they did so that it would not destroy the village. My parents tried stopping them, but the villagers stopped them, so the dragon spoke loudly and clearly and said that I had this power in me and it had called them here to collect me so I could join them and be trained.

"I refused, but there aren't many that can stand against a dragon and live to tell the tale. The dragon whose name I later learned was Sustanivo, roughly translating to "Beast", grabbed me up and flew towards these very mountains and no matter how much I struggled, he refused to let me go. For the next year, I tried finding a way out but kept ending up in other worlds or just being caught and thrown back in what they call 'Training world'.

"Then I got the brilliant, albeit stupid, idea to let them train me and then when I knew all their tricks, I could use it against them and escape that way. At first, they thought it strange at my easy acceptance. They just took it in their strides and increased my training program. Within a year, I was able to defeat their 'weakest' and a year after, I was on the same level with some of the strongest. It was about the same time that I realised I loved training and fighting with the dragons and exploring their worlds.

"And I had learnt of my villages demise by the hands of the werewolves 6 months after my arrival, and as I had nowhere to go, it seemed appropriate that I make the mountains my new home, because as far as I knew my whole village had been wiped out. When the dragons felt I knew enough, they informed me that I had a chance to go back into the real world and do some exploring if I wished to.

"I informed them that my only wish was that I could go and avenge my family. So, they let me go, and for a year while still doing the training, I searched for the werewolves responsible for the attack and deaths of my family and the village. I finally found their dwelling and I was planning my attack when I saw a man walk among them who seemed normal, and did not eat raw meat as readily as the rest of the pack.

Himself put it out of my mind however and continued watching, the one day in a village I was minding my own business when I saw the young man again. He was clearly more than human but supressed by where he found himself.

"I respected that and offered my hand in understanding, and that is how Shadick and I became friends, and together, we fought against the werewolf pack and defeated them. He also understood that I needed to be with the dragons as he had the wolves, but he invited me to join him and Astarte for lunch, and I ended up staying there for a few months.

"But through all of the ups and downs and the hardships of getting used to spending my life with the dragons, I learnt that everything happens for a reason. Even though we don't always know why we were chosen for something, it will always be revealed in good time, and when you are ready to know."

"But don't you still wonder what your life would have been like had you not been chosen?"

"I used to wonder yes, but then I realised had I not been taken away for training, I would have died along with my family. I wasn't strong enough back then to be able to stand up to them, and if it had not been the werewolves, something else would have killed me. I had not lived my life right; I had lived very hazardously. It had been a mixed blessing."

"That does make sense, and even though it doesn't always feel that way, it had its benefits."

Nodding and smiling, Chadromida continued. "The dragons sensed your uncertainty and spoke to me a few nights ago about this issue. They informed me that I need to speak to you and tell you my story and that you would feel better about your circumstances.

"They also told me that I should tell you that even they, the dragons, have felt that this is indeed the path chosen for you. Even when it feels like it is getting to much, you should stay positive because everyone gets their days where they feel that everything and everyone is against them. You should turn to your friends, and they will get you through all of it."

"The dragons sensed that I was the right person for this whole state of affairs?"

"Yes, and even in their worlds have they felt the change of energy and power. It makes them restless, and they feel the urge join the cause that you are fighting for."

"But they did fight alongside us during the last battle. Why would they not join it this time?"

"Some of them did yes, but there are those of their kind that have not left their worlds for millennia, and even they have felt the change."

"But what if the Fates made a wrong decision, Chad? I get that everyone is sensing the 'rightness' of this whole situation, but everyone makes mistakes, and I just feel so pathetic compared to the whole thing. I fell for Justin and I wholeheartedly believed his whole tale about his life and that he had feelings for me, someone powerful would not have fallen for his tricks."

"But you had your suspicions from the start; Shadick told me the whole story. And that is the most important thing, not if you fell for his lies or not. Trust me when I tell you that you are indeed the right person and that the Fates did not make a mistake."

Sighing softly and standing up, fisting her hands "It just all feels so wrong, I know I have all this power but I feel powerless. That no matter what I do it doesn't feel as though I am doing enough to improve the situation."

"I felt exactly the same way when I was forced to join the dragons and had to watch my life change right before my eyes and I had no control over it whatsoever. But in the end, I realised that I had control to guide it, although not completely be in charge of it.

And this is what the dragons were talking about when they told me that I can talk some self-confidence into you, I might not banish the insecurities completely, but I can help you see the significance you symbolise to the people around you and those who offered to help you in getting rid of the problem we have in the centaurs."

"I don't hold any significance to anyone."

"Do you think that people would have offered to join your

fight if they didn't trust you? That if they didn't believe in you, they would still be fighting and hanging on? They fight and hang on because of you Lex; they notice your strength and willpower and follow you because they know you are the only one that can bring them a triumph." Chadromida told her, pulling her up holding her as tears started flowing.

"I know that it feels impossible right now but I assure you that me, Shadick, Starlansha, Astarte, Amethyst and all your other friends will stand by you and support and help you. Even when things seem dire, we will always be there for you."

"Thank you, Chad I really appreciate the pep talk, it makes me feel better, and I am so sorry that I am ruining your shirt."

"Don't worry about it, just let it all out. I can feel that you need to let go; besides, there are a hundred where this one came from."

He laughed softly, wiping the tears away. "I'm sure there are a hundred more. Or it's called using your girlfriend to wash your shirts so that it feels as though you have hundreds."

"Fiancé, I'll have you know."

"Same thing, just a slightly different way to put it, and you know it."

"Yeah, you want to go down now or do you want to stay

here some more?"

"I'm not completely ready to go just yet. I still need some time to think."

"That's fine. I shall stay here with you for as long as you want me to."

"You really don't have to feel as though you have to; I understand completely if you want to get back to Astarte."

"She understands that I am here to make you feel a bit better about this whole situation. She is actually the one who sent me up here when Shadick started stressing and wanted to climb up here to drag you down, because he was worried you did something unintelligent like jump off this cliff."

"Tempting but I wouldn't, my friends would miss me too much if I did that."

"I will not tell Shadick you told me that. He will just make a big deal over it, and I don't know if it is entirely necessarily for that kind of reaction."

"I agree with you on that one, Chad, don't worry; I will just pretend that I just sat there and had no such thoughts. That I just had to clear my mind."

"I know this will sound a little weird, but it is written in the stars that this is your destiny and that this is exactly how things are supposed to turn out. That no matter how wrong it feels or how perfect it will turn out just the way that it's supposed to." Chadromida told her, squeezing her hand giving her a quick hug before touching a silver pendant around his neck.

"What is the necklace for?" Alexandria asked curiously.

"You will see." Chadromida said smiling, turning towards a massive dragon that had appeared on the top of the mountain. "It is my way of being able to call Nightshade here, as well as communicate with him if the need arises."

"Not that it is always enjoyable to listen to his whines about his life. Or to listen to him gush over his love, Astarte. Or how difficult it is to not slap Shadick about some of the things his friends do." The big dragon grumbled, rolling his eyes.

"I am not that bad, Shade! You are giving the lady a bad impression of me."

Laughing softly, Alexandria stepped forward and lightly touched the dragon's wing. "It is nice to meet you Nightshade; it is most definitely not something that happens every day."

"And it is nice to meet you 'Dearbhail'. I have heard a lot about you among my kind and from Chadromida over here."

"Dearbhail, what does that mean?" Alexandria asked, tilting her head slightly.

"It means 'Daughter of Destiny' in his world."

Chadromida told her matter-of-factly.

"I'm flattered, Nightshade; I doubt I've ever been complimented in such a way."

"It is only the truth; now shall we fly down? It will be getting rather nippy, and neither of you is dressed for that." Nightshade said matter-of-factly.

"Yes, you're right." Chadromida said, jumping onto Nightshade's back and then helping Alexandria up. "Now, hold on; it will be a swift flight."

Alexandria wrapped her arms around Chadromida's waist, closing her eyes when she felt the dragon's wings start to beat and he took flight. A few seconds later, she felt its paws touch the ground in an almost silent landing.

"Lexie, I am so glad that you're okay!" She heard Shadick's voice and then felt his hands on her waist, slowly opening her eyes.

"Shadick!" she exclaimed, jumping into his arms and causing them both to tumble to the ground.

"I'm happy to see you too, sweetheart, but you weren't gone that long."

"I know that you were worried about me, and just letting you know that I am perfectly well and that I missed you like crazy, even though I was away for no more than a few hours."

"I'm just happy that you are safe and seem to be in a

better state of mind than before."

"I told you she would be safe, big brother. When will you learn that sometimes listening to your little sister can be smart?" Astarte asked, pulling Alexandria up and hugging her tightly. "You almost gave my brother a heart attack, my dear."

"I didn't mean to worry any of you, and I am sorry if I did. I just needed some time." Alexandria said, leaning back into Shadick's arms and smiling at Astarte.

"Where is my thanks that I went to save the day? I went up there and risked my very life to bring dear Alexandria down here safely?" Chadromida asked mock, outrageously crossing his arms.

Astarte stepped forward, kissing his cheek. "You are thanked by the happiness I see on my brother's face."

"Then all is well." he replied, pulling Astarte closer while they laughed softly.

Chapter 23

Unicorn treachery

"I never thought that I would see Chadromida so happy. And I never thought that my sister would be the one making him so happy. From what I remember when we were younger, he irritated her to bits, and she wanted nothing to do with him." Shadick said as they rode back to Valencia.

"You would be surprised what distaste can hide at times. I mean, it isn't as though I always liked you." Starlansha joked.

"If I remember correctly, you actually did. Both you and Roslata..."

"Don't worry, you are free to mention her. I will not break down every time that I hear her name."

"I can't remember ever liking someone from the falls enough to 'lose' it. I was so concentrated on my training that I didn't want anything to do with guys." Alexandria said, smiling slightly. "Although I do remember the one night at a party, I met a young boy who completely swept me off my feet. And I do believe that Amethyst arrived just in time to stop things from going too far."

"Wait... I went to one of Valencia's parties where I met a girl, and things got out of hand. But we got interrupted by Amethyst."

Alexandria glanced at him, her eyes widening slowly as realisation struck her. His eyes seemed to get darker as he thought back to that evening.

"It can't be..." she whispered.

"I have learned that just about anything is possible. You were living with them at that point and obviously a young girl. And I was a horny young man that was forced to go to a party that I didn't want to go to."

"What are the two of you talking about?" Starlansha asked, glancing between them.

"One of Valencia's parties, she invited some of her human friends. Friends who of course knew about the magical creatures and could be trusted not to cause any trouble. That was my parents. We were invited as well, and me and my sister were forced to go with. Although I have to admit she was very excited to see the Faeries and other magical creatures so there wasn't a lot of forcing on her side.

"But for me, I didn't want to go and had a big argument with my parents about it. In the end, I went with but was determined not to have any fun because how could it be any fun? Not long after arriving, I saw a girl sitting at the top of the waterfall, and I went up there to find out who she is and why she seemed so alone."

"That girl was me..." Alexandria said. "It was one of the evenings that I was really missing my parents and just wanted to be alone but this guy walked up to me and kept talking to me. The next thing I remember is that we were making out like crazy people. I do believe that we would have slept together that night if it hadn't been for Amethyst and her then boyfriend stumbling into the clearing on their way to their own little naked party."

"We have met before! I thought you seemed familiar the first time I saw you at the waterfalls when I wanted to talk to Valencia, but I shook it off because I have seen so many people in my lifetime that I could not be sure where I had met you."

"I kind of drove Amethyst crazy over the next few weeks over the guy that I almost slept with."

"And why would she not tell you that the two of you knew each other when you met again?" Starlansha asked frowning.

"That's an easy answer... some of the attacks started back then so we were always busy and distracted, so it isn't a bad thing that she forgot about what or who almost happened that night. She was also an unwilling guest that evening because Valencia wanted her to be all Princess-like and meet the representatives of the different 'clans'. Something that she was not excited about at all."

"After that night, I always wondered whether I would see the girl ever again. But it seemed to not be fated." Shadick said smiling.

"And when I wasn't busy training and arguing with Amethyst, I wished that the guy would come whip me away from my worst nightmare."

"Just shows you what a small world it is that we live in." Starlansha said, laughing softly.

"It sure is."

"I have been wondering, Alex. What did you and Chadromida talk about at the top of Dargona Mountains?"

"He just reminded me of why I'm doing this thing. As hateful as it is."

"So, we get no details?" Shadick asked, frowning "Did he try and do something inappropriate?"

"Not at all! He just told me about some of his past and tried to make me feel better about everything that has happened to me in the last while. He informed me that even though I might still wonder why I was chosen, the Dragons apparently sensed me and knew that I was the right person for all of this. And when Nightshade joined us to bring us down to you guys, he just made it even scarier but better at the same time."

"And how was that old Dragon able to achieve that? As far as I know, all he does is complain about how Chad is useless."

"He called me Dearbhail. Which apparently means 'Daughter of Destiny' in the Dragons' world."

"Coming from a Dragon, that is a major compliment! They can be very fussy about whom they like or even trust and rarely calls someone by something other than their name. If they are even lucky enough for that. A lot of the time, they either ignore the person completely or insult them the entire time."

"I have heard that Dragons can be rather temperamental, not that I have ever met one before. Living in the ocean, things are completely different, and you meet other kinds of creatures." Starlansha said smiling. "I always wondered about them though, and wished that I could meet one."

"And is it everything that you believed that it would be?"

"I feel torn, I somehow imagined that they would be different. Not that I can tell you how different. Call it the imagination of a child."

"My father told me about Dragons and drew pictures for me, so I have always known how they look. Although I did not imagine them to be as gigantic as they actually are. Not that I expected them to be tiny... well, maybe some of them." Alexandria said smiling

"Did you expect them to fit in your hand and cuddle on your shoulder?" Shadick asked grinning.

"Something along those lines! Although I knew that you never get on the bad side of Dragons because they will incinerate you without a second thought."

"Lexie, your imagination is a strange thing. You thought that they were small, yet you believed that the small Dragons could incinerate you with one breath. I honestly don't see how that would be possible."

"Hey, be nice! I was a little girl, and my imagination went crazy after my father told me about them. It isn't as though I actually met one until now. It was just something that was like I imagined them."

"I seriously need to tell Chad about what you had believed of Dragons before the last few days. He will find it rather hilarious."

"Ignore Shadick, Alex. He is a guy, and he does not understand how the imagination of a young girl works. For a guy, if he hears Dragon, he imagines a huge beast that can squash you by just stepping on you, and the eyes are most likely white or something. For girls, we like to try and see the magic in creatures. For example, I kind of imagined that they would be more cat-like and longer rather than bigger. More snakelike and that they could crawl up the sides of mountains."

"And that! Something else that I need to tell Chad!" Shadick said, laughing loudly.

"As I said... guys are another kind of species, one that believes everything is as they see it and not as it actually is. Or believes that what they saw or think they saw is what it actually is and refuses to be told otherwise."

"I never thought that I would be able to ride on a Dragons back, but I do not regret it for one second. It was a very unique and awesome experience."

"The way the two of you are dawdling and babbling will make a day's travel last longer. If you want to talk to Amethyst about everything we have found, we will need to get a move on." Shadick said, slightly irritated.

"Oh dear... I do believe that we have hurt his feelings."

"No, it is not that. I am just getting a bad feeling all of a sudden, as though something is going to happen that will not be good for us."

"Is the feeling making you feel like Amethyst is in

danger?"

"It is not that specific, unfortunately. I just know that we need to get back now!"

Alexandria looked at him, then nodded and urged her horse into a run, hearing Starlansha doing the same. It was never a good thing when Shadick had a bad feeling about something, as it could only be something terrible.

They finally saw the walls of Valencia about two hours later, and she let out a breath that felt as though she had been holding it for hours. Now they could get to Amethyst and make sure that everything and everyone is still safe and unhurt.

"Look!" Starlansha shouted, and Alexandria glanced at the spot where she was pointing

At first, she could not quite figure out what she was seeing but then realised that it was a Unicorn flying around the Castle and seeming to shout down. From where she was, she could not be sure which one of the Unicorns it was, but she was convinced that she saw a black coat.

"We need to get there, NOW!" she muttered and shrieked softly as they were suddenly right in front of the Castle.

"How did..." Starlansha started, then stopped.

"I am sorry your majesty that I disappointed you in your

beliefs that all Pegasi are the good and docile kind. I am not one of them that will allow you to pet them whenever you wish to. I will not serve you as blindly as the other of my kind has been.

"I have been out of your control for years now but pretended to still follow every little thing that you have made me do because I was asked to do so by the Centaurs. Asked to find out what is going on and to report back and to try and push you into doing some things even if you did not think that it would be for the best. And guess what! You listened to every single one and I laughed behind your back.

"I will now return to the Centaurs and tell them of my success and to tell them of some of the things that I was able to make you do. And I will be heralded as a hero! Unlike here, where I was only treated like scum and nothing or no one important."

"If you believe that they will treat you like a hero, then you have completely lost your mind. They will only treat you like another informant, and the second they see that you aren't being useful anymore, they will have you killed. They are ruthless, and I thought that you knew that!" Amethyst shouted at the Pegasus.

"Markus, come down so that we can talk about this! There has to be a way to make you see the error in listening to the

Centaurs. You have never been a creature to just blindly follow someone without proof of what they want. And we all know that they just want destruction." Ashley shouted at him. "If you come down here, we can sit down and talk about everything."

"You mean that you will lock me up to ensure I cannot get back to the Centaurs. I refuse to be a prisoner for something that I believe in."

"Then please go to the Centaurs so that they can kill you because your 'work' for them is done. It will spare us from having to do it. And I can assure you that they will kill you once you tell them what you found out from staying here." Alexandria said calmly, getting off her horse. "And you can argue with us as well as yourself about how that isn't what will happen, but deep in your heart, you do know that it is true. And I think that you should just admit it so that you can die peacefully."

"How did you get here so quickly?!" Amethyst asked shocked.

"I don't think that now is the time to explain things, Am. Shall we keep it for later? When we aren't talking to a Unicorn backstabbing us?" Shadick said, standing next to her.

"And once again, you guys get lost in your own little lives when there is so much more going on out there that is a lot more important than your fickle in a group arguing and fighting." Markus said, then laughed. "When I approached the Centaurs during the first battle, they locked me up and wanted to make an example of me, until I told them that I could be of use. That I did not agree with what you guys want to achieve with all of this. I agreed more with them than I ever did with you, Amethyst. Your goals are narrow-minded, and you refuse to look further into what is possible."

"Our goals are narrow-minded?! The Centaurs are the ones wanting to rule over all of the Magical creatures and kill all the humans! We are trying to get together with the humans to make ourselves stronger." Amethyst said shocked.

"Don't waste your breath on him, Am. He has been twisted and manipulated by the Centaurs. And I now understand what my parents told me about the Centaurs getting information from the inside." Alexandria said, smiling slightly.

"Your parents are dead, Alex..."

"She saw their ghosts, but that is something that we will discuss later." Shadick added, putting a hand on Amethyst's shoulder.

"Markus, I will give you only one chance to come back to us without being locked up. But know that if you refuse this chance, we will put you on the same level as the Centaurs and you will not be welcome back here no matter what you do." Alexandria said, stepping forward. "Come down here so that we can hear about your thoughts and so that we can perhaps explain a bit more about our 'goals'. We will not throw you in a cell if you come down now. But if you leave here without listening to us, then you give us no choice."

"Nice try, Alexandria. I know that you are just spouting more lies! If I am to come down there, you will have me thrown in the prison, and I will never see the light of day ever again."

"I take it that your choice is to go to the Centaurs and be killed, just know that we gave you the option to come back and you refused it."

"I am getting tired of the lies! Now, if you will excuse me, I have better places to be and, in a lot, better company than present."

They watched him fly higher into the sky and disappear into the sunlight, and a silence fell around them that seemed about ready to burst. But nothing happened, and they kept watching the spot where Markus had disappeared, seeming to hope that he had just been playing around and would be back in a minute.

"Go to the gates and tell them that Markus has defected to the Centaurs and that he is on the watch list of dangerous creatures. And that no matter what he says, he is not allowed back in here." Alexandria said after a few minutes, "Tell them that for the time being, we are on lockdown. They shouldn't deny people access, but they need to be careful to allow just anyone in."

"Are you sure that we need to do that?" Shadick asked as one of the guards around them nodded and ran off. "Perhaps he is just having a moment of craziness. We are all allowed to have one of those every now and then."

"I looked into his heart and saw the darkness there. Whatever good was in him is long gone. And I remember when we were still talking about what our next move should be that he was very negative."

"We trusted him, and he broke that trust... are we fighting on the wrong side?" Amethyst asked despondently.

"He chose to break that trust, Am. His thoughts have never been all that positive if you think back on it. It has been a fight to make him see reason from the beginning. Do not blame yourself for his choices as you aren't the one that made him think that way."

"I think that we should go to the council room and talk about all of this. The rumours will start circulating soon about what happened here with him, and we need to ensure that truth comes out." Shadick said, looking at the villagers below them. "Panic will start spreading, and things might just get worse from there. I think that a public announcement should happen within the next couple of hours."

"Come on, Am. We need to discuss what we have learned at Dragon Mountains as well as what we will tell everyone."

Amethyst sighed and nodded before walking towards the Castle, her shoulders seeming to be weighed down by a lot of worry.

"I keep wondering whether there had been some kind of hint that he was about to betray us, but I can't seem to figure out where it came from. He still seemed happy, in a way, at least. But he never showed us anything but positivity." Amethyst said a few hours later.

"He gave us plenty of signs as well as a lot of negativity. We just refused to look at it because we had so many other things going on. So don't you dare blame yourself for something that is not your fault." Alexandria said, sitting down on one of the chairs.

"Did you notice how shocked the villagers were when I told them what happened? As though they refused to believe it."

"You are imagining things, Am. They were shocked yes, but they believed it. I am sure that a lot of them have seen how he acted around all of us."

"So, we did the right thing?"

"What do you mean the 'right thing'?"

"In letting him go..."

"Did you wish for me to shoot him out of the air? To kill him then and there?"

"No, I do not wish him death."

"Then we did the right thing. We have been saying from the very start that we won't force our opinions and thoughts on people. And that we will always be honest with everyone but that they are free to have their own thoughts. Do you have any idea what the rumours would have been like if we had killed him?"

"Would it have been worse than the ones currently flying around?"

"Yes, it would have been. The rumours would have put whoever killed him in terrible light, and they would have started questioning what kind of person you are for having allowed his death at the hands of one of us."

"But he went to the Centaurs!"

"They would have overlooked that little fact and gone straight to 'perhaps we are wrong for listening to her'. This way, they know that he was given a choice of returning without consequence or leaving but knowing that we will not let him back in. And you told everyone this during your speech."

"My mother would have been able to handle this so much better. This wouldn't even have happened to her if she had still been Queen."

"Amethyst, I think that there is something that you should know. Something that I hadn't known until I saw the ghosts of my parents."

"It is true that you saw their ghosts? Did you see my mom?"

"No, she wasn't with them."

"Did you see anyone else besides your parents?"

"Yes, I did... a golden unicorn named Inara, grandmother of Ashley. As well as an old man named Alastor."

"And what did they tell you?"

"Quite a bit. Like how Luanda is my half-sister which explains how she has visions. And told me about how the attack that killed them and how my mom teleported me to Valencia and how she knew what had happened. Along with a letter explaining about Luanda, but she never got a chance to tell me about any of it. They also informed me that there is a traitor amongst us, but they didn't know who it was. Except that he was of magical descent. Including something that explains a lot..."

"And what would that be?"

"I ask that you don't say anything until I am done with the explanation."

"Oh, alright then."

"My mother told me about something that had happened to her and her exact words were 'While I was expectant with you, Valencia and I were attacked in the forest by a couple of Centaurs. It was just me and her she thought I should get out while your father was hunting. They came out of nowhere and I got stabbed, we were able to chase them away and I would have healed myself but then realised that the sword had pierced the umbilical cord, and I was at risk of losing you. She offered to help with the healing, knowing that it would take a lot of power.' My father then explained further 'when they were healing you, some of Valencia's Faerie powers were mixed with your mother's powers. By healing you with so much of her energy Valencia inadvertently gave you some of her powers.'

"That is the reason why Valencia gave me the necklace of her wings. Because she had given me some of her powers when she healed my mother that day. I have no control over it right now, but it will apparently appear every now and then when I wear the necklace. Make me stronger than I would have been under normal circumstances.

"They also told me that 'Power is being taken from everyone in your camp, it is done in such a way that no one realizes it. So be wary, also know that if you are not ready do not start the war as you will be killed. You will know when the right time is to start.'"

Amethyst stared at her wide-eyed, her mouth hanging open slightly in shock as she tried absorbing what she had just been told. She closed her mouth and swallowed before opening it again but no sound came out, swallowing again before finally getting sound out.

"So, you have a half-sister, someone we figured had magical abilities but couldn't figure out how she received it. As well as you were given my mother's necklace because you have some of her powers, what did you not learn?" she asked quietly

"Whether you can forgive me..."

"Forgive you for what?"

"I know how much it hurt when your mother gave me her necklace, and we couldn't explain why she did it."

"When she gave you the necklace, I thought that it was some kind of sign that she loved you more than she loved me. Which is why I was so upset. But I can kind of understand why she gave it to you if she accidentally gave you some of her powers. And that is not something that was in your control, so there is no reason for me to be upset with you."

"Thank you for that. I was afraid that you would be furious, not just at me but at your mom."

"No, I'm not. There is no reason to be upset with anyone. How do you feel about what your father had done?"

"I'm not sure whether I am still in shock over what I heard or what, but right now, I don't feel that upset. Although I'm not sure how to tell her about any of that."

"You will not be alone when you tell her. I will be right next to you when you tell her. And yes, I do think that you should tell her about all of this, as she feels like a freak for not knowing where she got her powers from."

"That means a lot to me, and I appreciate your support."

"How did it feel when you saw them?"

"My parents? At first, I thought that I had hit my head when I fell down the hole, but then I was in my mom's arms and all worries over that went away because she was right there."

"She was able to hold you?"

"They said something about it being one of my abilities, not just being able to see ghosts but that I am able to touch them. A rare gift from what they said."

"I am so happy that you were able to see them. I know how much it hurt to not have them around growing up."

"I still wish that they could be around, but I now know that I survived that attack for a reason, and they do not regret it."

"Now, back to what they told you. They couldn't tell you more about the thing that is taking the power from the camp?"

"No, they couldn't. They tried though but said that it was as though something was getting in their way."

"Very well then, I will put some of the Creatures on it to try and figure out what is going on. Am I to take it that you will be the one starting the war this time around?"

"From what they told me... yes."

"Well, I trust you and know that you will not start something that cannot be carried through until we are all ready for it."

"It feels like everything is depending on me..."

"I can understand why you feel that way. And in a way, that is exactly what it is like, but you are not alone."

"And you will never be alone in this." Shadick said from the doorway. "Everyone here will stand behind you in whatever decision you make."

"When you first told me that you saw your parents' ghosts, I believed that you had completely lost it and the things you said did not make sense. But I now realise that I was wrong and I will stand with you. I should not have doubted you." Starlansha whispered, stepping closer

"We will all be there with you when you tell Luanda where her powers come from, and we will support you if she doubts you."

"You see... you have friends who support you no matter what choices you make." Amethyst said smiling

"Then why does it feel as though I will be hated if I make the wrong choice with the war?" Alexandria asked frowning

"Because it is a big responsibility to have on your shoulders. But as you have just seen... you aren't alone."

"We all love and trust you. So even if we may not be sure about your choices, we know that you have made the choices for a reason."

"It feels as though I am being crowned Queen or General."

"You kind of are, you are the General of all of the troops."

"Stop worrying so much over something that has not happened yet." Shadick said, walking towards her. "The Centaurs aren't on our doorstep... yet. So, there is no reason for us to fight yet. Although I do think that training sessions should be stepped up a little just so that we know we are all ready for what is coming."

"Shadick, would you please speak to the fighters and help

them if needed? I know that they have learned a lot already, but there is a lot more that they can be taught."

"If you want me to, then I will do so."

"What do you want me to do?" Starlansha asked, stepping closer. "I can't really help with the training, but I am willing to help wherever I can."

"The best would be to talk to your grandparents and make sure that they are ready for whatever is coming. Tell them that your sister has disappeared and that you are afraid that she may have joined the Centaurs. Be honest with them." Amethyst said, sighing softly.

"We have no proof that she joined them." Alexandria said shocked.

"I think that it would be for the best if we assume that she did, if she shows up back here, then we know that we were wrong, but for now, I think it is safer to not underestimate the Centaurs and the powers they may or may not wield. That would be stupid of us."

"I agree with Amethyst. It hurts thinking that she left us for them but it is a possibility." Starlansha said nodding.

"Alex, I think that for now, you need to figure out if you can call up the Faerie powers that have been given to you just in case, we need it. I know that you have the Elementals on your side but more power is never a bad thing."

"First of all, I think that we all need to have a good night's rest. It won't help any of us to be caught out by the Centaurs." Shadick said, grabbing Alexandria's hand.

"Very well then... tomorrow morning, I will call a meeting and tell everyone of our plans. But for now, I demand you all get to bed."

Alexandria sighed but nodded, hugging Amethyst quickly and kissing her cheek before Shadick pulled her out of the room and towards the darkness of their room.

Chapter 24

Water Slave

"You and Shadick just disappeared last night. I know that I said we would talk today, but I guess I was assuming that you would want to talk about Luanda and how you will be telling her that you are half-sisters." Amethyst said the next morning as they walked through the villages.

"I have no idea how I'm supposed to tell her the truth. It isn't as though I had some kind of crash course on how to approach family that doesn't know that you are family. Was kind of hoping that an opportunity would present itself, and I would just know that it was the right time." Alexandria replied, sighing. "And Shadick thought that you looked tired, which is why he pulled me away and to our room. He knew that I would like to talk to you some more or you to me but thought it best to save it for another day."

"Sometimes it feels as though he is in our heads and knows us way too well. Not to mention, the guards told me of the noises they heard coming from your room last night."

"Tell me about it! Although after everything that happened at the Mountains, he didn't seem to understand that I needed to be reassured that everything was still okay. Chadromida eventually told him to shut up, and he came to talk to me. They heard absolutely nothing."

"He is still a guy, Alex. Sometimes they don't think about what is important. All they see is the 'obvious' solution or even the words to say, then when the other person doesn't understand their point of view, it seems to freeze in their brains."

"And how did you get so smart when it comes to guys?"

"Oh, you know me! I get around a lot and observe people."

"That sounds as though you are a Faerie that sleeps with a lot of guys, just by the way..." Alexandria said, laughing softly.

"I learned quite a bit from Sachiel, I will have you know. He liked to talk about how guys work and how he couldn't understand why some don't just realise the obvious."

"When last did you talk to him?"

"Not since I told him that I was pregnant."

"Do you not regret it? Giving up Adriata?"

"You named her?!"

"No, I did not... Sachiel did."

"I thought that you would never mention that time in my life ever again?"

"You know what, Amey? I think that it's about time that you accept the fact that you have a daughter, she is over three years old now, and you still refuse to even admit that she is yours. Do you know that she has your eyes? It was one of the first things that Sachiel noticed about her when I handed her to him."

"And have you seen her or even him in the last while?"

"You know that I haven't. What with all the fighting and me being whisked away to learn how to fight I did not get much chance to go and see my own Goddaughter. I keep thinking that I will get a break so that I can go visit but it just doesn't seem to ever happen."

"Is that my fault then?"

"Amey, if you would just open your eyes, you will notice that people won't care whether you had a child out of wedlock! They would most likely accept her as one of us. She is half Fae, after all."

"There is no proof that she is half Fae! No rumours suddenly appearing from nowhere or even from Sachiel himself."

"Because as far as he knows... you want nothing to do

with your own daughter."

Amethyst opened her mouth to retort, but they were suddenly surrounded by a torrent of water. Frowning, Alexandria reached out to touch it and sighed as she felt the magic coming from it.

"Don't move, Amey. It is the last of my trials from the Elementals."

"Am I supposed to just sit back and watch this thing beat you up?"

"I am sorry if I interrupted your little argument. But I was getting rather tired of having to wait for you to stop arguing." a voice said sarcastically from within the water.

"Are you going to be one of those Elementals that talk more than actually fighting? Because I would rather get it over and done with. Not to mention your attitude is off putting." Alexandria replied.

A part of the water wall moved, and as it split, it changed into a ball and was thrown straight at Alexandria. Before she could move to stop it, Amethyst stepped in front of her and tried to stop it. In a flash, she was lifted from the ground, and the screams were almost unbearable. It seemed to happen in slow motion, slowly surrounding her wings and seemingly running over it, but pieces of her wings became part of the water that surrounded her.

Alexandria ran forward and jumped into the ball of water and grabbing Amethyst around the waist and pulling her out of the torrent. As she landed back on the ground, she noticed that Amethyst's screams had stopped, and the silence seemed to be magnified thousand times over. Not glancing down at her sister, she quickly stepped over her and threw her own ball of water at the Elemental. The Elemental froze when she noticed Alexandria's eyes and was about to comment on it when she was hit with the ball as well as another from behind.

In an effort to get away from the constant attacks Alexandria was throwing at her, she turned into her water form but it did not help. Alexandria concentrated on her life and pulled it out of her, slowly draining her of what she could feel flowing from her. She had hurt her friend and sister, and she refused to let that pass.

"Stop! You're killing me!" the Elemental shouted.

"You hurt my sister without a second thought, and that is unforgivable!"

"It is part of our laws that any creature that tries to stop us should be stopped, which is exactly what I did!"

"Well, guess what! One of your fellow Elementals was also interrupted by one of my friends, but he was not killed! He was restrained, and afterwards, he was released with no harm done to him!"

"I was just doing what I was told!"

"Then you should think about what your so-called superiors ask of you before actually doing it blindly. I will show you mercy where you did not show it to Amethyst. I expect you to support me in the coming war without questioning me or any of my friends... you will give it your all and not think about it twice. And yes, I will be telling the other Elementals about what you have done here today, and I can assure you that they will not be very happy with you either."

"But this is not how it works! We are supposed to fight until I see that you can truly use my Element."

"What is your name? And reveal your true form... before I decide to truly kill you!"

"My name is Creneis. I am a Nereid in form but as you know, I can take any form I wish."

"I do not care about which form you feel most comfortable in. I only ask your name, so I know who to curse tonight. Now send us back to where we were before I completely lose my temper. And before you start arguing about having to test me in my abilities, please remember that I was busy draining you of all your powers as well as energy. If I had not stopped, you would be dead."

Creneis lowered her head ashamedly and waved her hand

before turning into a stone, disappearing into her daggers. Alexandria blinked and looked around, noticing that they had been taken back to where they had been.

"Guards!" she shouted, bending next to Amethyst and lightly touching her face

"Mam?! What seems to be amiss?" a guard asked, running towards her.

"Help me get the Queen back to the Castle! And for now, do not question what happened; just assist!"

He nodded, shocked but quickly picked Amethyst up and ran towards the Castle, Alexandria on his heels, ignoring everyone who turned to look at them. She ushered him through the door and towards the medical bay.

"Put her down there and go find the best doctor that resides in the village."

She turned her back on him and looked down at Amethyst, her eyes drifting to her ruined wings. Instinctively she knew that she would not be able to save her wings at all, but she had to at least try and stabilize her. Sitting down next to her friend and lightly taking her hand, she closed her eyes and concentrated.

"Lex..." Shadick started but froze when he saw Amethyst's state.

As the energy filled her, her hair seemed to rise into the

air as though it was caught in the wind.

"Shadick, there is a slight panic in the village. Something about Amethyst being attacked?!" Starlansha said seriously.

He held up a finger, still watching Alexandria as she healed Amethyst. A few minutes of her radiating healing energy Amethyst finally stirred slightly, and she opened her eyes to look up at her friend.

"What happened, Alex? I can't really remember much." Amethyst asked weakly

"Creneis took her orders a little too seriously and attacked you when you tried to help me." Alexandria replied softly, letting her powers settle.

"I can't explain it, I kind of feel empty. As though I had something, and it is suddenly gone. But I know that you just healed me so I know that I am not hurt."

"Amey..."

"What is it, Alex?"

"I healed you, yes. But I was unable to heal your wings, they took the most damage in her attack. I tried everything in my power to heal it and to make it better, but nothing worked."

"My wings?!" Amethyst asked, shocked, sitting up and turning her head to look at what remained of her wings. "What am I without my wings? How can I be a Faerie if I do not even have wings?!"

"Your wings do not define who you are, Am." Shadick said, walking into the room.

"Have you ever seen a Faerie without wings?!"

"Yes, I have, when you showed us how you can retract your wings, back when we were still at Troll Mountains."

"Shadick is right, Amey. You still have your powers, and nothing can take that away." Alexandria said, smiling slightly.

"No! I cannot accept that my wings have been taken away from me. I am in just some kind of bad dream and will wake up any minute now with my wings exactly where they belong." Amethyst said, shaking her head.

"Could I perhaps ask that you leave the Queen alone for a bit? Just so that I can check up on her as well as her wings. I know that I am no match against you and your healing abilities Alexandria but I am the doctor and I think that it would be best if I were to look at the Queen." said a voice from behind them. "And you seem to be upsetting her more than necessary at the moment."

Shadick nodded and pulled Alexandria out of the room by the arm, glancing at Amethyst and sighing. Starlansha stared at them both, her mouth wide open and her hands on her neck.

"Were her wings really destroyed?" she asked.

"Yes, they were. The water Elemental seems to not have any brain of her own and acted without thinking for herself." Alexandria said, leaning against the wall and sliding down. "I really tried saving her wings but I can't really bring something back that isn't there anymore. I know that I brought Shadick back, but he was still there, in a way. Her wings were shredded."

"You tried your best, Lexie. I know that once she comes back to her right mind that she won't blame you for what happened. On the contrary, she will most likely thank you for at least trying."

"I'm not so sure about that..."

"What do you mean?"

"Right before we were attacked, we had been arguing, and she was not very happy with me at that moment. Me not being able to save her wings will just add to all of it and make it even worse."

"Unfortunately, the Queen will not be able to do much at the moment." the doctor's voice said, walking out of the room. "I looked at not just her health, which is perfect. But her wings as well, there is nothing no one can do to bring them back. Even if you had the whole world's magic, there is no way that her wings can be revived."

"What do you mean that she 'won't be able to do much'?"

Starlansha asked, still pale.

"She asked me whether you had just been joking with her about her wings being completely ripped. I told her the truthful answer, and she has gone into an emotional break-down of sorts."

"Is there anything you can do for her to make it better? Or to make her snap out of it?" Alexandria asked.

"I do believe that you are second in charge, miss Alexandria?" he asked, ignoring her question.

"Yes, I am, now answer my question."

"You should let the villagers know that the Queen is out of commission for now and that she has given the rule over to you, temporarily. There is no way for me to get her out of this break-down except talk to her and work with her until she gets better. But it will not happen overnight."

The guards stood around them as one sunk to their knees and bowed their heads. Alexandria glanced at them before looking at Shadick in shock. The doctor hesitated for a second before following in the guards' footsteps and sinking to his knees.

"Your majesty, the villagers are gathered and awaiting to hear from you." said one guard, still bowed.

Shadick walked a step behind her as they followed the

guards to the courtyard where the villagers were gathered. She was still shaking in shock and felt like she wanted to just turn around and run to her room and hide in the darkness. But she knew that Amethyst being out of commission meant that she had to step up and take the lead and decide what to do next.

"Please bow as our Queen steps out to talk to us!" a guard shouted and she stepped forward, trying not to freak out.

"But she isn't the Queen!" a voice shouted from the gathered group.

"Until Queen Amethyst heals, Queen Alexandria is in charge of ruling the village and all of us."

A hush seemed to fall over everyone as the truth sunk into them, and she stepped out from behind the guards. A twitch seemed to run through all the people and Creatures as they saw her before kneeling slowly.

"The stage is yours, your majesty." the guard said, inclining his head.

"What am I supposed to say?!" she whispered urgently to Shadick.

"Speak from your heart, sweetie." he replied, squeezing her hand.

Taking a deep breath and nodding, she turned back to the crowd.

"I know that you may not see me as Queen, and I understand why you wouldn't. And I do not hold it against you if you think that I will be useless at it. But this is what Amethyst wanted she isn't dead, neither is she anywhere close to it so there is no need to worry about that. She will return to rule you as soon as she is feeling better.

"That might not happen within a week or even a month but if we keep supporting her and sending her love, I am sure that she will get better. I will not go into details as to what happened to her but know that she is still alive, but she needs some time to heal her heart and her head. The doctors have looked at her and they agree that she is in no danger and they will keep working with her to help her.

"I have no real experience being a Queen and I honestly never expected that I would be thrown into this situation at all. There is a lot that I need to learn, and I will do my very best to not screw up. I just ask your patience and even your help with whatever comes next."

"What happened to Queen Amethyst?!" a voice shouted.

"Queen Alexandria said she would not speak of the events." A guard growled

"All I will say is that she had been attempting to help me when the other fighter took the fight too seriously and attacked Amethyst. I have dealt with her though and assure you there is no more danger from her."

"But she is still alive?!" another voice shouted.

"Yes, she is still alive, but what has really gotten to her is the fact that her wings were ripped to shreds. And if you do not know, a Faeries wings mean a lot to them, and some Faeries can't live without them and die. Amethyst is stronger than a normal Faerie though so she will be absolutely fine as soon as she is able to work through her loss.

"For her to do that, she does not need the added worry of dealing with the village. It is a very personal thing that she has to work on right now, which is why I have been named temporary Queen."

She glanced behind her and noticed that all the Faeries had joined her and were now standing behind her in support. Some of them were crying, while the others seemed stony-faced as they tried not to show too much emotion. If she had, had any doubt about the people and Creatures not accepting her as Queen, it was quickly thrown to the wind as she glanced around. Terri was walking closer to her, a grim smile on his face. The Unicorns stepped closer as well and bowed in front of her.

"Thank you, all of you for supporting not just me but Amethyst. I know that she will be proud of all of you if she finds out about your support towards me."

Shadick stepped closer and took hold of her hand in support, the pride shining in his eyes. A shadow suddenly fell over them, and they glanced up as a Faerie landed in front of them, the guards immediately jumping up to protect her.

"What is it Viora?" Alexandria asked frowning.

"The Centaurs are gathering!" Viora shouted at her, and as the words sunk into the people, chaos seemed to ignite around them, and the screaming started. It took her only a few minutes to calm the people down before she jumped to action to try and get everyone ready to move out. With the help of Shadick, Starlansha and some of the guards, they were able to get all the fighters together while the others returned to their homes.

"Shadick, you need to get a message to Chadromida, now. We will need the help of him and the Dragons." she told him seriously, watching Terri running through the crowd. "Star, you need to contact your grandfather somehow and let him know what is happening. They might be in danger as well if the Centaurs are moving against us."

"Your majesty, I found your daggers in your room." a guard said, appearing behind her as Shadick and Starlansha disappeared.

"Thank you so much. I was unsure whether I had left it in the room or lost it during the battle earlier today."

"It is only a pleasure, your majesty. I also checked up on Queen Amethyst, as you requested the doctor says that there has been no improvement since earlier, but he has been trying to get through to her. He also said that sometimes it seems as though she responds to some of the things he says, but it doesn't seem to last too long."

"Thank you for the information, I really appreciate it. And have you organised that two guards stay outside of her room to make sure that no harm comes to them?"

"Yes, I have your majesty. They are some of our newer recruits, but they are very promising and have been taking their jobs seriously. So, I trust them with my life that they will not abandon their posts. It is a great honour for them to be given this job of watching over the Queen. At first, they argued that they would be more help on the battlefield, but I was able to convince them that this job is just as important as being out there."

"Good job, and I trust your opinion. I would have requested more guards watch over her but unfortunately, we will need as many of the fighters as possible."

"I was able to get a hold of Chadromida. He is surprised that they are making their moves so quickly, but he will gather all of the Dragons, and they will be joining as soon as they are ready." Shadick said, walking up towards her. "I had to convince my sister to stay there as I do not want her to get involved in any of this. For that matter, I wouldn't want you to get involved in this but you are so deep in, and it seems like you are one of the few that can actually help us with this war that I know I cannot ask you to sit out."

"As much as I would love to sit out of this, I can't, the Elementals attacking me and testing me is proof enough of that." she replied, smiling slightly.

"Any news on Amethyst?"

"There has been no change..."

"She will get through this; you don't need to worry about her."

"I know that she is strong, but I have never heard of a Faerie surviving the loss of her wings. From what I was taught they either die immediately or go into a state of shock and never recover."

"But we are talking about Amethyst here; she isn't just any Faerie."

"My Grandmother informed me that the Sirens are on the move as well and that my grandfather has already gathered their troops just in case, they make a move against them." Starlansha said, running towards them. "She did not mention Roslata at all, which means that she is either dead or has really joined the Centaurs."

"She is not dead; I do believe that you would have felt her loss then. As for her joining the Centaurs. That will be her choice, but if she decides that she wants to return to our side, she will be more than welcome to." Alexandria said, hugging Starlansha quickly.

"The troops are ready, your majesty!" the General said as he ran up the stairs towards them. "On your word, we are all ready to move out to the battlefield."

"It is appreciated that you were able to organise the troops so quickly. Have you made sure that the gates will still be manned?"

"Yes, I have, your majesty. I have made sure that Valencia is still guarded. The horses have also been saddled for you."

"Thank you, we will go to the horses and then give the command to move."

The General nodded and ran back down the stairs. Alexandria watched him go, then took a deep breath and walked towards the waiting horses.

Chapter 25

The Second War

The two groups were gathered on either side of the battlefield. Whispering could faintly be heard from both sides as they tried to guess which side would make the first move. Tension building slowly as the armies relaxed in their battle formations, ready to jump and attack at the first sign of trouble.

Alexandria, Shadick, Chadromida, Astarte and Starlansha standing at the front of their group of fighters murmuring among themselves about what they should do next.

Shadick looked up as he heard a soft rustle of wings from the Centaurs side of the field, quickly turning to Alexandria and whispering softly to her before silently pointing to the group of Harpeas. She shuddered as she remembered the strength they had displayed when they had fought against them the first time a few months ago.

"They seem even more evil than that day when we were

attacked in the village." Starlansha voiced Alexandria's thoughts.

"I know what you mean; I was just thinking that they seem larger than before as well." Alexandria added.

"And the tension of this situation is getting to both of you. They are the same size and amount of evil as the day you are talking about. So just relax and get your mindsets ready for the battle that is ahead of us." Shadick said, hugging Alexandria tightly.

"Shadick is right. Thinking about the past won't make what lies in front of us any easier to face."

"I still can't believe that Amethyst went into shock at a time like this." Chadromida added frowning.

"The water elemental completely dissolved her wings when she tried helping me." Alexandria admitted sighing.

"What did you just say?!" Astarte exclaimed softly, her face showing shock.

"We were just walking through the village earlier this morning when we were suddenly surrounded by a ball of water. I tried telling Am to not interfere so she wouldn't get hurt, but it isn't who she is. When Creneis threw her first attack at me, she jumped in the way.

"It was as though in a daze that I watched her being bombarded by water and watched in shock as it destroyed her wings. I was able to pull her out of the bubble thing that she had been caught in, but there was nothing for me to do for her wings. I then demanded that the Elemental show herself so I knew whom I was facing, and a Nereid showed her face. I could have almost killed her in my frustration and anger but I stopped in time before actually doing it.

"Creneis was very shocked that I had almost killed her without a seconds thought but I told her that I showed her mercy. I then made her promise that she would help us during the war with no further questioning or argument as I had already proved that I could destroy her.

"She tried arguing that it wasn't how it worked, but I assured her that I had already proven myself and that she would either accept that she was now indebted to me or that I would kill her without a second thought. After a few more minutes of argument, she finally let us go, which is when I called the guards, and we rushed her back to the Castle. I healed her physical wounds, but there was nothing that I could do for her wings."

"But it is kind of an unspoken rule for all creatures that no matter what happens, no matter if it would strengthen your chances to win in a fight or a disagreement, that you never obliterate a Faeries wings; also there has not been a lot of reports of Faeries actually surviving without their wings."

Astarte said stunned.

"Not a lot of creatures have the ability to even harm a Faerie, even if it is just her wings. You can fight them, but they always rejuvenate up to a point. That is one of the reasons why Faeries live so long." Chadromida said shocked.

"The only time I have heard of a Faerie ever losing her wings was in a story my parents once told us when we were younger. And as far as I remember the story going, the Faerie didn't survive without her wings." Shadick told them, frowning.

"She is stronger than any other Faerie that we know; she will survive this as long as we keep supporting her and defend Valencia. It was always her dream to unite the humans and non-humans. She was ecstatic when the humans finally contacted us and wanted to help with the fighting." Alexandria told them, smiling slightly, then frowned and stepped forward. "So Balditha, are you going to let your army cower behind you and not attack at all? Or are you waiting for something to happen before giving them orders?"

"Perhaps we are the ones waiting for you to make the first move, dearest Alexandria. I do believe that we have enough information to know exactly what you are planning thanks to Markus." Balditha shouted, grinning, then turning to talk to Justren.

"I cannot stand this! Just standing here waiting for something to happen."

"Alexandria, just relax. It will happen when it happens. We just need to be ready for when that does happen." Shadick told her softly

Before he could put his arms around her, she transformed into a black bird and flew towards the Centaurs side. She was looking for the one Centaur that she knew would be able to start the fighting if attacked.

Alexandria spotted Diliante and swooped down right towards her, and just before she could land next to her, she transformed into her human form plunging her one dagger into the centaur's heart, in the same movement slashing the other blade across her throat before transforming back into the black bird flying away from the group as everyone surged around her trying to stop the bleeding as well as stop her from getting away. The moment she heard Balditha's angry shout, she knew that she had succeeded in what she had planned.

"Lexie, what did you do?!" Shadick asked as she landed next to them, fully human again.

"I made the first move, seeing that they seemed too cowardly to do so." Alexandria told them.

"Alexandria!!! You killed my wife! Now prepare to die the same way that you murdered her." Balditha's voice carried towards them, "And do not expect any justice or forgiveness!"

"You killed Diliante?! Have you gone completely insane, Alexandria? The fight will be even tougher than before!" Shadick said shocked.

"But now the target is on my back, not any of yours. Balditha will attack me and no one else, and we all know that Justren will be following in his father's footsteps. That will give you guys the chance to surge through most of the army and target the creatures that you guys think would cause the most problems." Alexandria told them, straightening.

"You just made one of the stupidest moves in the history of any battle, and you try to explain it away by saying you did it for us."

"I have given you the opportunity to make sure that the Harpeas and Minotaurs do not do too much damage to anyone. And I have to take out my frustration in some way and hurting her seemed like a good way to achieve that. And the extra part means that they are finally going to do something besides just stand there like statues."

"I do believe that you have finally lost it..." Starlansha said as the Centaurs started moving.

"She may have lost her mind, but her actions did achieve what we have been waiting for." Chadromida said shrugging.

"Ashy, I really wish that you listened to Chad and stayed

at the Caves and away from all of this." Shadick said, turning to his sister.

"He tried his best, but you should know me better than anyone, I will go where I want." Astarte replied.

"We need all the help that we can, so I am thankful that she decided to come anyway." Alexandria said, shaking her head. "Truthfully though this is not exactly the right place to discuss this. There are more important things to take care of right now."

Shadick turned back in time to see all of the humans and magical creatures racing onto the battlefield with shouts of readiness.

Chapter 26

Power of the Elements

Starlansha, Astarte and Shadick all raced towards the Minotaurs and Harpeas that were not too far from them making them scream. Their attention was instantly removed from those they had been attacking, and a shout of frustration was heard from one of the Harpies as its wing was slashed. Chadromida jumped onto the Falcon's back and indicated that the rest of the Dragons should start attacking the Centaurs as well. She watched in amazement when some of the Centaurs and Orcs turning on those they had been following.

It had all seemed to be rather peaceful not too long ago, and now you would not be able to hear anything but the clashing of weapons. Freya and Managwa rushed forward and bit at some of the Centaur's legs.

"I warned you that I would be the one to get rid of you. You were foolish enough to attack and kill my wife where I could see, so there will be no mercy for you." Balditha shouted as he ran straight towards her.

"Well, I only did it because you did not really seem interested in starting the battle." she replied, grinning, dodging his sword, then pausing slightly. "Oh right... I also killed her because she was a bad Creature who had been bringing nothing but destruction to this world for the last couple of years. But perhaps if she had not been involved with you, she would have been a good person. Unfortunately, we will never know if that is true because she refused to leave you."

"She was the one that encouraged me to go after what was rightfully ours!"

"Ah, I see! She had you by the privates, and you could not get away."

She crossed her daggers just in time to stop an attack from the Centaur. She used his movement against him and caused him to step back a few steps. Swinging the daggers around, aiming straight for his chest, she frowned as she missed. She just had enough time to dodge his next attack as he swung for her head.

Out of the corner of her eye, she noticed that half of the Harpeas were down, barely twitching, the life fading from their eyes as the Minotaurs stepped on them to get to the fight. She concentrated slightly and threw an energy ball at Balditha and, as he was distracted, swung one of her blades across his chest.

A growl told her that she had distracted him enough that he had not realised what her plan had been until the last second. She also knew that he would not fall for it again.

She stepped back and blew a small ball of fire at him while using the wind to make it float around, while she used the roots around him to go up his legs, ready to tighten the minute he seemed to want to retaliate. He smacked the ball of fire away and glared at her, she flicked her hand, and the roots and vines tightened and pulled him down. Fighting against it shouting at her in frustration, she made sure that he would not get lost just yet.

"With this I call the five Elemental beings to come and strengthen me and help me fight. With thy names you shall appear... first I call Jace, the one that represents Spirit!" she shouted, and with a surge of power, Jace appeared next to her grinning.

"I was wondering when you would be calling us." he said jokingly. "I was starting to wonder if you were ever going to need us."

"Secondly I call Meya, the one that represents Air."

Meya appeared on her other side and inclined her head to Alexandria before glancing at Balditha. "I never did like

Centaurs much."

"Thirdly, I call Necrontyr, the one that represents Nature."

Necrontyr seemed to appear from within the ground and his form was quickly formed by roots and vines as though it was an everyday thing. "Thank you for the introduction, sweetheart."

"Fourth, I call Claudia, the one that represents Fire." Alexandria said, a small grin appearing on her lips. "The one that represents her Element very well."

"Now that is a really nice compliment!" Claudia said, grinning as she stepped out of a sudden fireball.

"Lastly, I call Creneis. The one that represents Water. Also, the one that owes me the most."

Creneis stepped forward slightly and glanced at Alexandria then sighed. "I am here as promised."

"As you can see and hear, the battle has started. The leader of the Centaurs is right there, being held down by roots. I have no assurance that it will stop with him, but at least we can try. Will you help me fight and end all of this?"

"We shall." they replied in unison before turning towards her. "Accept us!"

She nodded and closed her eyes, concentrating on all of the Elements as they rushed at her. It was with ringing in her ears that she thought she heard Shadick screaming at her but there was no time to wait for him and to explain.

As the Elements powers surged through her it lifted her off the ground, and she was enveloped by a bright white light. Fiery wings appeared on her back while her daggers were transformed into that of water and air. Nature crawled over her body and created what seemed like a shield of some kind, replacing her clothes with vines and thorns. Slowly she was brought back down to the ground, and she glanced first at Shadick who froze mid-step, then at Balditha whose eyes had widened in shock.

"I did not believe that you would be able to control the Elements! I ignored the warnings from Markus, telling myself that it would not be possible." he muttered.

"Have I proven now that I am stronger than you could have ever believed? That I will be able to kill you without a second thought? As well as your useless half-breed son?" she asked in an ethereal voice. "Not that your opinion counts much for anything. Least of all whether I should prove myself to you or to anyone."

"You have proven nothing! Except that I have to kill you even more than before!" he shouted and broke lose, immediately jumping towards her.

She dodged his attack and threw a punch into his

stomach, which seemed to not faze him. She swung her blades at his neck, hoping that the momentum would catch him off guard but he seemed to sense it coming and was able to step back just in time. Vaguely she noticed Shadick fighting against Justren but there was no time for panic as Balditha ran straight at her before rearing up on his hind legs and kicking her away from him.

She slid back a few meters before she was able to dig her blades into the ground to stop herself. Rolling out of the way as he tried stomping on her, swiping her blades at his legs and catching his one hind leg as he tried moving out of the way.

A scream of frustration was heard as he raced after her again, ignoring his wounds. Swinging his sword down to her from over his head and she lifted her daggers to stop it as it swung down on her. He immediately moved his sword and swung at her from the side. She quickly jumped into the air and landed on his back majestically. But she was thrown off as Justren ran straight into his father and swinging his spear at her, which she could not dodge in time. A small line of blood appeared over her stomach from where his weapon had hit her.

"You have already murdered my mother! Do not think for a second that I or my father would be as easily killed." Justren shouted.

"Perhaps it was more a case of her just finally seeing a way to get away from the two of you, for good." she replied grinning

"Do not dare insult any of my family like that. She was a very happy woman with everything that she had ever wanted at her finger tips. As well as being loved by all of the other Centaurs!" Balditha said icily.

"Ah yes, she had too many lovers and was afraid that you would find out so she realised that it would just be easier to have herself killed than to go through all the trouble of having to explain to you that you weren't the one she wanted anymore."

"If she was still alive, she would tell you, while beating your face into the ground, that she was very happy with not just me but her only son! He did what none of the others could ever do."

"Oh, you mean lie to the one girl that might be able to kill him? As well as his father? And as it turns out, his mother."

"How dare you!" Justren shouted and ran straight at her ignoring his father's attempts to stop him.

Alexandria used her Fire wings to fly into the air to avoid his attack, quickly turning back to face him and throwing her Air blade towards him. As he tried dodging the blade, it caught his arm, and the blade sliced right through the artery his arm dropped to the floor while he screamed in shock.

Balditha grabbed her ankle and pulled her down, and she crashed to the ground with a small 'oof', quickly turning around and lifting her Water blade to stop his sword as he thrust it straight at her chest. Shadick suddenly appeared above them and smacked Balditha away from her and quickly helped her up, turning back on the Centaur growling.

"I do believe that your son might bleed to death if you do not get him out of here." Shadick said seriously. "Although I would not blame you for letting him die. It would spare you the trouble of killing him later."

"The arrogance of a wolf never surprises me!" Balditha shouted.

"Look around you, Balditha... your army has been taken care of and the ones that trust you blindly are still fighting but the rest are running." Alexandria said.

"We have beaten you, once again. And I am sure that the Dragons will be only too happy to rip the rest of your army to shreds." Chadromida said, landing next to them. "In fact, I know that they have been craving some Centaur blood."

"This is your last chance, Balditha. Take your son and retreat, as well as tell your army to retreat, and we will spare you. But if you refuse to go, then we will kill you without a second thought, and please take your bleeding son with you.

He has spilt enough blood on the soil." Alexandria said, stepping closer to him.

"Do you really think that we will just give up like this? Not fight back?!" Balditha shouted angrily.

"Oh, I am sure that in a few years, when you think that you have a big enough army you will come try again. But even you can see that you are being outnumbered. We took down your Harpeas as well as the Minotaurs that you had hoped would distract and kill everyone." Shadick told him. "We knew about their danger because you sent some of them to attack Alexandria earlier this year, so we knew that they would have to be taken out from the get go. We concentrated on them, and only a few got loose and attacked our soldiers."

"I will admit that I was rather hoping that they would take you out, Alexandria. They were given the command to not return unless they could prove that you had been taken care of. When they returned bloody and with no proof of your death, I ordered my men to take care of them as I saw them as weaklings. It did not make their kinfolk very happy but the message finally got through to them."

"Then I am very surprised that they still decided to stay and fight for you. If you cold-heartedly killed some of their own." Alexandria said.

"It is not always about what you know but about who you

control. You see, we took their King and Queen hostage and promised them that if they fought on our side that they will be kept alive. Of course, we killed them as soon as we had the 'contract' signed."

"Evil as always. I guess there is no chance that you will ever change." Starlansha said, shaking her head.

"Are you going to take your son and go? Or are you inviting us to keep fighting and beat you?" Chadromida asked. "Because I would prefer the latter, naturally. It just does not seem right to let the bad guys get away when their leader is right in front of us."

Alexandria glanced around as they were talking, trying to figure out why she felt as though they were relaxing for absolutely the wrong reasons. Her eyes caught a volley of arrows headed straight for them, and she quickly concentrated and transformed herself into a wall of vines just in time to stop the arrows.

She heard Balditha laugh and felt rather than saw him grab Justren and run back towards what was left of his army. After a few seconds, her energy left her and she collapsed to the ground back into her human form.

"Lexie!" Shadick shouted, kneeling next to her.

"There is no need to shout, Shadick. I am fine, just feeling drained." She said weakly

"How did you know that they were planning something like that?" Chadromida asked

"It was just a feeling I got."

"Well that was one heck of a feeling!" Astarte said as she ran towards them. "The Centaurs seem to be leaving although I'm not sure whether we should trust them."

"If it is anything like the last time, then they won't attack." Starlansha said. "Even if Justren technically killed Shadick the last time..."

"What?! Why was I not told about this?"

"Because Lexie saved my life literally. And I did not see why I should upset you when I was still alive." Shadick said, sending a glare at Starlansha.

"Sorry! I thought she knew." Starlansha said grimacing.

Alexandria giggled as she looked around at them. "Trust you guys to have an argument right after a big fight. After barely getting away from the enemy!"

"Are you feeling okay, Lexie?" Chadromida asked worriedly.

"I do believe so why do you ask, Chad?"

"Because your eyes just turned black."

"Everyone needs to get away from her as quickly as possible!" Jace said, suddenly appearing from out of nowhere.

"Do not question and do not argue with us!" Necrontyr

said.

"What's happening to her?!" Shadick asked standing up

"The power she absorbed from us is spinning out of control! She had no chance to practice, so there was no way for her to get stronger."

"We can't just leave her to die!" Starlansha said seriously.

"She will not be alone we will be with her. But if you do not get away from here, right now. You will be killed!"

"Trust us, please. I know that you guys do not know us but please. We are only trying to do what is best for you. As well as her." Claudia said. "We will look after her and make sure that she remains in control."

"Chadromida! Get yourself and your friends as well as the rest of the warriors away from here, now!" Falcons suddenly shouted as Alexandria seemed to start fading

Chadromida grabbed Shadick and Starlansha's arms and pushed them towards the edge of the battlefield signalling the army that they needed to move. As they all glanced back, the Elementals surrounded Alexandria and seemed to wrap their arms around each other. A strong wind started from out of nowhere and before they could figure out what was happening, a bright flash of light blinded them and when they regained their sight. Alexandria and the Elementals were nowhere to be seen.

<<<<>>>>

<<<<>>>>